"Ripley . . . has come up with a fresh angle to the serial murder game . . . clever and diabolical . . . This unusual debut thriller has a lot going for it."

"[A] gripping debut thriller . . . *Dexter* fans will enjoy the creepy vibe."

"A fast-paced, morbidly addictive novel of chilling infatuation. Ripley's impressive debut is a rich and innovative thriller."

"A wickedly smart thriller that manages to be both chilling and wry. The page-turning plot . . . is thickened by a great cast of characters and Nathan Ripley's fantastic eye for detail and dialogue. Just when you think you've got a grasp on it, the story twists to new and darker places."

"An unsettling exploration of obsession you won't soon forget . . . a first novel that fans of Patricia Highsmith's psychological thrillers and Thomas Harris's cat-and-mouse suspense will devour. I certainly did."

ANDREW PYPER, bestselling author of
The Only Child and *The Demonologist*

"Crafty and dark, Nathan Ripley's novel toys with the lines between predator and prey, his sentences as careful and considered as the crimes he depicts . . . a truly exciting new voice in the thriller world."

ROZ NAY, bestselling author of *Our Little Secret*

"Ripley's debut offers a twist on the typical serial-killer story . . . a unique spin with just enough creepy details to keep suspense readers interested."

Booklist

"It's not always easy diving into the mind of an obsessive protagonist, but Martin Reese's fixation on finding dead bodies makes for one heck of an addictive thriller . . . an original, inventive take on what happens when you go looking where you shouldn't."

JENNIFER HILLIER, author of *Jar of Hearts* and *Wonderland*

YOUR
LIFE
IS
MINE

ALSO BY NATHAN RIPLEY

Find You in the Dark

YOUR
LIFE
IS
MINE

A NOVEL

NATHAN RIPLEY

ATRIA BOOKS

NEW YORK   LONDON   TORONTO   SYDNEY   NEW DELHI

ATRIA
BOOKS

An Imprint of Simon & Schuster, Inc.
1230 Avenue of the Americas
New York, NY 10020

First Atria Books hardcover edition June 2019

ATRIA BOOKS and colophon are trademarks of Simon & Schuster, Inc.

For information about special discounts for bulk purchases, please contact Simon & Schuster Special Sales at 1-866-506-1949 or business@simonandschuster.com.

The Simon & Schuster Speakers Bureau can bring authors to your live event. For more information or to book an event, contact the Simon & Schuster Speakers Bureau at 1-866-248-3049 or visit our website at www.simonspeakers.com.

Interior design by Carly Loman

Manufactured in the United States of America

10 9 8 7 6 5 4 3 2 1

Library of Congress Cataloging-in-Publication Data is available.

ISBN 978-1-5011-7823-8
ISBN 978-1-5011-7825-2 (ebook)

To Rudrapriya Rathore

BEFORE A SHOOTER is a shooter, he's just a man in a room.

It's what follows that brings the background to the scene, to the way we remember it. The domestic dispute reports, the spotty employment record, the legal and illegal firearms history, the I-always-knew neighbors. Before all of that, he comes into the room with his gun, hidden or not, and he is just a man, and not the kind that anyone is used to noticing. Not remarkably handsome, and remarkably ugly only in retrospect. After what he's done.

On August 17, 1996, Chuck Varner walked into the Harlow Mall in Stilford, California, with a Beretta 92FS in his waistband holster. I was there, too.

Chuck owned an AR-10 with an expensive, post-manufacture scope, and had used it on the highway earlier that afternoon, but it wasn't suited to this final step. The radio—it was just the radio and television then, no digital feeds to warn us or lull us with repetitive news of imminent mass death—had said that there was a shooter, that death had come to some already and was likely headed to others soon. But the radio hadn't been able to say anything useful, anything actionable. The shooter was a man in a truck with a rifle. He'd shot from an overpass, and people had died. It wasn't the radio's job to guess what would happen when he parked the truck, when he set the rifle down and picked up a different gun. When he picked a building to use it in.

Chuck Varner chose the Harlow Mall months, even years before, seeing this panorama of waiting bodies and vivid lights in his fantasies and behind the paper targets in his practice drills. It was 2:30 p.m.— no one with a day job would be there, unless they were taking a too-late lunch, or a lazily long break. The adults were mostly stay-at-home parents or the unemployed, Chuck told me. As always, I listened, absorbed, knowing I would be tested later. And because it never occurred to me that he could be anything but absolutely right. The mall was also full of kids, retirees. Night workers like Chuck himself, but ones who drank heavily as part of their bat-hanging flipped schedules and therefore looked worn. Chuck collected conversations, speculated about potential future disciples, and made ambitious plans for his followers, until he realized that he didn't especially care to carry any of them out. He cared about killing.

Chuck never turned up anywhere in public looking strung out, haggard, anything but the upright leader of men that he aimed to be. He slept six hours every morning. Drank two cocktails max, no beer. Calisthenics, runs. At home, his family nurtured his routine with the full knowledge that it was the best way they could love him. That and listening to his gospel, following his drills and instilling his philosophy into the essence of their daily lives. Chuck could always count on his family. If Chuck read, or even if he watched documentaries about people like himself, he would know this made him an outlier, remarkable in a certain way: he was happy at home.

But that day, he didn't let happiness distract him from his purpose. From what he was there in the mall to do, looking tidy if casual in a black T-shirt with an unreadable band name overtop a skull logo, a costume that news outlets discussed in depth in the following weeks and months.

Even I wasn't a distraction for him: he'd brought me as a witness. It was my reward.

Because it was such a common sight in this mall, in any mall, it wasn't reported that the man who later held only a gun had come in holding a girl by the hand. Me. No one noted that Chuck Varner, before he became the shooter, had patted her on the shoulder, and gone up the escalator with her.

When I sat on one of the food court chairs that ran the length of the atrium railing, he left me and descended. When the first shot came, when the running, ducking, and panicking came a thick few seconds of disbelief and processing later, I didn't move. I didn't exactly watch, but I didn't look away. I knew that I was the only person in that building who had nothing to fear from Chuck Varner.

Chuck Varner was holding his daughter's hand when he walked into the mall. My hand. He took me up that escalator and told me that he loved me. He told me to walk away from the mall and go back to my mom once he was done. That everyone would be screaming and running, that no one would get in my way. He also said that if I didn't do just as Dad said, he would be very disappointed. That I should listen to him and trust that he was about to become everything that we'd ever talked about. He nodded at me as he went down the escalator, smiling and trying to do something with his eyes, achieving a look I'd never seen from him before. Then he got distracted and started touching the holstered Beretta through the thin fabric of his T-shirt, and by the time he reached the killing floor, I knew he'd forgotten about me absolutely.

I was seven years old. And I thought that Chuck won, that he did exactly what he said, that he updated the Bible in cordite and blood, and that no one would ever be the same. For my mother and me, that was true. Nothing was ever the same.

————————

The night I left her forever, my mother, Crissy Varner, stayed in the trailer while I left with Chuck's AR-10, promising to return. After Harlow Mall, we'd kept it hidden. The cops had the Beretta, but we had this—he'd dropped it off at home before his last run, and Crissy had buried it at the base of a hollow tree trunk. I'd shown the tree to Crissy myself: it was where I hid my little toys, the dolls that I'd pulled the hair out of and given waterproof clothing of my own devising, working mainly in ziplock and candy-wrapper fabrics. She hadn't taken the rifle out again until she, until both of us, thought we were ready to use it again as Chuck intended.

Almost ten years after Harlow Mall, I took the rifle from Crissy and hid it in pieces, each of them scraped and scrubbed clean. I was sixteen and doing what I thought I had always had to do: my duty, for my parents, the living one and the dead one. Crissy, alive. Chuck in the ground except for his words and his Great Act, the shooting that had ruled our lives—mine and Crissy's—until I buried the sections of the rifle in deep, widely spaced miniature graves across Stilford, each burial another step away from the trailer I'd shared with Crissy and Chuck's ghost in the vacuum that was my entire life. Until Crissy finally made me realize that I never wanted to kill, or control, anyone. Ever.

Maybe Crissy hadn't known that I wasn't going to come back to her when I left with the rifle in a battered Benetton bag. But she wasn't stupid. That's part of what made Chuck's hold over us so compelling—I knew that I wasn't stupid, and I knew that Crissy wasn't stupid, so it wasn't possible that Chuck's construction of the universe could be entirely wrong. We believed it. We chose his world every day that he was gone, every day that we didn't have to: we followed his code. The code he called Your Life Is Mine.

CHAPTER ONE

I STOOD OUTSIDE THE cinema, watching the crowd in the lobby, trying to get rid of what I'd just seen. One, then another of them, falling as they held their sides, screaming as the red started to show. Nothing like that was happening, of course. Everyone was just fine: I could see them moving, speaking. Just a crowd of people, New Orleans natives and our Los Angeles production and network team, drinking, having fun. Alive. But crowds still did this to me, twenty years after Chuck Varner let go of my hand. I saw the people falling, heard them dying.

I still didn't quite believe it, but I was standing outside a cinema where people had just watched, cried, and clapped over what I'd made. We'd only wrapped three months before. Editing-as-we-went had resulted in a rough cut that looked so good the producers demanded we leave it untouched for a slapped-together New Orleans premiere, this miniature gala event they'd flown in key industry and press to attend. As always, it was after postproduction when all the money they'd been telling us didn't exist happened to turn up.

"No one here knows who you really are," said a voice behind me. "Just me."

I pretended I wasn't entirely keyed up with fear and turned, smiling, tapping an inch of ash off the cigarette I'd almost forgotten was in my mouth. I'd dropped some, not much, onto the green bib blouse that Jaya had made me wear to the premiere to distract from my pilling but thankfully stretch-waisted black skirt.

"Sorry to sneak up on you," the man said. He was late twenties, like me, but built like he'd grown up with a lot more nutrition. A couple inches taller than most of the people in the lobby behind the glass, especially the crew that I'd used to shoot *The Marigny Five,* this historical true crime doc that was the closest I'd come, so far, to selling out. It was easy for someone to look tall compared to my crew: I liked using small men and women when I shot, a little team dressed in black who eventually vanished to the people I was talking to, began to seem like shadows in the rooms and homes where we filmed subjects telling us more than they wanted to.

"I think I can comfortably say that everyone in there knows who I am," I said. "I made the movie they just watched and stood up there while they asked stupid questions." He laughed, which wasn't the response I was going for. I was good at stepping on fear before it started, and I did it here again. The lobby was full of living people, with no threat in sight. And this was just a man trying his boring best to talk to me. Then he tried it again.

"I know, I was in there. But I mean I know who you really, really are." It wasn't the persistence that made my instincts flick on again—it was his smile. His anticipation. Like he actually had something to say to me, and I wouldn't want to hear it.

I turned away from him with an upward nod that I tried to make dismissive, but not a provocation.

"Whatever you say. See you inside, maybe," I said.

Jaya was by the food table, methodically working her way through a heap of green beans that was difficult to eat with the plastic spoons left over after the prescreening run on forks. Producing involved so much talking on the phone and in-person that she tended to shut down as soon as she could, leaving her quiet on premiere nights, changing her from the person who always did the approaching into someone who needed to be approached. This was the first premiere we'd done outside of New York or Los Angeles, not counting underattended screenings at whatever little festival would accept our weird docs and that we could afford to fly to.

Jaya had found this beautiful old cinema, the Carver, which was next to the fried chicken mecca that me and the rest of the crew had been hitting twice a week for the four months of production, eating enough bird that we had the production company do an all-seafood spread for this screening.

"You still glad we did this?" I asked Jaya.

"Of course I am. Did you see Programming Bruce's face? He thinks you're Errol Morris with sharper cheekbones and built-in commercial instincts. When you were doing your intro he was texting every press contact he has to set up on cameras with you."

"How do you know who he was texting?"

"I sat over his right shoulder so I could spy. Don't worry, I got him to turn his goddamn phone off before the lights went down."

"Yeah," I said. Jaya zeroed in on the ash stain over my left breast, pointing, and I shrugged. I'd smeared it in when I tried to brush it off. The blouse had already lost most of its structure from being subjected to the tonguing blast of humidity in my brief time outside, so the mark was no tragedy. Still, I worked on angling my bag strap to overlay the mark.

Before I could point out the guy across the room and ask Jaya to talk me out of my unease, one of the camera assistants we'd used came over and interrupted us. Nice kid, Maurice something. Jaya would know his last name, his parents' names, probably his social insurance number. He was wearing a T-shirt of so many shades of neon-approaching brilliance that my eyes dropped to the food table to avoid the strain of looking at it. I half-listened to him saying something quick about how great the show had turned out, before he started a hesitant sentence that Jaya interrupted six words in.

"You want to work on our next thing? I think we'd all like that. Way lower budget, and it's about a weirdo eccentric rich writer lady, I'm warning you in advance. Very different."

"I just want in on anything y'all do, you know?"

I turned up from my strap-fiddling at this, looking Maurice in the eye, which was a good thing, because he was nodding earnestly at me, actually tearing up.

"I've never made something good before. I love how you respected this city and the people this ghastly shit happened to, Blanche. Jaya," he added.

"Thanks, Maurice," I said. Jaya nodded, trying to look solemn, the effect hurt by the spoon she was holding straight up in her other hand, like a magic wand.

"Don't take this wrong," Maurice said, the kind of phrase that usually precedes a shitty statement from a man. "But I think you have this real grip on their trauma. What these people went through, victims or family, you just get it."

"I think that's a compliment," I said.

"I do, too," Jaya said, looking down in the hope I wouldn't notice how badly she wanted Maurice and me to keep talking. This was the kind of conversation I would have shut down before it started if it was just between her and me. It was why we worked together, as friends and beyond: we knew what questions not to ask.

"I would—I'd love to know how you do it. How you talk to people right," Maurice said. His expectant gaze and the fact that he'd worked insane overtime got me to give up a little bit.

"I treat them like they're more than the thing that happened to them," I said. "If you go in asking them how they dealt with this horrible thing, you'll get—every subject does this—they look at you to see if you already have an answer you're expecting. Bo Stallins, the brother of Chianna?"

"Yeah," said Maurice. "We shot him outside the dorms."

"Everyone who's asked him how he dealt with his sister being murdered wanted to hear one of two kinds of answers. Either the steps up to enlightenment he took, or the dark path down into addiction or rage or violence. And, because he's a built black man, most idiot reporters—"

"They want to hear the drug story," said Maurice. "The jail story. And he doesn't have that."

"Right. Straight arrow, has half a bachelor's degree, does the janitor job because it's union and part time, gives him time to write his atheist philosophical horror novels. And even those—those weird books of his, they aren't just his *trauma*. They're his imagination, his life. I get people talking about the whole thing first, their life, then the event that everyone else starts with. Right?"

Maurice nodded, and Jaya looked profoundly pleased with herself. It was clear to anyone who'd seen *Marigny Five* that it was mature work, despite initially seeming like my sell-out farewell to the difficult films I'd been making with Jaya since school. This was the first piece that didn't seem at all like an audition. And I hadn't wanted to do it, this odd, four-episode, doc-movie-show hybrid that had the camera assist in front of me tearing up, that had held the audience tonight in the best possible rapt silence. Jaya had forced me, and she'd been right.

The streaming network that wanted us to make the story of the Marigny killings gave us so much money that, when Jaya broke it down, we had enough beyond living expenses in our two contracts to get a start on the feature doc about Caroline Blackwood, the novelist, Guinness heir, and Lucian Freud divorcer that I'd wanted to do for the last two years.

"We have to do it," Jaya told me. "This is how weird movies get born. You seed them with money from the normalish things you didn't want to do. Plus, we can talk these people into distribution money up front for the Blackwood thing if they end up liking the show."

"I hate this serial killer crap," I said.

"These are killings that have nothing to do with you. Don't get mad at what I'm about to tell you, okay?" she said. "This isn't about Chuck Varner."

It wasn't okay and I did get mad. I yelled at her in the tiny office room of my apartment before calming down and apologizing, then admitting that she was right, even if she was an absolute bitch to have brought it up. We signed on to do the series the next week.

"It's pronounced 'Morris,'" Maurice said, but didn't look that put out. It was getting more crowded around the food table, with audience members and execs alike passing their third drink and needing to lay down some absorbent grease and carbs before they started to slur. Some of the Treme sidewalk traffic had made its way in and toward the open bar, too, and on my and Jaya's say-so earlier that evening, they were not being effed with by security.

"Oh, shit. How's it spelled?"

"Uh, M-O-R-R-I-S."

"Was I calling you that when we were working? The wrong thing?"

"Just a couple of times but it was unimportant, you know? I wasn't going to interrupt you for that."

"Next time interrupt the hell out of me, Morris," I said. "I'm not big on disrespect on my projects, top-down especially. I'm sorry. And I'm looking forward to the next time." At Jaya's insistence, Morris loaded up a paper plate.

"Who's the should-be-on-an-Australian-beach guy over there?" I asked Jaya, including Morris in my questioning glance. He shrugged. I was surprised I'd had to ask Jaya at all; I'd lived with her and her mom for half of high school and we'd been roommates for way too much of our twenties. She had a sharp sense of whenever I took an interest in a man, whether it was negative or positive. Morris backed into another conversation and Jaya set her plate with its delicious beans and frustrating spoon down. I resisted the urge to do a full visual sweep of the room, to make sure that everyone was all right, unhurt, still alive. Every time I indulged the fear was a setback, and I wouldn't let myself cave twice in one night.

"No idea," she said, looking at the man over my shoulder, then trying to wolf-whistle quietly through the gap in her front teeth. When we were teenagers she'd been able to do it perfectly, either factory-lunch-break loud or quiet enough just to get me and the rest of the kids sitting in back of Mrs. Stuart's English 11 to laugh when she had

Polanski's *Macbeth* playing for us in the darkened classroom. But the gap had widened slightly in the past few years, by micrometers, and her tongue hadn't quite gotten the hang of the new dimensions. What came out in the Carver lobby was a piffle of air and a shred of bean.

"Go ask his name," Jaya said. "Maybe he's press, or something."

"Maybe he came in for the free AC and oysters."

"Also likely." We were both looking at him without bothering to cover it up—he was leaning against a wall near one of the entrances to the screening room itself, doing something with his phone, his eyes sometimes flicking toward me. I'd felt them on my back when I was talking to Jaya and Morris.

"He had a weird line," I said.

"Like, creepy?"

"Sort of. Said he knew 'who I really was,'" I said, twitching my index and middle fingers as quotes.

Jaya laughed. "Something he heard between poses in yoga class and thought would work. You don't think it's just a line?"

I looked at her. Jaya closed her eyes for a second.

"You have to stop with this, Blanche. Chuck Varner's gone, no one thinks about him anymore, and no one you'll ever meet who matters in your life or in your work will ever connect you to any of this shit." Jaya was used to giving this talk and I was used to hearing it; not just hearing it, but needing it, ever since high school. She never got tired of telling me that Chuck was over for me. I kept trying to tell myself the same thing, but it was much harder to believe when I said it.

"It was just a line, Blanche. I do encourage you to be paranoid about any and every man being a scumbag, because it's not an unsafe bet, but that was just a line. Right?"

"Yes. Fine, you're right."

"So prove it," Jaya said, resuming her tangle with the beans, this time plucking them individually from the plate and crunching into them like french fries. She was fresh off a breakup with an editor named Cory Lutes, a really nice guy who eventually wanted more from her than half an evening per week. Every few months, Jaya or I pretended that we could have a functional relationship with a man and still have as much time with each other as we needed.

I walked over to the guy, making a stop at the bar for my third Old Grand-Dad bourbon, this one poured as heavy as the last two. When I reached him I plucked the phone out of his hands and looked at it.

"Whatcha doin'?" I asked. It was dark, on lockscreen. He hadn't been using it at all.

"Research on what I could say to you that wouldn't drive you away immediately this time. I want to talk to you."

"About who I really, really am and what we're really, really doing here?" I said. Programming Bruce and another exec, identically dressed in blue shirts tucked into whatever the upscale take on J.Crew chinos is, were making their way over to me, and I got ready to pivot—but there was no need. Jaya interposed herself and started talking to them, ushering them toward old Mrs. Bucknell, the eldest surviving relative of the Marigny victims. Ada Bucknell was the one who turned out to have been having an affair with the murderer, a brewery owner named Alec Mitchell. She didn't know who she was fucking, as she put it to us bluntly after an hour and a half of interviewing at her dining table, a looming crucifix and ten picture frames on the wall behind her, eight of which contained images of her dead sister. "If I knew the demon he was I'd have cut him open while he slept," she said. "Just cut him open and laid there next to him till the blood soaked all through the mattress and washed up around me."

When she'd said that, I thought of my father sleeping in the narrow bed in our trailer the night before the Harlow Mall shooting, and the little fixed-blade knife he'd gotten me for my sixth birthday. He'd encouraged me to sleep with it. In its sheath, of course. I thought of my small hands sheathing the knife in Chuck's heart as Mrs. Bucknell had talked to us calmly of her sister's murderer, and remembered why I hadn't wanted to do this movie.

Mrs. Bucknell was drinking a Tom Collins, looking profoundly bored by the humble praise that Bruce and the other exec were giving her.

"Yeah, who you really are," the man said, preventing me from finding out if Mrs. Bucknell would tell these two execs to fuck off, giving them a story that they'd tell back in the office repeatedly.

"I'm Blanche Potter, and I make documentaries. That's me. You want to do some spiritual probing? I'm not into astrology, I don't have a church, and I'm not successful enough to be a Buddhist or a Scientologist yet." I was daring him to say it, to tell me I was right and that Jaya was wrong.

"You were lying to me by word three of that sentence. How am I going to believe the rest?" He held out his hand, and for a second I thought he wanted me to take it. Instead, I gave his phone back.

"And word three was? Sorry, my short-term memory is pretty bourboned tonight."

"Potter."

I could tell he enjoyed watching my face change, but not until later. Moments like that, I'm still there, reacting, but also backing off, seeing it, logging the details for later.

He watched me recoil and then, before losing me, came in again. "I know your real name, and I know you're from Stilford, and I know who your dad is. So that means I know more about the real you than anyone else in this room except for your intrepid Indo-American pal, right?"

"Fuck you," I said.

He laughed, but not for me—for the people near enough to have heard me curse at him. He was spinning my "fuck" like it was the deadpan punch line to some anecdote. I wasn't happy, definitely not, but I was satisfied. This was it. I was right. Jaya was wrong. Chuck Varner was here, and he would never leave. I thought about that sheathed knife again, how it used to feel nestled into my belt, just where Chuck Varner holstered his Beretta. I found my thumb grazing the spot, just at my right hip.

"You are just pals, right?"

"In high school they used to ask if Jaya and I were 'dykes together.' Try saying it that way. Has the benefit of frankness and makes it even clearer that the speaker is a moron."

"Whoa, sorry. Look, my name's Emil Chadwick, and I'm not here to pry unnecessarily or step on your life, Blanche. You want to go somewhere else? Get a drink?"

"With a blackmailer? Sounds fun." As long as I could keep my tone up, could keep any tremble out of my face and any scream from spilling out, I could control this man. I had to believe that. I could control myself, and I could control this situation. I looked back at Jaya, who had moved away from Mrs. Bucknell and the execs, and was taking a second of peace, her jaw relaxed and eyes closing in a slow blink that showed how tired she was, how hard she'd been working.

"I'm not going to blackmail you. If you come with me and hear me out, that is. If you don't, then there will be some information in circulation—" Emil made a swirling motion, taking in everyone in the lobby, all these people who were essential to my work and life

"—that you will not want in circulation. I'm giving you an opportunity, Blanche Varner. A grasp on your own future. So, yes, I'm blackmailing you to sit down with me and listen to what I have to say, I suppose. That's it."

I held up a hand to him, then turned and went over to Jaya to tell her I'd text her as soon as I got to wherever I was going with this guy, and would continue to text her every ten minutes to tell her I was safe for the next hour. Nothing to worry about, I told her, and she grinned at me, happy I might be deciding to get laid.

"This is a perfect time for some casual whatever. You did such a good job onscreen that you could only mess things up by hanging around here and talking to the moneymen, anyway."

"I'm just going to talk to him, no casual anything," I said, waving and walking backward a couple of steps to alert Chadwick that I was on my way. I kept the quaver out of my voice. I hated hearing the name Emil Chadwick had said to me, in this beautiful lobby, in this cinema where we'd just screened a piece of my work that I was starting to realize was the best thing I'd ever made. I didn't ever want to hear that name again, be called that name again, anywhere, but especially not here. I wanted him out, and that meant I was leaving, too.

"Wait," Jaya said as Chadwick and I reached the doors of the Carver. We turned and she took a picture of us, Chadwick seeing what she was doing in time to smile. Jaya walked closer to us and took a close-up of him.

"I could get my agent to send a headshot," he said.

"I'm just making sure that you know that I know what you look like, and that the cops will, too, if I don't get answers back to my texts to Blanche tonight, mm-hmm?"

"Jaya, it's fine," I said, holding the door open. The humidity sucked at the AC around me.

"Fine by me," Chadwick said. "Caution's smart. Everyone likes smart."

"I wasn't looking for your approval," Jaya said. She pointed at the snapshot on her phone, pointed at Emil's face, and waved goodbye to me.

We cabbed to a place called the Fela Cafe, right back in Faubourg Marigny. The street was lush, even more than most in that city. Citrus fruits of some sort on the sidewalk, thick green leaves and vines on everything. Getting out of the car, we passed two assertive-walking girls wearing bras a size down, faces scared in that uniquely touristic way that I'd learned to shed my first month in LA. One of them looked at me and half-smiled. Chadwick emphatically didn't check them out, keeping his eyes a half-foot above their heads.

"It's safe here," I said to them. "Have a fun night."

"You should have waited a few years if you wanted to blackmail me. I don't have anything worth taking," I said, scanning the cocktail menu and settling on something called a Kentucky Rain. Chadwick got a pint of Dixie. The drinks I'd had at the premiere had evaporated out of my bloodstream when Chadwick first used my father's name, and I needed to replace them.

"You're being modest," Chadwick said. "There's plenty you have that I'd like to take. Your profile, your skills, your future. And I don't even want to take-take them—just borrow them for my own work."

"Which is?"

"I write stuff."

"Oh god," I said, hating that I was starting to feel at ease, hating my hope that Chadwick was the kind of creep I was used to from the business, not the kind that only Chuck Varner had prepared me for.

"I'm not some sort of parasite or aspirant. I've got a book finished already, which I can tell you about—"

"Pass."

"But I'm easing into your field, now. I want to produce a documentary that comes out right on the heels of a feature article, each feeding the other, unpacking a crime in the past and in the present."

The cocktail arrived in front of me and was holy-shit good, strong and smooth and a reminder that I should stop pretending that I liked the cheap whiskey on ice that I'd been drinking for most of my adult life.

"You aren't doing a very good job of not sounding like an amateur or a parasite, Emil." I drew strength from insulting him, but it wasn't enough. A hand raised to hail a server out in the courtyard looked like Chuck Varner's in the way it pointed, lazily then with a sharp summoning twist, the way he used to signal me to run over to him at the end of a drill that I'd messed up. I looked down.

CHAPTER TWO

―――――

B LANCHE," CHADWICK SAID, as soon as we sat down at the bar. "You really do look like him. Better, of course. You should be in front of the camera more, you absolutely have a face for it. But you're definitely Chuck Varner's kid."

It was cool inside and the bartender, who had both a neck tattoo and a bow tie, was close, two good reasons that I hadn't chosen the courtyard just behind us. I was able to test bow tie's listening skills right away, too.

"You call me that again and I'm out of here, got it?" Chadwick smiled and the bartender looked over at me, a quick eyebrows-up question that I answered with a nod and open-handed "it's okay" gesture.

"How about every time I say 'Blanche,' you promise to mentally tag on your real last name, so you know what we're really talking about."

"I'm getting to the point. I want this to be about your dad. About Chuck Varner's killing spree and its aftermath. My article will be about the shootings and what they predicted about our America, right now—I've already talked to an editor at *The Atlantic,* she's interested—and the doc's about the aftermath."

"Someone already wrote the book on this. A pig named Jill Gudgeon."

Chadwick's cheeks pulled upward in a tiny flinch that he converted into a smile. His good looks didn't sit on him well—the gym muscle, the tan, and the too-blue eyes, all were like features he was trying on for a few years before he could comfortably sink into soft, pale invisibility. "We both know Gudgeon didn't get it right, though. Especially her writing on you. You come across a little—"

"Creepy. I know. All children who are half-smart come across as creepy when you write down what they say."

"So Jill Gudgeon got your voice right?"

"Selectively, yes." I was lying. Jill Gudgeon had gotten me exactly right. My memory, shaped by Chuck Varner's drills on recall, concentration, and calculation, had kept my childhood alarmingly intact, and I remembered those talks with Jill Gudgeon. Her ghostly thinness moving through our trailer, in dresses that cost more than all of our furniture. The questions, delicate and subtle, that I eventually started to answer, only realizing how subtle she was being when my intelligence and experience caught up to her years afterward, when I read about myself in the book my mother had forbidden me from opening as long as I lived with her.

"So it's accurate, but you still hate it?" Chadwick asked.

"Of course I hate it. It kept Chuck Varner alive when he would have just been another forgotten shooter." Which is exactly what my mother hoped the book would do, exactly what she conned that smart Vassar-schooled writer into doing for her. "It glorified Chuck Varner, made him into some sort of avatar of working-class struggle turned to evil. White-trash Lenin with a rifle. He went from a couple of weeks in the news cycle to having his mug shot on T-shirts," I said. Chuck would have loved the T-shirts; Crissy relished seeing them in the wild, said that their value as a teaching tool was incalculable. "Made him a folk hero to the right kind of loser. So a big no-thanks to all of this, Emil."

"I'm with you," Chadwick said. "You have to see that. I think Gudgeon's book is trash, too, and of the worst kind. Pretentious, highbrow garbage, the kind that pretends to take a somber look at the American vileness that crime comes from so that liberal arts majors and society wives can *tsk* disapprovingly while they glory in the blood and poverty."

Chadwick looked as smug as the book he was describing, but it didn't make him wrong. "Borderline right-wing and definitely misogynistic take, but I get your point," I said.

"If you're hearing any misogyny here, I assure you that it's just my feelings toward Jill Gudgeon that you're picking up on, not your gender in general."

"It was the 'society wives' thing."

"Oh. Sorry." He held up his hands in an inadequate second of apology. "Listen, Gudgeon's not important here, other than as a counterexample of what I want to do with our project. Look, just for example."

Chadwick pulled out his wallet, a streamlined fold of brown leather, and dug around in the compartment behind his credit and debit cards, among the receipts and customer loyalty cards that normally took up this netherzone. He took out a card that had once been red, but was now a dusty pink splotched with white, like diseased skin. When he flipped it over in front of me, I had to control my natural recoil, pretending that I was just rearranging my skirt.

"I got two of these on eBay. This one was in the worst shape, already lost its value, so I carry it around for moments like this."

Chadwick looked proud. Ugly proud with a grin too big for his face, the way Chuck Varner looked when his first order of these cards came in from the print shop. He'd told me that I could keep two for myself but only if I put a hundred of them under windshield wipers outside the movie theater. No one would stop a cute five-year-old girl from flyering, he said. He'd patted me on the head. Chadwick looked like he wanted to pat me on the head, too, when I finally leaned forward to read this visiting card from the past.

The Varner 6

1. Chaos is our natural state. Violence reminds us of that.

2. Leadership is essential, even in chaos.

3. Obedience = Faith.

4. Spread our laws through action: keep your allegiance secret.

5. There is no justice or peace in civilization. Only in chaos.

6. The only order in chaos is death.

"That Jill Gudgeon was able to miss out on this in her book," said Chadwick, shaking his head, "that she breezed over the manifesto that your father mass-printed—well, that just shows the caliber of research she was willing to put into the project. She told Crissy Varner's take on the story effectively enough, I suppose, but that's it. Gudgeon never understood what your father was trying to do—to spread tentacles, to install believers in a grassroots way at first, and then take his teachings national through the Harlow Mall shootings. Gudgeon was shortsighted, and that's why she didn't understand what Crissy Varner was telling her."

"And what was that?" I asked, knowing what he was going to say.

"Chuck Varner was a cult leader, not just another spree shooter. You know and I know that he was more than just another killer. At the very least, he was an impatient Manson, let's say, one who liked to do his own wetwork."

"Keep your theories in your doughy head," I said, quickly realizing that I was whispering. "And take this poison away. Manifesto, god. It's fucking nonsense. Crazy, evil nonsense," I said, louder. The fleshy card, its edge damp from condensation, started to waver in my vision as I remembered Chuck Varner making me stare at it until I could recite it back to him, word for word. Each mistake meant I had to run around the trailer park five times, one for each year of my age. He'd deliberately left off the seventh rule: that had to wait until later, it couldn't be part of the initial pitch. It was where he explained what faith and obedience meant. The seventh rule was what he said to Crissy and to me every morning and every night. Your Life Is Mine.

Chadwick slid the card into his shirt pocket.

"I'm sorry. It was impolite of me to dive right into speculating before asking you more about what you think. You feel like leaving, don't you?" Chadwick asked.

"Absolutely." I looked into the courtyard for the rest of the body that had been attached to the arm that reminded me of Chuck Varner's, then forced myself to look back at Emil Chadwick. I couldn't start losing the focus that had kept me steady for years, right when I needed it most. I buried the fear in the same place I kept the memories, let it descend from a boil to the constant simmering horror it always was.

"If you do, I want you to know that's fine. I'm not restraining you here in any fashion, of course. But I have an article ready to drop that details your personal history and suggests, in a fairly ugly fashion, that you are exploiting the Marigny killings as a slow build to your own true crime opus, which is going to be an apologia for Chuck Varner and for the media's treatment of spree shooters in general. I have a contact at the *Times* who owes me and might allow me to slot it in as an opinion piece on true-crime-media-gone-wrong, maybe piggybacking off the most recent school incident. So that's what happens if you don't hear me out."

"You're a total piece of shit."

"I can be. But I don't want to operate that way. I want to go the *Atlantic* route, and I want us to do an honest, fully formed piece of work together. After my feature article is polished—an honest one, about how you transmuted trauma into your work, we work together on a movie. We talk to Varner victims, the families. Your origin story, made by you."

The drink was too good to throw in his face, so I took Emil Chadwick's phone off the bar and sank it into his half-finished beer. He yanked it out and started shaking it.

"Jesus. Shit," he said.

"You want me to go from two decades of no one knowing I had anything to do with that monster, to me making it some sort of explanation for my entire life?"

"It is, though, Blanche. Chuck Varner's a big part of your story. I know Jaya would agree—she must have been pushing you toward doing this story in little steps since you started making these movies together, no? Maybe even since you moved in with her and her mom, what with what happened to her family?"

"No." I stared at him. "Jaya has as little interest in exploiting her father's death as I have in exploiting my father's killings. And there's a big difference between what Chuck Varner did and Mr. Chauhan taking a dumb mugger's bullet. Jaya's dad didn't ever make a step wrong. Chuck was despicable." I started pressing on my hip bone with my thumb again, willing a knife or a gun to fill my hand, Jaya's name in this creep's mouth now worse than hearing him say *Varner* over and over again.

"It's two sides of murder, but it's still murder, right? I know you two are both reaching toward something in your work, that it's happening now. You can't keep away from true crime because both of you *are* true crime," Chadwick said. He set his disabled phone down, giving up.

"Try a bag of rice," I said, wiping my forehead, trying to push the violence I was imagining out of my brain.

He kept going with his theories. "You come from where you come from, you emancipate from your mother, you immediately make best pals with your sidekick whose dad wasn't a shooter but was shot—"

I thumped a fist onto the bar. Chadwick twitched and shut up.

"You think because her dad died that we have some sort of divine bond that was driving her to trick me into making a documentary about Chuck Varner? You truly are a moron, Chadwick. We're friends because we're friends, not because we're in the Dead Dad Club."

"And you're telling me that your distancing yourself from the Varner name doesn't ring out to you a little like someone running from the story she was always meant to tell?" Chadwick asked, taking a sip from his pint that he paused halfway through, remembering and maybe tasting the phone that had just come out of it.

"I ditched the name because of how little it meant to me, not how much."

"Look at the movie you just made. You were born to document and explore murder, and you didn't inherit your eye for that from Mom. Condolences on that, by the way."

"What?"

"The inheritance thing? I thought it was pretty elegant and clear."

"No, 'condolences.'"

Chadwick started worrying at the phone again.

"That's what—that's what I was talking about when I said 'a crime in the present.' The investigation we'd—the Stilford police haven't called you?"

"No one back there has my information. No one. I made sure to burn the trail from my old name to this one any way I could, legal and otherwise."

"I can't believe this. I'm sorry." For the first time since the movie theater, Chadwick almost had appeal again, because he looked authentically lost and sorry. "I'm just going to tell you straight: your mother died last month. Not naturally."

Chadwick didn't only tell me straight, he told me fast, stuttering in his haste to get the sentence out. I stared at his glass of beer until it started to blur. A creep of nausea started somewhere below my stomach.

"I just saw her," I said.

CHAPTER THREE

H I, BLANCHE. HUMIDITY'S awful, isn't it?" Crissy
Varner said. The crew was all still in the house, packing gear
after our final B-roll pickup shots. It was the end of our last day of
shooting. All I had with me in that Marigny street was endless heat, a
bougainvillea bush, and this specter in front of me.

Crissy looked almost the same as she had the year I left home. Just
barely older, showing only in her hair, which had grayed out from the
shade it had once been—the same brown as mine. Poorer, maybe, her
clothes more worn and frayed than anything she would have walked
out in public with when Chuck was alive, or when I was with her. Jean
shorts, a raggedly customized red denim vest, and one of Chuck's *Entombed* shirts, so dryer-scarred that the design and logo had peeled
and cracked into a wordless red-and-blue enigma that I only recognized because I could see it stretched over my father's chest in my

memory. I was holding the Pentax I used to take on-set photos with, sitting in the open bed of the truck that belonged to our New Orleans fixer, Jerome. He was arguing with a cop one block over, explaining which permits we already had and which ones we didn't need, while we made our gear as invisible as possible.

The heat, a late-May boil of the air that shimmered even if you were completely sober, which I wasn't, made Crissy look unreal to me until I noticed her shabbiness. That's not the kind of thing you hallucinate—Crissy looked good, just not as good. I convulsively pressed down on the shutter like I was pulling a trigger, but the camera was dangling at my side, pointing at the enormous trunk of a live oak across the street.

"No," I said. It was all that would come out, until Crissy spoke back to me in the same taunting voice she used when she was teaching me an oh-so-obvious lesson, the same persuasive, patient wheedle that Chuck used when he was teaching me to aim and shoot the .22, first at cans, then at things that moved until I stopped them from moving.

"'No' what, Blanche? You can't say it isn't humid out here. It's just a fact. We're breathing so much vapor we could be underwater."

"It's 'no,' I don't want to talk to you. No, get the fuck away from me, right now."

"I know you don't want to talk to me, Blanche. I got that impression from the paperwork you had sent over after you left," Crissy said. Her eyes looked placid, in a way they almost never had when I'd been with her. As though all the rage had evaporated out of them, that her lifetime allotment of emotion was used up and she was left with either peace or emptiness.

"You really didn't need to be so official about it all," Crissy went on.

My tongue had withered in my mouth, become a dried, sour fruit that I couldn't dream of speaking with. Not being able to talk made her words soak into me with permanence, like I was listening to a sermon in a quiet church, not this bird-teeming, lush street in a forever unquiet city.

"Almost got yourself downright adopted by that Hindu family. Ran out of time, I guess, growing up as fast as you were, not being a minor anymore. Or did you ask them not to try? Thought that dropping Chuck's name, our name, was distance enough?"

"Don't come any closer," I managed, using stock TV-police-warning words as an incantation to get myself talking. Crissy seemed to have no intention of moving. I could tell, with absolute clarity, that this was how I would look in twenty years, when I caught up to the age Crissy was right now. I had Chuck's eyebrows, especially since I stopped plucking them into unnatural arcs, but Crissy's eyes and the rest of her face, jawline aside. She was squeezing that little cherub's chin while she talked to me, a nervous habit she managed to make look both thoughtful and mocking. She was standing four sidewalk squares away, the cement between us agitated and broken by the insistent roots of trees. When I told her to stop, she held her hands up and sat down right where she was, getting into a cross-legged meditative pose, lacing her right foot up and over her knee with her hands.

"I won't do anything you don't want me to do, Blanche. I never have, not since you left me. I didn't come for you, I got the message. I understand that you have been loyal to me in your own way."

"Stop," I said, shuddering hard enough that the camera slipped out of my sweating hands, the strap catching on my wrist before it could slide to the ground. "Stop talking like Dad, you fucking crazy bitch. Stop it."

"I could never talk like your father," Crissy said, sounding as meditative as she looked. The *Entombed* T-shirt was sweat-stained, but I couldn't fault her for that in this temperature. It was the white salt rims of all the previous sweat stains around her neck and armpits that made me wonder what she smelled like, when she had dropped out of the game of decent society altogether. She couldn't be holding a job in that state. "Only Chuck spoke like Chuck. Only he was capable."

I knew that. I didn't think it was true, but I *knew* it, on the level that you internalize and know things when you are a child and are given no choice to believe otherwise.

He was empty, but when he was rolling, Dad spoke like a god.

"He wasn't perfect," Crissy said, though, cutting into my thoughts. "I bet you think that I believe him flawless, your dad. He wasn't. When it mattered most, he didn't even know what he was."

"Which was?" My mind finally started working well enough that I reached for my phone, sitting next to me in the flatbed, and tapped out an SOS text to Jaya.

"A leader, Blanche. A king of men, a prince, someone who should have been at a pulpit his whole life, not behind a gun for a couple hours. He should have left that work to his followers, but he was just so eager—so purely committed to the message—that he made the worst mistake he could have."

"What was that?" I glanced down. Jaya had answered my text with a "?," which made sense, because I'd never sent her an SOS text before, and also I'd spelled it "AOS."

"You can look at your phone in a minute, honey, I'm almost done. Chuck took himself away from the world. His mission was to *assign*, Blanche. Like he did with you, with me. He taught us, prepared us, then lost patience with how slow we all were on the uptake. We were weak. You're weak, Blanche."

"You still waitressing, Crissy? Does talking like a complete nut-case hurt your tips?" I hopped down from the flatbed and walked around to the passenger door of the Chevy, never taking my eyes off my mother, her cross-legged docility meaningless to me. Chuck had taught us both how to draw a pistol from any posture.

I opened the truck door and the glove compartment, hoping that Jerome was the kind of fixer who drove around with a gun. No. Trash, receipts, and a knotted sock full of coins—useful for short-range road rage, but not for anything I might have to face from Crissy.

"Stopped last year, Blanche. I live simple and saved enough for the time I have left. Plus, I stopped having to worry about you costing me anything except pain." As though this little prod had made her aware of her current physical discomfort, Crissy stood up, massaging her knees a little before straightening up.

"Fly back where you came from, Mom. Crissy."

"I left you alone after you went because I knew you wanted it that way. I have to admit you were a great help to me, and I missed you so much when you left. You loved me. I let you and Chuck down, letting you go, letting that family take you in and help you pretend you were something else, but I knew it was what you wanted. You couldn't bear the burden any longer. You lost patience, that's all. Like your father did."

"I don't want to hear this crap ever again. I'm within screaming distance of ten friends and at least one cop." I couldn't help hearing Crissy, though. And she was getting through. My right pinky and ring finger started to shake, the way they did when I was getting nervous, or when I was about to cry. Chuck tried to teach me how to control the shake, said it would prevent me from being a great shooter unless I could get it under control.

"Still wouldn't be fast enough for what you're afraid of," Crissy said, walking a step toward me. "Not that you need to be afraid. You, of all people, should never be afraid. Chuck and I both made you *know* that. You're the most important piece of all of this, Blanche. You have to be there for the next one."

"What 'next one'?"

"For when it happens again, Blanche. Do you think that just because you left, just because I was feeble, one time, that this would all stop? You should know that's impossible." Crissy smiled at me, moved her right hand a bit. From the way she was holding her fingers I knew she wanted to brush my face.

"Your Life Is Mine is bigger than us. It's bigger than our world. We're going to do what Chuck Varner did. We're going to let the bullets loose again. You have to be there. You just have to. It's history."

"Get away from me," I said. I climbed into the truck through the passenger door and started it, with the tailgate down, my phone rattling around on the flatbed until I finally braked five blocks later and it flew off to shatter on the sidewalk. When I drove back to the house twenty minutes later, the crew was on the sidewalk with our gear, Jerome yelling at them to stow it before the cops rounded the corner again and we got a fine that would devastate our already tight budget. I got out and Jaya saw my face. She hugged me, diplomatically turning me away from the crew so I could cry for a second. They respected my work, after these weeks we'd spent together, but men on set are always looking for a way to stop respecting your power, your choices. Jaya and I both knew that. I lied and said a man had tried to drag me into his car after asking me for directions.

I knew that telling anyone, especially Jaya, about what Crissy had said about another shooting would make my mother real and present again in a way I couldn't handle. So I didn't.

CHAPTER FOUR

C HADWICK WAS STARING at me. If he'd kept asking questions while I went over those last moments Crissy had forced on me, I hadn't heard them. A few moments had passed while I was switched off in front of him: that much was clear. There was a fresh beer in front of him, in a can this time, and a small pile of napkins in front of me.

"Are those for me?" I asked Chadwick.

"I thought you might need them," he said. "Your lights went off for a second there."

"Silence isn't crying, Chadwick," I said. I still wasn't entirely back; Chuck Varner used to tune out like this, too, losing himself in fantasies when Crissy or I were talking to him, expecting us to wait until he was back to resume the conversation. When I would phase out in front of Jaya, she'd think I was doing something ineffable, something creative, in my mind. But mostly I was trying to get away from a memory of Chuck, or Crissy, or both, and couldn't until I'd relived it.

I hadn't cried for Crissy Varner since the last day I'd lived in her home. Even then, I was crying for myself, for how much I'd lost to her and Chuck. Hearing the news of her death from this stranger who also came bearing alcohol and a pile of absorbent paper, my body's only response was a weird ache in my jaw.

"I didn't think you were going to cry," Chadwick said. "Maybe spit on me or something."

I took the last of my Marlboro Lights out of my purse—I bought a case at the beginning of every shoot, and forced myself to make it last. I pointed at the courtyard, holding up the smoke, and the bartender shook his head in sympathetic apology, patting the pack of cigs in his own breast pocket.

"Out front. Sorry," he said.

I pushed my stool back, realizing as my shoes hit the floor that I was drunker than I thought, but not enough to worry about. I left more money than my drink plus tip cost, but not enough to pay for Chadwick's. Chadwick followed me, of course, but stayed under the canopy when I crossed the street to the citrus tree, poking at one of the fallen fruits with my toe. I couldn't tell whether it was a small grapefruit, an orange, or some sort of deformed lemon. The skin was pale green, alien, like something hastily painted for an old sci-fi TV show.

I'd started calling my mother "Crissy" when I was eight, and she had never corrected me. For a second I had another vision of her so vivid it made reality vanish—all I saw was Crissy, putting her makeup on to go to work out at the bar, moving her lips in rehearsal of banter with customers, seeing me behind her in the mirror and turning to laugh, surprising me to the point that I didn't think to laugh with her until she'd already stopped and turned back to her mascara job.

I stepped on the thin green skin of the fruit on the pavement and it burst, pink. I lit my cigarette and walked back to Emil Chadwick.

"Go on."

"Your mom was shot with a small-caliber handgun. Home invasion, they said."

"Trailer invasion," I said, seeing if some deadpan would knock away that pain in my jaw.

"They got the kid who did it. Some opioid crisis statistic."

"You have a name?" Chadwick shook his head, but I could tell he was lying, holding back until I gave him something or begged him. Whoever the kid was, he wasn't just some home-invading stranger. That would be too random, too tidy, too much a part of the Chuck Varner preaching of chaos, and not the actual chaos that Chuck and Crissy made: violence that they themselves fueled, that they carried out. Crissy must have known this kid, the shooter. She would have taught him, tried to make him her instrument. And he'd killed her. She could never just die by accident. Not her.

"We'll pay for the ticket when you go down there," Chadwick said. "Me and my backers—which I already have, I want you to know. This is all paid for as long as you plan on bringing a camera."

"No."

"Blanche, you *are* the story I'm doing. You, your dad, your mom. You can either be in control of it, or you can be the Difficult Subject in my movie and my article."

"What happened to the napkins and sweet concern, Emil? You have to stick to whichever act you pick, or your subject is guaranteed to be difficult."

Chadwick took out his wallet and dug around for a card again. This time, it wasn't the Varner Six.

"Here," he said, handing me a Stilford Police Department business card for a Dan Maitland, with an additional number written on the back and cell in brackets. "This is the only person who's been able to give me any information at all about your mother's death. The department there is an organizational nightmare and they're at the crest of a ten-year steady rise in crime. So now you have a contact. Helpful enough for you?"

I took the card, turned and blew smoke away from Chadwick, and started to follow it, walking through the cloud and picking up speed.

"Blanche," Chadwick called. I stopped, didn't turn. "Happy birthday, Blanche."

"It's not my birthday."

He had nothing to say to that.

"It's the anniversary of the Harlow shootings, Emil. The important part of research is getting it right when it matters."

"Your mother told me it was your birthday," Chadwick said. I could tell he was shaken for a second, as though he were surprised Crissy would venture to lie to him.

"She told everyone that my birthday was the day of the shootings. But only her. So you talked to Crissy?"

"Months ago, once. Yes. You want to hear more, come back in and sit. You need to, Blanche. I don't think your mom is the end of this, not for a second. Lives are at stake." Chadwick wasn't walking toward me, but he reached with his right hand, then let it fall, not knowing what gesture he could make that would summon me back. "People could die."

"And I'm sure you hope they do," I said, walking away. I wasn't going to let Emil Chadwick see me cry, for obvious reasons, and for a less obvious one. He'd think I was mourning Crissy Varner, which just wasn't true.

I was crying because I felt safe.

CHAPTER FIVE

THE DAY CRISSY Varner got back from New Orleans was also the day she died. When she was looking at the gun, in the few minutes she talked to The Boy, wondering if she was supposed to beg to stay alive, wondering if she had planned this far at this level of detail, she decided that he hadn't waited for her to see Blanche one last time before killing her. The Boy wasn't the tactical type, more of a grand-design fellow. Which was one of the things that made him both a flawed and perfect successor to Chuck: they were just alike. While this moment wasn't a surprise to Crissy, it hadn't come when it was supposed to. But it would still work.

She'd set down her one suitcase and taken her sneakers off, and was walking toward her bed when she noticed The Boy's Timberlands on the mat by the door. He wore these boots year-round, like a lumberjack or a drug dealer. The Boy had vain habits, a desire for a precisely constructed look, but Chuck had suffered from these as well.

"Hi, Crissy," The Boy had said. He was in her bed, lying down, and from the sound of his voice, just woken from a nap. "I found a way in."

"Do you need something from me? I was going to update you on Blanche tomorrow, but I suppose I could now. But I'll be keeping it short. I need sleep. I need to prepare, and so do you," Crissy said. The air felt impossibly dry after her brief time in Louisiana; every breath felt like it was going to start a nosebleed, not much different from the arid, oxygen-light mix of air on her discount flight back.

"Aren't you going to ask me to get up?" he said. He was still in the darkness, but she could see his socks. White, clean, new.

"I shouldn't have to."

"I know. 'Get out of my bed unless I'm in it with you.'"

"I've been helping you. Helping you get rid of something that bothered you."

"Yes, my disease of virginity. My thanks, good lady. But that was just the first time, wasn't it? What about the rest? My transference lessons, right? Physical education."

Crissy forgot about her weariness and, for the first time since leaving Blanche, remembered her authority. Now wasn't the moment to let go of it; The Boy would need to remember her this way. And she needed the dignity of it, the command, in order to really make her way through these moments with the strength others had always thought she had, and that she eventually accepted she did have. Crissy walked the few steps toward the bedroom's faux-wood sliding divider and wrenched it open.

"Why are you talking to me like this? I suggest you think, very carefully, about your response, and about all of your behavior. If you are drunk or high, I will forgive it this once. We are on the edge of a major step forward, and—"

"Yeah, the Your Life Is Mine Olympics, around the corner," The Boy said, sitting up. Crissy was momentarily ashamed of the state she'd left the bedroom in. Clothes on the floor, a slightly overflowing trash can. Either she'd left the fan on or he had turned it on when he'd come in—it had blown some of the contents of the ashtray onto the floor by her desk, right onto the up-facing cups of her second-favorite bra. The shame snapped back into anger that The Boy had violated this space.

"You're mocking the most important gift Chuck Varner gave the world, which you happened to be lucky enough to be given in turn, and you're violating the sanctity of the home that I shared with him, and that I've opened to you. You leave. Right now. Exactly this minute."

The Boy got up from the bed, a fluid motion in which he barely used his hands and never used his elbows. A great distance from the wriggling, rolling movements Blanche used to get out of the same bed, after the distortions that time and a career on her feet had manifested in her spine.

He'd grown up beautifully, had taken every physical measure and discipline that Crissy told him Chuck would want. He'd obeyed and it had resulted in this sharp, dangerous form, a shape that needed to be draped in baggy clothing to ever look harmless. The Boy, standing naked in his socks, was what Chuck had imagined, yet had never been able to forge in himself. But Crissy had. She'd cut this stone out of the soft young flesh that had turned up at her door in 1996.

"Why aren't you dressed?" Crissy said.

"My clothes are in a bag by the door," said The Boy. "Don't worry, it's not sexual. Quite the opposite. It's to ensure cleanliness."

"Oh." He had thought of details that she wouldn't have thought of herself, necessarily. "This is why you're catching me right off the plane."

"You're armed every day of your life, and I don't want to have a shootout. Just an ending. Getting you right after airport security is my way of making this—"

"Cozy. For both of us." This is where the begging should start, Crissy thought, before feeling a pang of pride so severe it could have been arrhythmia. She wasn't worried about herself, not at all. "You have to promise that you're not just abandoning all this, the way Blanche did. That's the only thing I couldn't take, and you have to re-member that it's the only thing that—"

"Don't tell me, Crissy, what Chuck would want. You never even really saw him work. Doesn't that ever stick in your head? You're a placid, smug sow. You think you're his, his John the Baptist. That his project is graven in your soul, that it's your purpose. But no. This life is just an accident. It's all that you can do. You stumbled into an im-portant role through no virtue or talent of your own, and here we are.

"You're a waitress with a power complex. A flake of scrap paper that blew near a flame. Exactly the kind of empty, idiotic woman that thinks she's a creator when she's only a vessel. Your purpose was me. Me and Blanche. And you've already half-failed.

"Chuck would want me to be with her, but it's me who has to bring her back in, not you. You couldn't even anchor her to her path when she'd seen Chuck's greatest hour, when he'd shown her how it could be, and how we could get there. The blood. She's seen the blood, so she knows. It's you that disgusted her, you that drove her off the path. You've only ever been a petty criminal, Crissy. A dumb accomplice. You're exactly what we don't need."

Through the insults, the accurate ones and the ones that were baseless, woman-hating garbage, fueled probably by websites that Crissy had ordered The Boy not to visit knowing that he would seek them out as soon as he was alone and that they would help to shape him to a purpose, she cried. What she would keep to herself, what she would never share, is that the tears came from an ecstasy of fulfillment. Of having done everything exactly right, of working this situation for over twenty years just the way that Chuck would have wanted her to. A solution to Chuck's absence that was so elegant she had always felt his hands behind The Boy, pushing him toward his fate along with her.

The Boy didn't ask her anything about her tears, in the end. He didn't ask her anything at all. He stood in front of her and told her to kneel, to demonstrate her acceptance. Crissy wondered for a second if he was hard, if he was going to ask her to do something to him before he killed her, but shook the thought out of her mind as disrespectful—not to The Boy, but to Chuck. To Chuck and herself. This creature with the gun and the rage was their creation, the perfected child they hadn't been able to forge genetically. He was so angry, but so controlled, twenty years of anger and teaching and focus coming together. He really was Chuck's creation, as she had ensured he would be. The Boy took the gun out from beneath the pillow, pointed it, and asked her to look at him.

"No," she said. She closed her eyes and imagined Chuck, tall and naked, holding this ugly little gun, wishing that it was his sweet Beretta. He loved that gun.

The Boy kept talking as Crissy prayed to Chuck for peace.

"This next one is going to be what Chuck dreamed, Crissy. Not just a few people shot and a couple of days on the news. Blanche and I, we're going to make enough bodies to convert anyone who's paying real attention. They're going to hear Chuck's name. They're going to hear his message."

Crissy kept praying, in her own way. Every evening since Blanche left, for an hour, she had tuned out and communed with the Chuck she remembered, before he became a prophet. When they were young, before Blanche, before this constricting set of rooms where they would both live the rest of their short lives, before the project became the only thing that Chuck wanted to talk about. To her, at least. He probably had spoken of other things, to other women.

She spent all her praying time in the before. Crissy ambled through a memory that placed her and Chuck on the bench outside Raleigh's Books & Records, kissing and daring each other to throw ever-larger rocks at the big display window. Crissy started them moving up incrementally from the nail-clipping-sized pebbles around the feet of the bench to slightly larger rocks, but it was Chuck, storming off into the park as though he was mad at her and returning with a grin and a palm-sized stone that he calmly sailed through the plate glass before grabbing her hand and starting to move as the alarm wailed, who ended the game. He always ended the game.

In the cramped, hot, ugly, and unchanging trailer, The Boy was still talking. As though he would never stop, the way Chuck could just keep talking and talking when he came to grips with his role, when he truly began to believe in himself.

"You're not Chuck," Crissy said to The Boy. It did stop him talking. "Even Chuck wasn't Chuck. But he was better at all of this than you are."

Crissy didn't know if she believed what she'd just said, but it was nice, for a last moment, to be unsure of exactly what it was she believed. Chuck, or someone, or no one, granted Crissy silence, after one incredibly loud sound.

CHAPTER SIX

DIALED JAYA AS soon as I stopped believing in the safety of a Crissy-free world, which took about two minutes. I didn't turn to see if Chadwick was following me, but in the traffic-free silence that set in one block north of Fela Cafe, I would have heard him coming.

"He knows," I said when she picked up. "That Chadwick guy just drilled me about Chuck Varner for an hour. I don't want this, Jaya."

"I know he knows," Jaya said. It was quiet behind her—either she was in the washroom at the Carver, or she'd ditched the screening. A flush gave me my answer. "I looked him up. It's his mom."

"What? It's my mom. Crissy's dead, and I had to hear it from some exploitative fuck who wants me to help him make a movie about it."

"Oh, no. No," Jaya said. "Wait, let me get outside."

I heard the rush of voices as she walked through the lobby of the theater, heard her name called out a couple times. I'd walked four blocks, clearing the paved roads and entering a little field between several squatty buildings: small disused factories and an old school converted into offices and apartments. There were loud frogs and old train tracks around me, tall grass and puddles. I sat on a broken parking median.

"You ready?" I asked.

"Yes. I'm so sorry, Blanche. I love you. I'm so sorry."

"You know exactly how broken up I am about this, Jaya. I wouldn't have chosen to hear about it this way, and you can be absolutely sure the cops in Stilford are going to know that, but I've been free of that woman for years."

"It's still—I mean, she was your parent, you grew up in her home—"

"Jaya, you were born with parents. I had genetically similar creatures in my home. This is not a mourning thing, it's a fact thing. Crissy's dead."

"I understand," Jaya said.

I didn't think she did, and I wasn't ready to do the amount of explaining I would have to for Jaya to truly understand what Crissy was. In over ten years of the closest connection I could imagine having, I'd never been able to speak fully to her about what Crissy was. What I was, even.

"What's this stuff about Emil Chadwick's mom?" I asked. There was a pause that the frogs filled with their mindless, thrumming music.

"Jaya? Still there?"

"I don't want to load more on, Blanche."

"I don't think the condescension of the only friend I have in this fucked-up world and business is going to soothe me."

"Emil Chadwick is Jill Gudgeon's son. That's why he knows all about you. His mom wrote the book on it. On you."

"That bitch," I said. Of course. Jill Gudgeon had written to me once when I was at USC, sending the letter c/o my department, addressing it to *Blanche (Stella) "Potter."* The department secretary, a trim, aging man named Tom who often provided students with usefully embarrassing anecdotes about our professors, recognized Gudgeon's famous name in the return address, but didn't get the *Stella* reference. He'd only read Gudgeon's Warhol book and her memoir of AIDS in early '90s Castro, SF, which I had also read and had to admit was pretty good, even if she had no business being the one to write it. I threw the letter away unread, first opening the envelope and inserting a banana I had in my bag, crushing it into the text and tossing the mess into a campus dumpster.

"Which one?" Jaya said.

"They're both bitches. His mom at least gave up trying to rope me into a follow-up." The frogs had gotten louder, the force of their croaks loud and unified enough to become choral. An amphibian soundtrack behind this discussion of reptiles.

"I looked Chadwick up after you left. He used to write scripts for podcasts, which, I guess everyone has to start somewhere, and he started his career trying to bury that connection to Gudgeon. Except when she opened doors for him to get work, I assume. He got floated a book contract a couple months ago. That's the gossip. Mix of a mom memoir and true crime gossip."

"Jaya? You were right. This is too much. I'm going back to the hotel for the night to process this shit. I have the minibar and half a bottle of NyQuil waiting for me." There was a shake in my hand, the one holding the phone, and I steadied it using one of the mental tricks Chuck had taught me, shutting my eyes for three seconds and focusing on my pulse. The flutter went away, but the feeling of Chuck's hand on mine didn't.

"Please. We can't be flip like this, Blanche. Not now. We have to talk for real, okay? She was your mother, and no matter—"

"No matter what, Jaya? I can't—you of *all* people know this about me," I said, stamping my right foot hard when the nervous shake turned up there. "That thing was my mother and Chuck Varner was my father and that's *why* I'm talking to you like this and not sobbing about how it all hurts. If I start with that I'll never do anything again, do you understand?"

"I do," Jaya said.

I let a buzzing silence build, thought about saying more. But I couldn't, not without losing it.

"I need to get to Stilford," I said. "I'm changing my LA flight as soon as I hang up with you."

"I'm coming with," Jaya said.

"Not right now. You can't. I need you to make sure they don't take our next movie away. I'm not going to let Crissy derail the life we made together, now that we're finally actually doing it. So you get back to LA and tell Rod and Jarod—tell them I'll do another one of theirs right after they get us development funding for our Blackwood movie."

"I'll do that if it's what you need from me, but I don't like leaving you to go back there alone. So then I'm driving up to Stilford, Blanche. Once we get your business sorted, we can give an inspiring talk in our old AV class, get Mr. Walley crying about how big of an influence he was on us," Jaya said, doing her best to get some jokiness into her tone. About forty memories of our years in high school together converged on me at once, and I slid down the median I was sitting on, settling on the cool broken pavement.

"I love you, Jaya. I'm going alone for now, but I will need you, you're right." Even if this wasn't true, I knew Jaya needed to hear it. And it might have been true.

"You going to stay with Mom? You better."

"No," I said. Padma Chauhan's house was the first and last sane home I'd had in Stilford, since moving in a few weeks after leaving Crissy's trailer for good, after a series of planned run-ins that confirmed Jaya and I as friends. It wasn't hard—Jaya was reeling from the very public loss of her dad and her newfound celebrity status at high school, where murder gets you quicker notoriety than a leaked nude. I knew I could help Jaya and that she could help me, and Jaya's mom was so shattered and suggestible at the time that taking on another kid, first unofficially then legally, seemed as good an idea as any in a world where waking up barely made any sense anymore. We all pretended our way into being members of a family.

"She's going to be pretty hurt," Jaya said.

"That's where you come in. Tell her what happened, why I need to get my head around it before I can cross her threshold and hang any of this shit on her. I want to be able to smile and hug her and mean it. She'll get it."

"Blanche." Jaya's voice shrank, the way it did when she was about to get more sincere than either of us could handle.

"What?"

"Would you think about not going there at all? You said it, you know—she's not even really your mother anymore. Can't we just forget it? Let it go, let the city handle it?"

"It wouldn't be right, and you know it. Think about what Padma would say."

I didn't add that it wasn't the past that I was going there to seal up—it was the future. The future that Crissy Varner had opened up with the follower she'd found. The one who'd killed her. The one who almost certainly wouldn't stop at her.

"I want you to be around for the next one," Crissy had said, just a few blocks from where I was now.

Now you won't be around for the next one, Crissy, I thought, thinking of the bodies hitting the tile floor of Harlow Mall twenty-two years ago. She'd missed that one, too. Crissy was always jealous of that, and didn't do a good job of hiding it. That Chuck had made me his official living witness, not her.

I kept walking after I hung up, shunting from memories of high school to those of Jill Gudgeon's dry, cool hand around mine in the Harlow Mall, when I was a little white-trash kid who had never seen the ideal crescents of a manicure that close up. The stuff I said that day to freak her out, all the real things that Chuck told me, I can still remember, and while Gudgeon changed all of Crissy's speech into a Manhattan-imagined pastiche of uneducated rube dialogue from the South and the West Coast, she didn't tamper with the way I spoke to her. The quotes were right, just everything around it was sick. Gudgeon spun me, made me story. Used that awe-stricken prose of hers to make me the inheritor of Chuck Varner's crazy, some sort of low-income Damien just waiting till I was tall enough to see through the window of a bell tower with my junior three-quarter-sized scoped rifle.

Emil Chadwick had his mother's eyes, I thought, as I looked over my shoulder for a moment to see if he'd followed me. There was no one there.

A frog hopped out of the grass, onto the sidewalk in front of me. I lifted my foot and thought for a second about crushing its soft-boned body with as much ease as I'd pulped that citrus fruit before I left Emil Chadwick behind. It hopped back into invisibility in the grass before I could finish the thought, or the step.

CHAPTER SEVEN

Excerpt from Last Victims: The Varner Spree Killings, *by Jill Gudgeon. Morris & Connington, 2000.*

The little girl is all limits. I've come here and talked to her mother every day since I arrived. Eighteen and a half hours of tape. But Stella, which is what I'll call this daughter of Chuck Varner's: she's a closed bud, waiting for the bees to leave.

I am the bees, and that's plainly evident to me when I'm talking to the mother. Crissy McKee, or Crissy Varner, as she insists on being called. She had her name officially changed after the shootings, making herself Chuck Varner's wife in death, saying that it was that way when he was alive, anyhow. "I was and am his wife. In flesh and in spirit." The daughter doesn't go by McKee or Varner at school, Crissy says. "I'm 'nonymizing her to the public. But at home she knows who she is."

The girl is made even smaller by her system of containment. I saw her looking through my bags at the front entrance the first night I drove into Stilford from Los Angeles, when I came by Varner's house before checking in to the hotel. His home is a trailer, just as I had envisioned when I read about the killings, about Chuck Varner. I was ashamed then of how classist it was of me to assume. While much of the population here lives hard, most of them do so in dilapidated homes, in apartments that advertise weekly rates and have thick-chested men who collect the rent in smudged envelopes that jingle. But Chuck Varner did indeed live in a trailer, and I like to think that when I saw him there in my mind, it was insight and not prejudice that lent me the vision.

There's no air-conditioning, or if there is, Crissy doesn't use it. Dogs, a few chained and some roamers, bark intermittently outside, provoking shutups from their owners. Crissy asked me if I wanted a drink and I said yes, as I always do when I'm offered alcohol and I'm away from my home, from my own child. Crissy didn't ask me what kind, just made me what she was drinking: gin with three teaspoons of frozen Minute Maid lemonade concentrate, a bit of water, and ice. I knew innately that this was Chuck's drink, his personal cocktail. An oversweet punch.

Stella stole all the tapes from my bag on my fourth day in Stilford. I didn't bring it up with Crissy when I made the discovery, in her Datsun pickup, its color a delicate interaction between the original maroon and overtaking rust. My journals were still in the purse, both of them, the rubber bands undisturbed, as though written words were protected by Stella's code of privacy and acceptable violation in a way that the spoken ones on my tapes were not. If I really were prejudiced, I'd have assumed that she just couldn't read yet: but the girl's mind is incandescent, a glow of intelligence in her haunted home.

"This is where he took the first one," Crissy said, pulling over on an overpass. She mimed reaching into the back for a rifle, a particular rifle—Chuck's AR-10, long since vanished into whatever canal or sewer Crissy said he'd tossed it into in 1996, in the hours between the highway shooting and Harlow Mall.

There were no cars coming toward us, nothing behind—for a glimmering moment, in the warm Malick light before the sunset, I felt afraid of her. The highway beneath the overpass wasn't much used, even though it was newer than the one we'd driven there: a disgraced remnant of the state and city's infrastructural reach in a direction that citizens and commerce hadn't wanted to flow.

Crissy could be withdrawn on most topics, and stunningly ig-norant on others ("If we go round the sun once a day and spin the whole time, you think anyone could drive straight?"), but on Varner's massacre, she was voluble. Sometimes I thought her igno-rance was playacting, her truncated words and gaps of knowledge flitting masks that her intelligence burned through whenever she forgot herself. She was absolutely eloquent when she spoke of the combination of chance, psychosis, and artillery that had allowed Chuck Varner to murder eleven people in Stilford on August 17, 1996.

"Chuck used to lie under the tarp of his truck with his rifle for hours. Every day. Top peak-heat days, especially, when it was hard-est. He loved that. He'd practice being invisible, vanishing totally, and I'm telling you, he made it. I'd know he was out there, parked right in front of the kitchen window, the barrel pointed into the room. Stella playing with her dolls between me and his Ford—all I could see in back of the truck was cinder blocks, rebar, some, you know, light bumps. Nothing big enough to be human, nothing moving. Chuck was skinny, you know, beautiful skinny, but no one could get flat as he was back there except by magic or hypnotizing anyone who looked that way, in a snap.

"If I stared long enough I'd still never see him, but I would see the hole."

"The hole?"

"The black at the end of the gun. It's darker than the rest of the dark around it. If you concentrate long enough, you can see it. Chuck taught me that."

Crissy broke into this odd, gothic timbre after a few minutes of talking about Chuck, but these were clearly her own words, not some leftover programming of Chuck's, like the treacly lemonade cocktails. She's good with language, good at seeing. Not as bright as her daughter, but perhaps she once was. I began to grip what it was that Chuck needed from both Crissy and Stella, how they fit into his aspirational project. Crissy provided both structure and absolute faith. And if Chuck had held on to this world, if he'd anchored himself as the leader Crissy insisted he was instead of losing himself in murder, Stella could have been his ideal acolyte. A more appealing teacher than her father, whatever the lesson was. Crissy had tried to explain her dead husband's thoughts on chaos, his "Your Life Is Mine" lyrical nonsense, but she never managed to articulate what made Varner's code at all special, or even a code, as opposed to a scattering of cool-sounding one-liners.

The tiny cab of the Datsun was sweaty, despite Crissy's window being rolled down and mine entirely absent, kicked out last month from the inside by Crissy's pistoning thighs and calves, her feet in Chuck's steel-toed construction boots, a cheaper workaround to fixing the broken roll-down mechanism, she said, adding that she'd make a new window out of packing tape when it wasn't summer anymore.

After ten minutes of silent waiting that Crissy didn't explain, a hatchback appeared on the highway below us. Crissy grinned and clapped once. Then remembered herself, who she was with.

"So he would have done it today, too. What he told me when he got home afterward is that he posted up here intending to wait fifteen minutes, exactly. 'A clean fifteen,' he said, and if no one, no car showed up in that time, he was going to take the AR-10 apart, drop off pieces along the twenty miles of road back to town, turn up at the hospital construction site, and ask for work starting the next day. Decide what to do about his teachings after a couple of months of thought-killing hard work. But someone did show."

"He came home after the first shootings?"

"Sure," Crissy said, uncertain for a moment, then back into the flow of her telling. "After he got rid of the rifle, he came back to talk to me, to Stella, a last time. I told the cops, they knew it. Just not the papers. He didn't tell us he was going out again to do anything, though."

"Didn't you guess? What else did he do at home?"

"Talked some and split," Crissy said. She didn't elaborate, but smiled again.

The Dillons were the predecessors to Varner's performance in the mall. George Dillon, a sixty-three-year-old ex-Army North Dakotan and devotee of the lost highways of America, took the one and only round from the rifle. It splintered on impact with Dillon's skull, flowering, steel shreds twisting off and passing through June Dillon's cheek and up into her brain. George was dead before their car hit the guardrail, but June, a city heritage and restoration advocate with a mail-order yarn business, didn't die until after their car flipped and flamed up.

At the mall, Chuck used a Beretta 92FS, an effective, frequently police-issue gun that was still modest next to the portable cannons widely available in California gun stores. He killed his last nine in a forty-second stroll through the main concourse. Each shot was close, as Chuck nestled the muzzle into rib cages, backs, stomachs, the bodies acting as silencers, powder burning polo shirts and halter tops. Mel Kronstein's polyester shirt would have melted into his lower back: a witness saw it flame up, but the blood that gouted out extinguished the blaze.

I was, all this time, being slow-baked in Crissy's car, thinking of my own child at least once a minute. Listening to Crissy, back into full eloquence now, talking Chuck alive again with every sentence. Chuck, who pressed a gun barrel into the warm bodies of two small boys and one girl as compact and pure as his daughter, Chuck who found the surface over organs that he wanted to pulp into malfunction, who pulled the trigger and made those bodies cold.

"That's what people have to remember about Chuck," she said. "He wasn't 'an independent actor'—what he called it. Chuck read a lot of JFK/Oswald stuff—I'll show you the folders he made at the house. He had so many good ideas. But for his own work, Chuck was making sure that it all fit with fate. There was every chance that the Dillon man and his wife wouldn't come by when they did—but they did."

A black Trans Am topped the horizon on the highway Crissy and I were still staring at, and she laughed. I did, too. Not spontaneously, but to lock our connection in deeper. Crissy trained her pointing index finger on the Trans Am just as it was about to speed below us.

"Pop," she said, displacing the bang I'd been hearing in my head since we left Stilford.

———

As I sat on that overpass with her murder-channeling mother, Stella was listening to my voice on the garage-sale *DuckTales* stereo in her tiny bedroom. When we returned, I found her and pressed Eject, Scrooge McDuck shaking a downy fist at me from above the tape. Stella assented silently to the reclamation, sparing me the trouble of asking for the others by opening a shoebox hidden in her laundry hamper.

I took the rest of my cassettes, wondering briefly if they'd been wiped, taped over with Art Bell broadcasts or FM hard rock. I recognized, looking at Stella, who had turned to face the wall above her desk so she didn't have to look at me, that the girl gave up the tapes so quickly because doing so meant I wouldn't have a good reason to stay and talk to her.

———

On Saturday, Crissy Varner had a noon to midnight shift at the bar where she worked. She de-Varnered herself with a tartan skirt and surprisingly good makeup. "There's a sitter usually," she said, "but I figure since you have a kid anyway, you know how this all goes." We, all three of us, knew that Crissy was lying: no one ever sat for

Stella. Small, internal, so quiet she seemed either developmentally delayed or rich with ancient wisdom, she took care of herself on Saturday and for most of the rest of the week.

"Of course, Crissy. That would be a waste. I'd love to stay in with her, I could get some notes typed up."

I took Stella to the Harlow Mall, the sign a vivid teal swoop visible from the highway. When we drove closer, I could see the garlands around the base of it, both fresh and rotted. There'd been a minor scandal in the news when Harlow had their security guards clear away the memorial blooms six weeks after the shootings. They were replaced, and since then, they'd just had to stay there, without any signage. We went in, and I reached for Stella's hand simply because she was there and the same height as my son. She took it.

Stella knows what her father did, Crissy has told me. Sometimes I wondered how much Stella knew: more than her mother had revealed to me, I was sure of that. I'd been consumed by a wish to see her moving in the space of Harlow Mall, alive with commerce—DVD players, sneakers, swimsuits—and the ghost of Chuck Varner's closing act. The management had replaced all the tiling in the atrium after the massacre, when every media outlet in the country outside of prime-time network television ran aftermath shots of the blood, pooled and sprayed over the green floor, the mingled liquid of victims that had to be pressure-washed off after staining the public consciousness. The new tiles were pale yellow. Scuff magnets, but far from the crimson and mint of our collective slaughter recall.

Stella was carrying a small clutch purse, a thrift-store find that would have netted fifty dollars in a vintage store in New York. She let go of my hand and walked a few paces ahead of me, and I was ready to catch her if she ran. She stooped to pick up a dime I hadn't seen, feeding it into the little mouth of her purse. I let her keep walking: I was only obliged to watch her, and I could see her. She cleared a small crowd of shoppers, young Asian girls, entering a small oasis clear of people but rich in sun from a skylight. She stopped, and I could sense that she was waiting for me, in the way that I used to wait to be approached at parties, at bars, when there was a particular man nearby that I wanted to meet. Looking slightly upward, absent, not really in the room, floating just out of reach. I went to her.

"Daddy was smarter than you," she said.

"Oh yeah?"

"And smarter than all the people in here. He called it the collection house, this place. He would get me a cinnamon bun and talk to me for a long time, away from Mom. She didn't know anything. She still doesn't know anything."

"What would he talk about?" I asked. Stella was looking into the dark of her purse, poking at the dime there, and the hair clip with frogs on it that I'd watched her put in before we left the trailer. There was no dirt or lint in the lining, just perfect black.

"He'd talk about these people. How they might think they wanted to be here, but they didn't really. They didn't want to be anywhere. He said he was going to help them."

CHAPTER EIGHT

I SAID WE DON'T know where the decedent is *right now*, Ms. Potter. That likely means the remains are in transit, and not even between facilities, just midtransfer in the morgue and as-yet-not refiled. The info'll pop up on my screen the minute you leave, probably."

Officer Dan Maitland leaned back in a chair that clearly wasn't his, pulling his shirt down and taut, with a conclusive nod. We were far from concluded. I put both my hands on the desk, near a framed photo of a family that I could tell wasn't Maitland's, and stood up. My phone was recording all the audio in case I wanted to use this conversation later as a reference, for when I dumped all the parts of this that I was ready to tell on Jaya and we decided what to do.

"Finding the body is important, and yes it is ridiculous to say that out loud. But it's also beside the point of what I asked you, Officer. Was the autopsy perfunctory, or did you actually look for a cause of death that wasn't necessarily in line with what you arrested that kid for?"

"There was a bullet in her head, Ms. Potter. I'm sorry to put so fine a point on it, but that's what we saw at the scene, and that's what the autopsy extracted. And the suspect isn't a kid. He's a seasoned small-time criminal who escalated petty theft into a spate of bolder break-ins, and then graduated to home invasions. We have a lot of that around here these days, I'm afraid. Most of the time it doesn't go fatal, thankfully. Not thankfully in your mother's case, I mean—"

"I got it. Am I going to get to speak to him? Or is he going to be mis-filed, too, maybe via getting nightsticked to death in his cell?" I said, seeing in Maitland's eyes that I'd pushed it too far with that last comment. Worse, it made me feel bad, because he seemed hurt, not angry, which in turn made me angry again for caring about the idiot feelings of the man who was standing in the way of me confirming, with my eyes, that Crissy Varner was dead. Maitland looked like he still had a bit of innocence in him, though he must have been working through the rising flames of opioid hell and cutting his teeth on the kind of thorny Stilford domestics that happened every weekend, in which the caliber of firepower under the mattress was sometimes the only limit on how bad things could get within the four walls of a rotted-out relationship. Maitland was small, about my height, lean, maybe half-Hispanic. His eyes were a light enough brown that they could almost pass for yellow under the hostile and artificial office fluorescents, which were better suited to illuminating oral surgery than a conversation.

"It's far from typical for our department, or any other, to let family members speak to those suspected of murdering their relatives. So, no, you won't be speaking to him, except via some pretty remarkable circumstances."

"Is it typical that I also don't get to speak to the detective in charge of the case? That I've been handed off to a, no offense, lower-ranked stand-in?" I did mean offense. I wanted to see Crissy dead, badly. I needed to know the exact reality I was contending with, and this little functionary was standing in the way. This was another trick I had for controlling myself, one that Chuck hadn't taught me, but that I'd taught myself after escaping him and Crissy: as long as I was focused on the one problem in front of me, the rest of the horror around me couldn't collapse in. It had been surprisingly useful in getting my movies made. And right now my one problem was finding Crissy.

"This—the department isn't asking for indulgence, but some level of understanding is required for us to communicate effectively here. There is a detective on this case, Ron Pargiter, and he's excellent. I assure you that he's overseeing every detail of your mother's case, and that I'm checking in with him frequently, but the volume of homicides this year is such that our detectives have been using qualified officers for detail work, while overseeing the investigations as a whole." Maitland emphasized the last few words, pulling his lips into a flat, serious frown that looked completely ridiculous.

"So any open-and-shut killing that seems vaguely drug-related and doesn't involve anyone making over $50K a year gets offloaded to the nearest uniform cop," I said. Maitland's lips opened and I had a vivid sense of how many times he would call me a cunt when talking about this encounter after I left. When it was clear he wasn't going to answer, because it was equally clear that I'd gotten it exactly right, I went back to the suspect.

"I'm not speaking to this suspect—what's his name, anyway?"

"Vernon Eagle Reilly."

"God. He never had a chance at not being permanent trash with that name," I said, still standing but trying to lessen the tension by a few percentage points so Maitland wouldn't go into full informational lockdown.

"Maybe he should have changed it," Maitland said. The wall behind him was papered with Missing posters, a fairly even blend of young women and young men. Some had small blue ballpoint checkmarks in the upper right corner.

"I have no intention of speaking to Reilly as a bereaved daughter. I'm going to speak to him as a journalist and documentarian, for the purposes of a film that I'm making on the death of my mother." I took over stare-down duties from Maitland.

Maitland sighed. A long one, an older man's sigh.

"If you're recording me, Ms. Potter, you are doing so without my permission. And I don't want to have any legal dealings with you, because frankly, as I've said, we're stretched thin as it is."

"I know that," I said. "I lived here for eighteen years, Officer."

"And then you left," Maitland said, a little edge to it. "Things aren't the way they used to be when you were—"

"Fine. So the city went bankrupt a few years ago, so as a direct result you can't find my mother's body, and you're an underqualified officer working this case, and you're pretty sure that you're going to hang up any investigating from here on out because problem solved, there's someone in jail and that's that."

"We strongly believe that the suspect in custody is the person who killed your mother, Ms. Potter," Maitland said. "Is there any particular reason you're reluctant to accept the man who was seen with a gun outside and inside the residence where your mother was found dead as her killer?"

"Because it's not simple with her," I said, speaking before I had a chance to think. "It was never simple with her, just like it wasn't with my dad. Did you do that much research, at least? You know who you're looking at? Whose body you lost?"

"I'm aware of your family history."

I've noticed something with people when they talk about mass killings—not just Chuck's, but any of the ones in schools, Manson, Jonestown. There's disgust, there's shock—but there's also a note, a tiny note, of reverence. Not for the killer, but for the event. Maitland hit that note of reverence, more than I thought a cop familiar with the banality of murder would, casting his eyes down for a moment and touching his eyebrow in what looked more like a miniature salute than a scratch as he went on speaking.

"There's no chance that I, or anyone else in the department, would hold what your father did against you, or use it as a reason to treat the investigation of your mother's homicide with anything less than our maximum—"

This had me halfway to the door before I knew it was happening. I turned, grabbed my purse strap, and starting pulling down on it, hard, keeping my hand there so I wouldn't stick my finger into Maitland's face.

"I'm not begging you to do your job even though my dad was a piece of shit. I'm telling you you're not looking deeply enough into this. Did you check, thoroughly check, to see if this Vernon Reilly had a preexisting relationship with my mother? Did he know her?"

"They may have crossed paths, but there was nothing significant. Nothing he's told us, nothing we can verify," Maitland said. He was starting to get the look, not in the eyes, but in the hands and brow, the skin just above his cheekbones and below his eyes, that you get used to chasing in interviews when people are deliberately holding back from you. Chuck Varner had taught me to look for it when I was in the first grade, made me sit in the passenger seat of the Chevy and study him talking to teenagers outside the 7-Eleven, the way he would lean into them when they started to scratch their faces or pretend to squint up at the sun or down at the pavement. Chuck would shoot me a quick smile when his subject first started to cave, when the opening was made. When people are pursued, they start to fuck up. Then they start to apologize. Then you can ask something of them.

But being a cop, Maitland probably knew all of this, too. Soon his eyebrows and forehead were smooth, and his hands were invisible below the desk.

"Crissy wasn't stupid, Officer Maitland. She wasn't altogether sane, and she was a bad mother, but if she wanted to hide her ties to someone that she had planned something criminal with, she would do a very careful job of concealment. And I'm telling you that the person who killed her is someone she would have known in advance. If Reilly isn't that person, then you have the wrong guy."

"Ms. Potter, do you have a specific reason to believe that your mother was murdered by someone in particular? Have you had recent contact with her?" Maitland, trying to wrangle back control of the interview, had altered the tone of his voice, coming across with a reasonable impression of a smooth, conversational interrogator.

I shook my head, sure now that they hadn't made even the slightest effort at an investigation away from the crime scene: Maitland hadn't checked Crissy's credit cards, seen her flight to New Orleans.

"So there's absolutely no chance that your mother was a victim of a random break-in, of which we had about twelve thousand last year? There's no chance that she was in her home at the wrong time, that she said the wrong thing, that some skeeve with a burnt-out brain killed her because it seemed like the simplest solution to his problem? No chance of that?"

I was quiet, and eventually, I sat down again and let Maitland finish his small lecture, while I evaluated whether there was any sense to what he said. If he wasn't going to listen to me, I could at least listen to him to find out exactly how stupid or how smart he was.

"We want order, Ms. Potter. Humans, not just police departments. People like you and me want situations to make sense, we want life and death to come with reasons. Sometimes we lose a grip on what we know just at the moment when it'd be most useful. Like with your mother, here. These situations—these crimes that have no reason, nothing personal, just an alignment of economics, bad luck, and a bad person—they don't have any order to them. You add grief to all of that, and well . . . all that's what you're having trouble with."

I had my answer. Maitland was at least as dumb and lazy as he was condescending, and he had no intention of putting in an extra second's work on a homicide case that he'd borrowed as training-wheels practice from an equally uncaring detective. Especially if the cost was only the freedom of a repeat offender with a silly name.

"Okay," I said.

"That's all?"

"As in, I'm going to process what you said and there's no point in me answering you right now, Mr. Maitland. Officer. I'm going to get back to the more directly useful interview work I've been doing."

"What interviews would those be?" Maitland asked, looking at the ceiling. He'd missed a line of dark stubble to the left of his Adam's apple, and another patch at the right angle of his jawline.

"Chatting with your citizens about murder, police competence levels, that sort of thing. Local color." I hadn't done any such thing, but

I wanted to leave Maitland with something unpleasant. He did look pained.

"I'm sorry to hear that you haven't found this conversation useful. And I know it's frustrating that we can't bring you to your mother's body right now, but I promise that we'll resolve that situation quickly. Is there anything further you'd like to know about the case at hand that I can answer for you, Ms. Potter?"

"You say Reilly had an escalating break-in pattern. Are you sure this is his one and only murder?"

"We have him on some assaults, no murders. Mostly scraps in public, the kind that would be barroom fights if the parties involved were drinkers instead of users."

"You don't think it's worth looking into whether this killing fits with any home-invasion-type shootings recently? Whether my mom's one in a line?"

"There's no call to put any zoomed-out conspiracy theory on it. Your mother was an unfortunate victim of unfortunate circumstances and a desperate man who had already committed three smash-and-grabs at the same trailer park. He was witnessed entering the scene, he's our perp, and there's not much of a story there."

"I'm going to tell you something that you're not going to listen to, Maitland. But I am going to say it out loud in this police station so we can both know that I did what I had to do and said what I had to say."

"Please, Ms. Potter. And I can tell you that I am 100 percent listening. I understand that you're bereaved, that this added stress—"

"I'm not bereaved. Think a hostage is bereaved when the person holding her gets shot in the head? I'm there right now, but before the relief part enters into it. Because I don't know what happens next, I just know that this isn't over. I don't mean the grieving isn't over, I mean the killing isn't. Okay?"

"I understand but do not exactly agree, Ms. Potter."

"If my mother was killed for a nonrandom reason—if she was killed by someone who had any interest in Chuck Varner, and in his cult bullshit, then there will be more killings. Probably all at once. Probably a spree." I didn't tag on that Crissy had visited exclusively to more or less warn me that there was going to be another shooting, because I didn't want to give this fake-caring cop any reason at all to keep me under watch or to forge a reason to put me in jail. Not that it seemed like he'd be willing to make that effort.

"I'm hearing you, Ms. Potter. I really am, and I care about what you're saying." Maitland ended with the universal cop slang for "fuck off": "We'll look into it, I promise."

"Give me a call when your computer error that misplaced my dead mother like she's an order of highlighters is resolved, all right, Officer? I never wanted to come back to this place and I don't want to stay for an hour longer than I have to."

"I don't blame you for that. Obviously I wasn't on the force when it—when your father—happened, but I was around. A kid. And for all this—I want to apologize. For not finding you, or following the paper trail on this. We knew your mother had a daughter, I just didn't know it was you. I've seen your movies."

"I didn't know they got around up here," I said.

Maitland grinned. "Your moving away doesn't make Stilford Mars, Ms. Varner. Ms. Potter. We've got computers, we've got VOD. We even have a populace that takes an occasional interest in matters be-yond college and pro ball. I thought *Mainline Dosing* was very good. I just wish you'd make something like it here in Stilford so I could make a better case for us showing it in schools."

"I make documentaries, Maitland, not War on Drugs PSAs for you to scare ethnic kids with," I said. He flinched again—not with his body, not even with most of his face, just a drawn-in movement of the skin just beside his tear ducts.

"You don't seem anything like what I thought you'd be, Ms. Potter."

"What gave you any idea of what I'd be, Officer?" I asked, guessing the answer before he could come up with one himself. "Jill Gudgeon's book? You read that piece of shit?"

Maitland simultaneously apologized and confirmed with a small nod.

"It's a true crime book set in my own city. I sort of had to, Ms. Potter. Why'd she call you Stella in the book, other than to protect your identity, of course?"

"Blanche, Stella. *A Streetcar Named Desire*. She was both lazy and wanted to make it as easy as possible for everyone to guess my real name. Anything else?" I wasn't about to offer anything more up, not from the past, at least. I could already guess how Maitland would tell this at some cop bar—*She's Chuck Varner's daughter, for real. Something off there.*

"We'll want to ask you questions," Maitland said. "Time and place stuff. I have no doubt that you're accounted for and out-of-state during the time of your mother's—happening—but I need to type something into the file."

"Get me the body and I'll get you your information. And I want to sit down with Reilly. I'm going to talk to him whether you facilitate it or not."

CHAPTER NINE

OUTSIDE, WALKING TO my rental, I considered driving right back to LA. It had been a bad summer for forest fires, and the smoke that had settled into the valley Stilford shared with a few other cities, towns, and the agricultural heart of California was hazing the air, making breathing a caustic experience. Five hours to the south was my existence as it stood before Crissy embedded herself back into it with her death. I could regroup, make phone calls. Get Jaya to hold me and promise not to talk for an hour, minimum. Order delivery to the shitty apartment I was going to be gentrified out of unless my paychecks started catching up with the neighborhood. I could turn off the lights, flush my phone down the toilet. But it was useless to go back until I buried this, the way I hadn't when I went to Jaya's house instead of dealing with Crissy directly when I was sixteen. I could have stopped her poison—Chuck's poison—then.

"Your Life Is Mine," I said to the steering wheel. Chuck used to sing it in a death metal rasp in his truck, pounding the steering wheel, once slipping and snapping the windshield wiper toggle right off. He'd let me tape it back on as one of my special jobs, giving me a Payday bar when I was finished. Dad. He told me to only call him "Father" or "Dad" when I was four, said that "Daddy" sounded creepy.

"You were the creep for thinking any way that made it creepy, Chuck," I said. A memory shot back while I changed lanes, of him ripping my booster seat out of Mom's Datsun and throwing it farther than I thought any human who wasn't on TV in a uniform with a ball could throw anything, the little cushioned hunk of plastic bouncing off the closed lid of the trailer park dumpster. He didn't want teenage boys thinking he had a baby—it didn't match with his recruitment talks.

"They can know I have a family later, but not right away. The boys, the girls, both of them. Can't give that game away. They get close enough that they get into the car, Crissy, means that they want a new father, one who'll concentrate on them, on teaching them, on loving them. I'm offering these people unconditional love and a chance to control their own futures. They need to see me as singular, and in some cases, that means single. Unattached."

Crissy nodded that night. I think I remember Chuck's voice, his words, so well not because I was bright, but because he'd so often begin and punctuate these mini-manifestos with violence. Always just a gesture, always just objects. He never marked us, Crissy or me.

And I remembered that speech about the car seat, every word, because I knew he was lying. He wanted it out of the car so he could pass himself off as single, yes, but not to potential followers. He'd tell the women he talked to when we went on our little nighttime ventures while Crissy was waitressing that he was the visiting cousin who'd gotten saddled with babysitting, but he didn't mind, because look how cute, look how docile.

I was excited to spend some time with Chuck. He'd usually get me ice cream or lemonade while he trawled for women on the beach boardwalk, wearing a half-buttoned cotton short-sleeve, always blue, over his permanent white tee. He had a teenager's narrow, shallow chest his whole short life, as pictures proved. To me he always looked enormous.

When Chuck had luck with a woman he'd get me a second ice cream or lemonade and drop me off while he went with her to a hotel. I'd never told Crissy. Chuck's command not to wasn't voiced, but it was clear. I was afraid of breaking a promise to him. Almost all of his promises, in some way, demanded silence. The cheating, the base pettiness of it, was incompatible with the Chuck we kept alive in our home afterward. She probably knew, anyway. It wasn't something she ever would have told me.

I turned the key and reversed away from the station, almost grazing a cop cruiser I didn't notice in my blind spot.

CHAPTER TEN

T HE BOY WATCHED Blanche leave the station and get in her car. The Boy, The Boy. He was still wary of using this name, either as a self-referent or, even worse, passing it on to others to use on him. But Crissy had insisted that this was Chuck Varner's preferred name for his messiah, for The One Who Would Come After.

Lying in Crissy's bed one night, about five years before he killed her, they'd talked it through in detail. It was one of their Proximal Transference nights, another Chuck Varner term that had fallen away between them as they started to sleep together more often. But in the beginning, Crissy had told The Boy the story: she'd come home from work early once, and seen Chuck in bed with a girl from the high school that Blanche would eventually attend.

"The girl looked nothing like me, that's how I knew that Chuck was being straight with me. That and that he always was," Crissy said to

The Boy. "She was this little skinny nothing with black hair, very dusky, almost, you know. Just not Chuck's thing. He told me that physicality could be a part of teaching, especially to the young—that knowledge, the true knowledge, could pass through naked bodies in proximity. That just being in bed together didn't mean anything coarse. That congress had multiple forms."

The Boy hadn't thought to laugh when Crissy had first told him. It was exciting for him to lie down next to Crissy Varner's nude body, an excitement that had been enhanced by the need for total control: he had to stare at the ceiling, to listen to what she said with absolute attention, ready to take one of her pop quizzes at any moment as he stared at the odd false wood-grain wallpaper on the ceiling of the trailer. They'd lain together, had their "chaste congress," for two years, before Crissy allowed it to become something else. Always initiated by her, always with her in control. Every time they lay down together, he had to stay limp until she touched him, or risk being ejected for a full month, a penalty that Crissy had only had to enact twice. The Boy was proud of his ability to control himself, to manage a body part that was as disobedient as the heart or lungs for most men. But not Chuck's Boy.

That name was what they spoke of on that evening five years ago. "Chuck's Boy." It seemed undignified, The Boy tried to suggest. Not the name of a leader.

"The Child is the Father of the Man, Chuck always said. The dignity is in your purity of purpose. Especially raised as you have been."

"Didn't he also use 'The One Who Would Come After'? Doesn't that have more weight to it, Crissy? I'm asking for the followers we don't have yet, not for myself," The Boy said, his hands flat on the even flatter mattress beneath him, a relic that lay upon the slats of the trailer's bed like a length of single-ply toilet paper resting on railroad tracks.

"You're asking out of pride. Out of a need to escape the boyhood that Chuck Varner wanted his greatest descendant to always dwell inside. That need is your devil, do you understand? Blanche couldn't find the humility to know and dwell in her place, and that's how we lost her." Crissy's speech always became more formal when she was upset, and reading emotion was where the mattress's paucity was useful. The Boy wasn't allowed to look Crissy in the eye when they were in congress, sexually or otherwise, but he could feel her shake with pleasure or twitch with grief through the cotton and latex. When she talked about Blanche, the mattress moved with sobs that were choked back before they could even become sounds, let alone moist ones.

"Do you think we could get her back?" The Boy asked. He almost risked taking Crissy's naked hand, touching the naked thigh next to it, but didn't. He let his smallest finger graze her left hand, as though by accident.

"Blanche could never properly leave. She's bonded to Chuck and her fate in a way that's beyond me, and definitely beyond you, to understand," Crissy said. She didn't take The Boy's hand, but did rest her palm on his cock.

"But will she come back of her own will? Do we need to bring her back?" The Boy asked, not knowing until he said it that he was making a plan. He put his hand over Crissy's, suggesting movement. She swatted him away and put her hand back where it was, still.

"Life will bring her back. Not a request, not a phone call, not an invitation. Life, Chuck's plan. I promise that. To you, that promise is a prophecy, but to her, any promise from me sounds like a threat.

Because she's weak. She's not like us, Blanche. But Chuck couldn't have been wrong about her. She was just part of his one mistake: dying. Blanche needed more time with Chuck to become what she needed to be."

Crissy got up and hovered over The Boy, knowing that as soon as she sank down onto him that neither of them would be willing or able to keep talking. She waited until The Boy gave the right answer.

"Chuck is still here. He's alive in us. Blanche will have more time with Chuck as soon as she understands that. As soon as she's with us, she'll be with her father again."

Crissy eased The Boy inside of her and he started to have sex with her, with total physical presence, tailored to the often spoken and detailed demands of the only woman he had ever been with. But for the first time, his mind wasn't in the act at all. Fucking Crissy wasn't a pleasure or a duty anymore. It was no longer part of Chuck's plan.

Crissy hadn't known it, but Chuck must have always known about this phase. The Boy couldn't have come to understand the plan so well unless it had been ordained. Crissy had just issued Chuck Varner's orders to bring Blanche home, and there was only one sure way to summon her.

Crissy, that day, had ordered The Boy to kill her without even knowing she had. That was how they could bring Blanche Varner home. To her proper place, at the center of the great, definitive killing, the one that would finally cement Chuck Varner in the American mind and the world's consciousness.

Outside the station, The Boy watched Blanche Varner start her car and started his own immediately afterward. Blanche Potter was such an odd name to choose, he thought, but perhaps not as odd as The Boy. When they were together, she would revert back to her true name, and he would finally graduate into his. As soon as he made everything clear to Blanche, The Boy would start to call himself by his true name. In barely more than a day, when the next great demonstration was complete, he would call himself Chuck Varner. And the world would listen.

CHAPTER ELEVEN

I WAS AIMING FOR my first home, and not the motel pass-out I badly needed. They were in the same direction, the trailer park just off the West Side Freeway, but I blew past the Arcadian Inn and kept going to the park. Jaya called while I was driving, making my cell rattle around in the cup holder's parking meter change. With an immediate purpose, I wouldn't panic. Without it, I'd end up wide awake on that motel bed, thinking about rifles in towers, handguns pressed into people in a crowd who would, at first, think they were only being nudged.

They'd renamed the park: Underwood, it was called now, a nice new blue sign out front that looked deliberately retro, like living in this place was a quirky decision and not the result of insurmountable financial hardship. When I passed the gates I saw why.

"Sweet rebrand," I said, driving past gapped rows of RVs that flanked the entry path, leading up to the central office that old Mr.

Kindt used to haunt, chasing boys and girls around the park with strips of mosquito-blackened flypaper while laughing. He was mostly friendly, we thought, but his interest took on a nastier edge when the kids verged into teenagehood, enough that Maddie Ryder's dad had once had a baseball-bat talk with him. Alfred Kindt, bald and with a pate that was always peeling, never properly able to take on a tan, had no interest in me until the After Chuck era, when he talked about our fictional bond to any reporter who came asking.

"Dead by now," I said to myself, just before Kindt came out onto the porch, scratching flakes from his skull into the backward tiara of white hair that still circled his head. He didn't wave at my car, just watched me drive toward the back of the place, where I was confident I'd find something closer to what I'd grown up in.

Yes. Past the tourist RVs, past the new and hey-not-so-bad mobile homes, was the place I remembered. My old home, a rotten core of ten overpriced and barely maintained, week-to-week renter trailers, the economic engine that kept the lights on in the landlord's house. Kindt's boss, whoever it might be now, didn't make credit checks on renters in these rectangles, these human storage units. You just paid at the beginning of the week, every week, or were evicted on the spot. Kindt would have movers, of a sort, waiting behind him as he roved around, taking the envelopes. The whole time I lived in the park, from four years before Chuck's death right up to age sixteen, there had never been a Monday morning without a forced eviction.

Farther down the drive was where the lifers lived. Twenty mobile homes that hadn't gone anywhere for decades and wouldn't go any-where until they were disassembled. Chuck used to call it *Septic Acres,* referencing a disaster that happened when I would have been about three. One of his running jokes with Mom.

"With Crissy," I said, biting the word off. Crissy. Emil Chadwick would be delighted to hear me sinking into the forced habits of childhood, giving this family treatment to the woman I'd been forced to grow up with. Another chat with Chadwick and I'd be calling Chuck "Dad" again.

I parked in front of lot 7B, if that was what it was still called. If the address was on the door, it was covered with one of the ten or so strips of duct tape that blocked entry, as though the cops had run out of the yellow crime scene tape that now hung, snipped, from the four posts that had been erected around the trailer. The duct tape looked like a Kindt touch.

The grass was high back here, and as I got out of the car, I stopped, staying quiet for a moment to see if what I'd noticed was just temporary. It wasn't. It was quiet out, even though it was four p.m., prime time for the kids to be tearing around out here, letting their parents sleep it off or have sex or, in the case of the roughly 40 percent of steady, sane, substance-free families, make dinner, watch TV, and prepare a balanced lunch to be loaded into a paper bag for the next morning. There were working poor families in this place, normal folks with aims for themselves and their children. Pretty much what Crissy and me looked like to anyone who didn't know about Chuck, who didn't hear Mom talk about him: a waitress with a forty-five-hour workweek and her precocious latchkey daughter. Just a pair of decent people working toward a brighter future.

If anyone still lived in the three trailers near Crissy's—and the recent McDonald's wrappers and Del Taco bags suggested that it wasn't totally abandoned—they were older. Quiet, no kids, small interior dogs. The new No Dogs signs that had dotted the property had been obeyed, by the sound of things: no barks, no coils of shit, even back here.

I hadn't consciously taken my video camera out, but it was in my hand—the little Pentax I always had with me when we were shooting a project, the one I used to pick up B-roll ambience that I'd play for myself at night when I was thinking about shooting the next day's subjects, whether they were interviews or places. It helped me see better, watching what I'd shot and walked around in on a screen back in my apartment, or a motel room. Nothing seemed real, or at least multidimensional and fixed, until I'd seen it this way.

I circled the trailer, watching it on the monitor. It had gotten a paint job since I left, a cerulean that had likely been closer to the sapphire blue of the Underwood sign before a few relentless years of sun had eaten the color up the spectrum. I breached the line of the cut police tape, getting close to the walls and windows of the place I'd grown up in, where I'd listened to Chuck Varner speechify and my mother praise him, where I'd wondered how much I'd have to disobey him to get a dose of the violence that he talked about carrying out against the people who'd wronged him every day—the beatings and the coffee-burnings, the acts of vandalism and minor terrorism that he bragged about to me before the big day. I'd never tested him, not once, which seemed impossible for a child. But it wasn't. That level of awareness of danger, of caution, didn't just come from being smart. I used to think it came from faith, from the knowledge that Chuck was righteous, that his violence was something he was entitled to.

But after living with the same feeling with Crissy for the next decade after Chuck's death, I came to know that that kind of awareness wasn't born of belief. It came from being terrified, from morning until bedtime, of knowing that only by stepping exactly right in every waking second around the person that you thought you loved were you guaranteed to survive.

I tripped over a car battery I hadn't seen in my sideways amble around the trailer, but fell like a true shooter, holding my right arm and the camera up high above my head, twisting my body so my back would hit with full impact, keeping the Pentax unscathed. A patch of starved, yellow grass scratched against my lower back as my T-shirt rode up. Twenty years ago there was a good chance it would have been a broken bottle.

There was a flash above me that I thought was the camera firing off a shot when I gripped it to make sure it wasn't broken, but I knew the light was too small and localized when I was collected enough to sit up again. It was a glint off glass in the hills west of the trailer, probably off a dirt bike's windscreen. I could see little trailing dust clouds from a few bikes buzzing around over there, one thing that hadn't changed since I was a kid—I remembered Billy Vaughan asking me if I wanted to ride on the back of his as a twelfth birthday present, saying no, and grabbing the bike for a ride of my own as soon as he got off and had his back turned.

Wiping myself off, I went to the side of the trailer. Someone, not too long ago, had spray-painted something four letters long in green that had then been poorly covered up by some rollered-on dull brown house paint, the same shade as the fencing that separated the lots from each other in the RV section at the mouth of the park. This part of the trailer faced the hills and the eventual sunset, and the bright afternoon light allowed the neon of those four letters to shine through the paint: Ylim. Your Life Is Mine. Crissy never would have put this on her own home; it wouldn't benefit anyone. So someone else had: a Varner true crime fanboy, at best. A follower at second-worst. And, worst and most probable, Crissy's killer. In black Sharpie just below the window, someone had written "Psyco Bitch." For that one, the suspects were infinite, limited only by how many people the unwashed last version of Crissy had encountered who were accurate judges of character.

I shot video of it all, then walked to the trailer door, climbing the few steps. Someone, probably Kindt, had rubbed soap on the windows on this side to prevent anyone who wasn't going to make a little effort from looking in, and no one had. Just to the right of the door was a puffy sticker, pale pink and featureless now. It used to have a rainbow and a unicorn on it. Crissy had gotten it a few months after Chuck was gone.

"This is for you, Blanche," she'd said, still in that abstract voice she'd used for a while after Chuck died and before she'd built herself into the apostle she believed he'd want her to be. That hadn't truly happened until her interviews with Jill Gudgeon opened her up again, got her thinking about Chuck's Path, about our future. In the year between Chuck's death and Jill Gudgeon's first letter, Crissy had been a ghost, almost silent, barely looking at me and certainly never touching me unless she had to. After Jill Gudgeon, Crissy found a way to live: by becoming Chuck's ghost.

I owed Jill that, at least, both sides of it: she'd brought my mother back for the few years I was going to have to endure her anyway, making the occasional nice days we had together possible, as well as putting Crissy back on the road that had ended with her dead in this trailer. I pulled the sticker off, gently, but it tore anyway. Crissy must have superglued it up there: the cheap adhesive this thing had come with would have dissolved decades ago in this weather. On the back of the sticker was a key, just where Crissy told me I'd always have a secret spare.

I tried it on the door and it opened right away, swinging inward on hinges that moved too easily, like something had come loose. The stink rushed out at me first: decay, but not human. Garbage. Red light from the sunset behind me poured into the trailer, bringing dim illumination to the mess.

"Hey," a man said, from the dead silence behind me. I made a weird grunting noise that would have been a scream if I were better hydrated and dodged into the trailer, turning around when I was in the kitchen, realizing I was scrabbling for a knife only when Mr. Kindt came in with his hands up. He laughed.

"You don't have to worry," he said. "Didn't call no one. Recognized you. Next of kin. Remember how I set up that pool for you and the other littles back too many years now?"

Despite his decent vocabulary, Kindt was the ideal form of a certain kind of Northern California male, a sort of nostalgia-trash they don't make here anymore, and that for a long time must have been a simulated fusion of Vietnam vet and Haight-Ashbury these men cobbled together from images they'd seen in magazines and on TV. His belt was a piece of rope, his jeans ancient but clean, the shirt blooming with tropical flowers that had never grown on this planet. He was standing closer to me than even the confined space of the trailer called for. I did remember the pool he'd set up for us kids back then, and how Crissy didn't let me swim in it after the first time, telling me it wasn't up to the dignity Chuck would have wanted from me to splash around with our neighbors barely dressed.

"Hi, Mr. Kindt. Can you give me a little room?"

"Sure can. I just stand close because of my hearing, don't like making people speak up. I can just stand back here a pace and lean if you're willing to yell, though. Was it Darla? No. Rose."

"Blanche," I said.

"Can't forget a pretty name like that. Kind of thing that a slave ought to be whispering with a 'Miss' in front of it while she waves a fan over you." Kindt did back off, but I kept tight against the counter, set the camera down, and moved my right hand over to my back pocket to grip my phone. If I had to, I could bring it down hard onto the bone just under his eye. I'd done that once to a mugger when I was drunk and stupid enough not to just hand over my bag, maybe ten years ago. He'd taken the purse anyway, but left bleeding.

"You remember me, Mr. Kindt? I'm impressed."

"I remember all the old residents, even if they come back looking different. And you were here until you were what, sixteen? Turned into a lady quick, left us all in your dust."

I let that hang in the air. Kindt flipped the lights on, illuminating the conditions of Crissy Varner's former existence. "They wouldn't let me clean it up," he said.

"Once they got the body out."

"And the brains and the splash, yeah," he said. "Sorry," he added, not looking up at me. "I knew it was that Reilly. Told the cops about him lots of times, even called in when I saw him roaming 'round earlier that night, sort of driving by slow in his Pontiac. They don't listen to me."

"They did afterwards."

"What?"

"They listened to you. That's why Reilly's in jail, right? Because you put him there."

"I didn't put no one anywhere, just said what I saw and that's that." Kindt got trembly around the lips, like he was one question or poke away from divulging something closer to the truth. If he was all Maitland and Co. had to go on other than some security tapes that didn't come anywhere close to covering Crissy's trailer, I would be even less friendly during my next drop-in at the station, and insist on seeing this Pargiter, the detective who had dumped the case off on Maitland.

Kindt had been coming closer to me again as he talked. He hooked a right in the narrow chamber and sat down on the unmade bed, which wasn't curtained off as it was when Crissy and I lived here. The curtain was now a brown plastic divider, drawn tight to the wall. I'd always cared more about privacy than Crissy had. She never worried much about nakedness, and once Chuck was gone, no other man set foot in this place while I was there. Other than Jill Gudgeon, barely anyone had—Crissy just learned to fix anything that broke, or left it broken.

"Get off that," I said. "Stand up."

"What? This here's a rental unit, sweetie. I'm the one to be telling you where you can and can't go," Kindt said. He circled a hand around on the mattress as he spoke, not exactly in an inviting way, but close enough that I wanted to jam the heel of my Converse into his gappy teeth. I gestured to the side of the trailer.

"When did that graffiti turn up? The letters you painted over?"

"Dunno. Sometime after your mom died, I guess. Asked the cops if I could at least clean that up, they said yeah."

"Did they come down and take a look first?"

"Nah. I just told them it was some letters, nonsense, that we have kids tagging every goddamn thing around here unless I'm on night patrol with a floodlight."

"Who'd you talk to? Got a name on the cop?" I asked, but Kindt didn't answer, poking instead at a crusted orange food stain in the carpet with his toe. The unique glow of powdered cheddar from mac 'n' cheese.

"They took both my spare keys for their investigation, too—didn't think to look around for whether your mom had a spare, or I would have been in here to do the proper thing and get this place in decent shape again."

"Ready for turnaround to the next renter as soon as possible," I said, more bitter than I thought I'd be at this place I had no nostalgia for being passed over to another tenant as though it was a place to live, and not a tomb for Chuck Varner's cult and my childhood.

"If you want to get cynical about it, Blanche. Now can I have that key you used? Don't think you've got any right to it."

"When I'm done, Mr. Kindt," I said. The cheese stain was illuminated by light pouring in the window that faced the hills. Kindt was between me and the window now, so I passed close by him as I walked over, looking out at a view that I had memorized from the time I was tall enough to see out of this pane of glass until I escaped. Kindt was within groping distance of me, but that meant I was in punching range of him. It wasn't the light that was drawing me to the glass: it was its cleanliness. Absolutely pristine, inside and out, not a smudge or a smear, as though it had been freshly Windexed. It was neater than anything else inside or outside the trailer.

Then I saw the flash again, up there in the grass of the hill. And this time I recognized it for what it was: sunlight off a lens. I dropped to the carpet and grabbed Kindt's arm, pulling him down with me. The echoing blast of a gunshot was the first sound I heard after the air came blasting out of my lungs in a cough.

CHAPTER TWELVE

W E COULDA STAYED on the bed if you wanted to move
things along."

"Shut up," I said. The glint and the sound should have come with
a bullet, or at least the sound of a ricochet, but there was nothing. A
light layer of sweat had slicked over me, the way it had whenever I
went outside in New Orleans, but this time there was an animal scent
of adrenaline in it. Any of the times I'd gone shooting with Crissy,
using an old SKS while we both thought of Chuck's hidden AR-10,
I'd instantly get this sweat going and try to conceal it from her, hoping she would concentrate on the accuracy of my work at the target,
hoping that having the gun in my hands and no one else's would help
me take hold of the fear that I'd never been brave enough to confess
to Crissy, and had never talked about with anyone else. I couldn't hear
a shot, outside of a movie, without seeing Chuck walking into those

first couple of people in the mall, and caressing them into his gun, before the bangs had everyone running. You'd never guess how loud a gun could sound in the echoing architecture of that mall.

I'd seen the light bounce from the scope, before coming into the trailer. That glimpse when I fell. There had been no attempt at shooting me then, when it would have been easy, easier by far than trying to nail me in this trailer through a window, no matter how clean the glass was. That shot was an invitation, not an attempt. A starter pistol for whatever was coming next.

Or maybe he had just hesitated the first time and missed the second. I stayed on the ground when Kindt started to get to his feet, about to warn him when he cut me off.

"This ain't normal mourning," he said, adjusting his rope belt and taking a packet of Eclipse spearmint out of his shirt pocket, likely the closest he ever got to a toothbrush. "You think your mom's accident is on some sort of repeat cycle? I'd have a hard time getting renters out here if everyone was crime-scene allergic. This break-and-enter shit happens a lot but that don't mean you've got a high chance of getting murdered just by coming in the door. Vernon Reilly came here to rip her off, didn't think she was gonna be quiet about it either before or after, so he did what he did. It's sad, but that's that. Maybe she talked back, or maybe he was so squirrely from the drugs that he shot when he didn't mean to, but it pans out the same. It's over."

"You didn't hear that gunshot?"

"I don't hear shit these days, that's why I look you in the face when I listen to you. I got about 20 percent hearing left, and only in this," Kindt said, flicking his right earlobe.

"Even mostly deaf, you can hear a gunshot."

"I can hear a backfire, I can hear kids setting off fireworks, and I can hear gunshots, sure. There's plenty of all three out here most days, and if I collapsed every time one sounded, my knees would be even more gone than they are." Kindt squatted and wiggled a bit, testing his joints for lawsuit potential.

I headed to the door of the trailer, telling him I'd see him back at his office within the hour. Enough time for me to get to where I'd seen the light career off the glass, or for me to get murdered or taken away or violated by whoever it was up there.

"Lemme guess," he said. "I call the cops if you're not back by then?"

"No, you call them now," I said, giving him Officer Maitland's card. "This is probably the one you've been dealing with up until now, right?" Kindt grunted, leaving the trailer. He started walking back to his office, crossing the open yard, and wasn't harassed by any fresh gunshots.

Before making an approach to the hills, I stopped to check another of Crissy's hiding places, this one for items too large to be hidden behind a puffy sticker. It was a hollow compartment behind the coat hooks just to the left of the door inside the trailer. The wall-mounted unit looked like it had been badly installed, sticking slightly out on one side, but it had actually taken Crissy seven tries to get it stuck on perfectly. I remember the day she did it, keeping me out of school with a fake cold so I could assist her. She'd been wearing one of my old T-shirts as a bandana, and when it got too hot as we worked, she stripped down to just her bra and jeans. Finally she got it just right, a recessed hiding place that would look like a widow's fumbling home improvement job to a cop.

I put a hand into the little dark space behind the wall mount, feeling the intervening decade of dust inside before pulling back and taking a pen out of my pocket, which I used to poke around first. The pen came back furred white, but without any mousetraps snapped around it. I reached in for the ziplocked object Crissy had entombed in there in 2004.

Taking the small, holstered Ruger SP101 out of that filthy bag, checking the cylinder and feeling the weight of it, marked the first time I'd held a gun since I'd helped Crissy hide the rifle before I left this place for what I thought was forever.

"I hate guns," I reminded myself, to contradict the intense wave of comfort and security I felt when I slid the holster onto my belt and slipped outside.

In that way she had of somehow appearing when I was about to do something stupid, Jaya texted me. I saw her name but didn't read what she sent, pocketing the phone and letting it buzz with a few more ignored texts. I started walking around the trailer, feeling how opened up it had gotten here since I was a kid, how the trees had either vanished or seemed more sparse now that I was an adult. I'd made the six trees back here into a thicket in my memories, but they were spaced out and gave a clear view of the hill that I was walking toward, through desiccated patches of grass like the one that had scraped my back when I fell.

I started running the camera again, bracing it against my collarbone with my left hand as I climbed toward where I'd seen the flash. My right hand I kept free and close to the Ruger. My thumb was twitching with the remembered motion of working the revolver at the range.

"Chuck would have hated that I didn't buy another Beretta, but this one just felt right," Crissy would say, as though this was somehow an element of defiance that normalized her wholesale acceptance of Chuck's cult rules and claims.

Other than the dead whisper of Crissy's voice, I heard nothing behind me, but there were sounds farther up on the hill—scatterings, rustlings. Not animal sounds, I didn't think, but probably not human ones either.

The trees here did match up with my memories, thick and close together, the canopy that overhung the rough path adding extra darkness to this sunset hour: I could still see well, at least in front of me, but I couldn't make out what, if anything, was on my left or right. I started to cast the camera around in those directions, after adjusting for the lower light. It could see what I couldn't, but not in time for it to be of any use to me up here.

The forest broke into the tiny clearing I remembered from all the times that Crissy had brought me up here on her practice runs, and from when I'd brought my own friends to play and, eventually, to make out.

There was nobody here: just the source of the glimmer. I walked close enough to the tall branch the scope was hanging from to see and recognize its pitted, scored surface, the brown-painted metal so naturally worn it almost looked like the pockmarked skin of a man. The lenses, though, were pristine. Chuck had found it at a pawnshop when I was with him, on a day when he was supposed to be picking me up from kindergarten and driving me to the illegal day care that Mitzi Winslow's mother ran. I'd been four, and even then he'd tried to explain to me what a score this purchase was, how amazing it was to find something this high-end in such a broken-down little shop. We'd hidden the scope and rifle before he took his last drive to Harlow. Crissy and I had buried both deep in the woods behind the trailer before the police did their full toss of our home two decades ago, first carefully disassembling the rifle, coating the components in oil, and wrapping each one in a piece of aluminized Mylar before putting everything in a PVC pipe section that she capped and sealed. Crissy described the process to me in great detail at least once a month, when we walked out to the burial site. The rifle was used one more time after that, and the next time it was hidden I dismembered the thing and spread it all over town. There was no reason for this scope to be here, looking as well-preserved as it did now.

"How the fuck did it end up out here?" I asked, watching the scope turn in the soft breeze, hanging from invisibly knotted fishing wire. For a second, I thought someone might answer me, from closer than I could handle without screaming. The rifle, or whatever had made the shot I'd heard after I brought Kindt and myself to the ground, wasn't anywhere to be seen.

I heard a tiny *spang* noise and felt a sting in my arm at exactly the same moment. *I'm not shot it would hurt more it would hurt more,* I thought at least forty times as I turned to look at my right arm, moving it up to see the spot where I'd felt the bite. The camera started to slip off my arm as I reached under the strap—I set it down next to my boot, seeing a new, tiny hole in the strap. There was a corresponding bleeding hole in my arm just above my elbow: a tiny circle stopped by the object that had made it, a BB ball. I fell flat on my stomach and watched the trees where the shot must have come from. BB guns were close-range, so he must have been in the—

"There," I whispered, when I saw the dual glimmer of eyeglasses in the nearest tree stand, a double-vision visual echo of the glint off the scope. What happened next wasn't me, it was panic and training I'd never wanted. It was Chuck, it was Crissy. I rose to one knee, pulled out the Ruger, and snapped off a shot at the spot where the glasses had been a second earlier. The explosion, a menacing and fatal version of the little BB whisper, filled the clearing, just before I screamed. Murderers don't carry BB guns. Kids do. I lowered the gun and ran to the little thicket of trees, breathing hard enough to doubt the last sound I heard up there before I called Maitland. A laugh. Not a kid's, a grown man's delighted, charmed laugh, the kind of sound people make at dinner parties, not after they've been shot at.

There was no one in the tree stand. No kid, nothing. I squeezed the BB out of the flesh of my arm, letting it drop into the grass. I walked through the forest in a straight line, looking for the round from my Ruger, finding it finally in the smooth branch of a manzanita tree. Chuck had known a lot about trees, for some reason that he'd never told me, and may have identified this particular one for me on one of our walks, years before. I put the Ruger in the holster and squeezed it like a crucifix. My heart started beating normally within a couple of minutes. I tried digging out the bullet with a pen and almost got it, then decided that more destruction would be necessary to cover up what had gone on here before the cops arrived. Shooting a gun that didn't belong to me at what was probably a teenager with a sadistic streak wasn't going to get any cops on my side, or off my back, if it came to that.

I kicked at the thick tree branch until it broke off, disgorging my bullet. I pocketed it, then bashed the branch into smaller sections, rubbing each section against the bark of other trees, sanding off any traceable shape of a bullet hole. Drudging, stupid, probably useless work. But it cleared my head, and also let me listen, while plausibly occupied, for that laugh again, or the sound of a child's gun.

I didn't hear anything.

———

"You're not making a movie of this. Not now," Maitland said, squatting on his haunches and looking into the tree above the hanging scope, from far enough away that he wouldn't be yelled at by the technicians he'd promised were coming. He had big cyclist's thighs that bulged out his uniform pants, constricting him.

"This is my tourist camera. I don't shoot anything serious with it."

"Right." Maitland stared at the scope in the trees, squinting into the sunset, cutting glances at me.

"It's off, anyway." I was dangling the camera from my arm—more precisely, it was hanging off the BB-shot portion of my arm, which was now beaming pain signals directly into my brain. But the hole was nicely concealed. The Ruger was holstered at the base of my spine.

"You were right to call me first. Best we'll be able to do tonight is tape this off, bag the scope at least, see what's in the tall grass tomorrow."

"Really? Is that the best you personally can do? Because it's maybe not the best the actual detective assigned to this case can do, and he's my next call."

"Flashlights are great but not for this kind of bushwhacking, Ms. Potter. You can call Detective Pargiter right now, but I'm pretty sure he's with his family, and his response would be to send me out in his stead. And, like you see, I'm already right here. Taking care of this."

"Are you?"

"Fact stands, we need daylight to make this kind of search."

"And there wasn't any daylight when my mother was murdered? Not then or any of the days since? Some sort of global warming localized long eclipse that disallows basic police work from happening?"

My phone buzzed and I checked the text, as much for the time it would allow me to think of more clauses to add to my rant as to see who it was: Jaya.

recording everything right

I typed back

f you for assuming I would, and yes, I am

The lens-capped Pentax was indeed tracking audio from its sling. When the forensics team—just two men, neither of them booted-and-suited—turned up, Maitland waved me off a few feet, brashly, but with some pleading in his eyes. He'd earned one small point by finding a cartridge, a .45, nothing to do with the kind of rifle that would go with that scope. Whoever had been up here fucking with me had fired, probably into a tree, and left the oscillating scope to do the rest of the scaring.

Just like in an on-camera interview, there's a time to lean back, to surrender something so you can retain the subject for later. I got the sense that if I continued to chew Maitland out in front of these new arrivals, both older and stockier men who didn't defer to him in any visible way, the mustached one in front even leaning forward to wipe a leaf off Maitland's lapel, I'd lose any chance to squeeze information out of him. So I backed away, waited off to the side like a good distraught-but-distanced daughter.

"You agree that this is strange, Officer?" I said, when Maitland made his reluctant way back over to me. I could tell by the puzzled look one of the two had shot him that he'd chatted to them longer than he needed to. I was glad I'd had a jacket with me in the car, because I was finally using it—not to ward off a chill, but tied around my waist to ensure that the holstered Ruger stayed invisible to Maitland.

"I do, Ms. Potter. A little strange. It's not that unusual for a weapon, or parts of a weapon, to be abandoned at a short distance from a crime scene, however. Perps panic."

"I heard someone up here. I heard a shot. And you're not saying now that my mother was shot with a scoped rifle, are you?"

"Heard's not seen, Ms. Potter. I would need a little more."

I was tempted to show him the hole on my arm and the purpling bruise around it, but held off. That would put me two questions away from admitting that I'd sunk to a knee like the militia freak my parents had trained me to be and fired a lucky miss at what could have been a child. Or what could have been a man who was still in these trees, watching us.

"This is the kind of thing that Chuck Varner meant when he talked about chaos, Officer. Most of his preaching was just garbage nonsense, boring down-the-middle male rage, but he cared about the chaos part. How chaos isn't just random violence, but coincidence. That's when life can feel most chaotic, when things that you aren't controlling keep falling into place, one after the other, and you feel as though you're being driven somewhere. Do you get me?" The dangling scope was the kind of Varner touch that Chuck would have thought was definitive: a piece of history that should have vanished turning up exactly where it shouldn't be, right when the only living person likely to recognize it was near.

"That's not Vernon Reilly's scope, Maitland. It's Chuck Varner's." I was willing to risk this part of the truth to see if Maitland was capable of doing his job at all. If he even wanted to.

"What?" Maitland grabbed my arm reflexively, and I stared at his hand until he let go. He'd gripped the uninjured one, thankfully. "Sorry. Sorry."

"I know that scope. I was with my father when he bought it. I assume Crissy hid it somewhere after the day of the shootings."

"Where do you think she would have hidden it?" Maitland whispered, with an eye toward the forensics team.

"How the hell would I know? I've spent a decade-plus trying to forget how she thinks," I said, not about to reveal that I'd hidden evidence from investigators, even if I had been a teenager at the time.

"If you're right about it being Chuck Varner's, that . . . that would be a strange thing," Maitland said, rubbing the underside of his chin with his thumb, a nervous-thinking tic that I bet he hated.

I decided to stop keeping my voice down.

"This is a strange thing no matter where this scope comes from, isn't it? You think my mother is killed in some random home invasion, but I show up and someone happens to threaten me with a gunshot and this obvious reference to Chuck Varner." The forensics guys had turned to watch us. "That's not *normal*, Officer. Whoever killed my mother was up here, he was—he was fucking with me, and he's counting on you being too dumb or too stubbornly dedicated to closing this case to move on this."

"Move on what? On your vague suspicion that you're being pranked?"

"More people are going to be killed. Because you're not doing your job."

"I'm not going to be condescended to by you, Ms. Potter," Maitland said. He pulled out a notebook with a black vinyl cover and a tiny pen holstered in the binding and scrawled out some digits and a name. "You call Ron Pargiter," he said, handing me the paper. "You tell him exactly what you think I overlooked, at your convenience. Just don't think I'm going to entertain this type of treatment from someone I'm trying to help."

I held my hands up for a second and sighed, and then brushed them on my jean shorts. I looked down at my legs for the first time in a while: they were scraped up from my dive in the trailer. They looked like my legs used to when I ran around this forest on weekends, mostly chasing the kids who didn't want to play with me at all, before Chuck told me I was too good to be playing with trash like them anyway. It was a lesson I took to heart, and by the time he was gone and I was old enough to start changing my mind, only the weirder, more aggressive boys wanted anything to do with me. One of them, Tommy Oliver, a black-haired boy a couple of years older who I'd had a crush on, had thrown a jar of pee on me right on this hill once, after inviting me up for a lemonade party with the other kids. I'd wiped the piss off, then broken the glass in Tommy's hand by squeezing his fingers around it as hard as I could. No one would have thought an eight-year-old girl could have been that strong, not even me.

And right now I decided to be strong enough to put up with this cop's sulking in order to get what I needed.

"Sorry. Sorry, Officer, I haven't dumped the adrenaline from when I saw the—when I saw the light coming off the scope. Tell you the truth, it reminded me of when my father used to practice his stupid stealth drills up in these hills. He gave me the other half of a set of walkie-talkies, made me track him with binoculars from inside the trailer, and got me to guess where he was every five minutes. I thought it was really cool, then. Before he'd done anything. Seeing that flash off the scope, it took me there."

I watched Maitland relax as I bullshitted this apologies-for-my-hysteria act and understood that he wasn't just resistant to the possibility that he'd been wrong and that there was more to Crissy's death than a mishap with a meth head. He was diametrically opposed to entertaining anything I said as having any potential of truth. I was Chuck Varner's fucked-up whacko daughter who moved on to become a liberal shithead Hollywood bitch, and those two factors ruled out his being able to do more than nod patiently when I talked.

"I get it," he said. He put a professional hand on my arm. "Not absolutely, but I see the idea. It's hard. And that's why it might be best if you get away from this for a while. Have some dinner, go to bed. We'll run tests on this round and on the scope, see what we can find out." He hooked his thumbs into his belt, gazing at the two techs finishing up their tape-off of the scene.

"If you say so," I said. "If you don't mind, I will call Detective Pargiter, just so I can tell him what I told you, all right? I understand that this all sounds like speculation to you, but if this is someone's idea of a prank, it's a prank related to a mass shooting." I looked into Maitland's eyes, and, for the first time, saw a sharkish, predatory dullness in them, not just the disinterest of a bored cop.

"You call him, sure. He won't pick up until he's on the clock again, so you might just want to get some sleep for now, Ms. Potter."

I made my way back down the hill, and it wasn't until I actually saw Kindt that I realized why he had listened to me and called the cops instead of following me up the hill. I should have wondered, since it was out of keeping with the hovering watcher I remembered him as; he should have been sniffing around the cops and me the whole time we'd been up there. Even a normal person would have been hungry for the kind of out-of-the-ordinary spectacle my little find made.

Kindt was stepping out of Crissy's trailer, and I froze just out of his field of vision, counting on my stillness to keep me hidden, even though I was in the middle of an open field. He'd left at least forty-five minutes before, so he had no call to be there, unless he'd just finished a marathon bathroom break.

But he was carrying a box: a little box, one I recognized. Blue, plastic, covered with Ninja Turtles and G.I. Joe stickers. Mine, my childhood pencil box, from before Chuck had gone on his spree, a piece of my past that my mother had said was missing, had even hit me for losing, decades back. Mine.

I stayed put, watching Kindt make his way back to his trailer. I ran then, hiding in my car and waiting until I saw him pull out in a yellow hatchback. Keeping my lights off until we hit the highway, I followed him.

CHAPTER THIRTEEN

―――――――――

EMIL CHADWICK HIT the buzzer at his mother's building and waited. She had extra keys, but he hadn't proved himself worthy of one yet. "Not till I've trusted you for 730 days," Jill Gudgeon had told him, her latest psychoanalyst/lover nodding in approval from across the too-goddamn-big-for-Manhattan living room. It was his dad's bled-out divorce money that bought this place, Emil wanted to say. If she had any right to make rules about the apartment, it was a right mitigated by blood. That settlement wouldn't have been so fat if Emil hadn't been a minor during the divorce. Anything hers should be his, at least a bit, except for whatever her royalties had bought. And for at least a decade, that wasn't much. Mom might be able to rent a studio in Queens with the income from her old books and a half-dozen feature articles a year, if she was lucky. But she was better than lucky—she was smart, and had divorced the right person. The buzzer made its assenting chime, a sort of new age tinkle that sounded like a heavenly cash register, and Emil went through the lobby and up.

The loft was unlocked when Emil tried the knob. Jill Gudgeon was alone, typing furiously at the coffee table she was kneeling in front of. She held up a finger to pause Emil: she'd probably been typing for about as long as Emil had been riding the elevator. She always seemed to be intent on work whenever Emil arrived, but hadn't published a book for almost two decades.

"The cop texted me. Insists on using some weird third-party Chinese service, so the messages come through garbled as hell."

"One second, honey."

Emil let her have the second, walking to the kitchen and giving a light kick to the cabinet that concealed Jill's boyfriend's beer fridge. He opened a Brooklyn Lager and waited. Jill finally closed the laptop and smiled her concealed-triumph smile, the one that let everyone know she'd just unknotted a great human mystery by correctly arranging syllables in a sentence.

"So," she said. "A cop. I never had much luck with them, myself."

"Gotta start with cops. Look for an easy one and pump. All he wanted from me is to get Blanche Potter in touch with him, and he'd keep me up to date from there."

Jill Gudgeon stood up and walked toward Emil. She was almost a foot shorter than him and slim, wearing her usual off-white layers, different shades of eggshell above cream slacks. People, usually young woman students and writers, recognized her from her decades-old author picture all the time when Emil was with her, especially if they were anywhere near Columbia or NYU. She always took Emil's arm then, but never introduced him, leaving these women to think of him as perhaps her lover, perhaps her son. His face wasn't recognizable, yet.

"You didn't tell me how it went with Blanche. The important talk, Emil. You skipped over it entirely, which is a pretty certain clue, I'm afraid." Jill reached past Emil and picked a tiny apple off the kitchen counter. He knew that she'd just be holding on to it as a prop for at least a few minutes, would never take a bite in the middle of an interrogation like this. It infuriated him.

"She didn't go for it, Mom."

"Go for what?"

"Working with me, going down to Stilford as a duo. She's there right now on her own. Just took the information and ran with it."

Jill *tsk*'d, then surprised him by starting on the apple. She finished the whole thing in about six elegant bites, then gestured at him with the core. "'The information.' Her dead mother, Emil. God, I can already tell how badly you went wrong with this. How totally off-base your approach must have been."

"Mentioning you was what really drove her away," he said, walking past her and sitting on the couch, taking gulps of his beer with what was probably a sullen look on his face that he couldn't quite cast off.

"Are you trying to be hurtful?"

"Yes, but it's also accurate. She doesn't have pleasant memories of you, Mom."

"She can't have *any* pleasant memories of that time, Emil. Or the years before or after it. It's—she's—really a miracle, you know? To emerge from that swamp of trauma not just as a functioning person, but as an *eye*, a curious, roving investigator of what's around her— well, it's just miraculous. If she turned that eye on herself I think she'd crumble in moments, of course, but that's not weakness. It's sanity." Jill had put the core down and waved her index finger at the coffee table. Familiar with her "fetch" gesture, he picked up her laptop and made a joking feint at tossing it to her before walking it over to the counter. Jill opened it and began typing, likely a version of what she'd just said.

"You can't turn it off, huh?"

"Language is language. You use it and it uses you."

"I mean the performance, Mom. I'm trying to talk to you. I'm trying to get your help."

Jill stopped typing and looked at him, anger sharpening the few lines around her blue eyes before she shook her head and laughed. "Not everything is for your benefit. I'm on to something here. For the first time in a good couple of years, I have something that I need to write about, and I have you to thank for it. So, of course I'll help you, but that doesn't mean I have the patience to be insulted before I do so."

"Fine." This was as good an apology as he was going to get from his mother, and this "fine" was about all Emil was capable of offering up as well. This detente of acknowledged but undealt-with nastiness joined a lifelong catalog of similar exchanges that were behind them, stretching back to Emil's earliest years of being verbal, shortly after his mother had returned from Stilford with the recordings and notes that built *Last Victims*. Jill's publisher had insisted on *The Varner Spree Killings* as the subtitle, but she still thought it was coarse, an interpretation that ruined all the multifaceted brilliance of the two words she'd opened Blanche Varner's story with.

"It really is all Blanche's story," Jill said.

"What?"

"You have to understand that first if you're going to approach her intelligently, and if you're going to tell this part of the story properly. It's not about Chuck Varner shooting people. That's *backstory*, Emil.

It's relevant, it's important, but it's not the story. I didn't realize that until I'd spent days and days with the little girl that she was."

"The killings are the real story, Mom. This isn't some memoir-drifty-literary journey. Crissy Varner's been shot dead, Chuck Varner's daughter makes movies talking about everyone's fucked-up problems except her own, and I have a pet cop that's come close to telling me that there's orders from above not to look into Mommy Varner's murder. It's about killing and about looking away."

"Looking away. That's it, Emil, don't you get it? The story is what Blanche turned away from, what she turned into. Haven't you noticed how *odd* she is? How cold, unreactive? Unless she's changed. That's her father in her, not just the experience, what she's been through. I'd never met a child like her, so remarkable, so frightening. I hope she hasn't changed."

"You don't know what the story is this time, Mom. Maybe you didn't know back then, either."

"What do you mean?"

"Chuck Varner was never dead for Crissy Varner. Or for Blanche. He's alive still, in that trailer, and in that city."

Jill Gudgeon laughed at this, a full-throated, rasping laugh that made it impossible to believe that it had been decades since her last cigarette.

Emil clenched his right fist inside his jeans pocket. "Right, Katharine Hepburn, I get it, it's funny. You talked about Crissy's obsession in the book, I know, but you didn't get to any of the practicalities. Her planning, Mom. She was the one who got me to reach out to Blanche, to use a movie project as a lure. That was in our very first conversation. She said that Blanche needed to be back in the city, and that no matter what, it would happen. Blanche in Stilford. Like it was a prophecy.

And Blanche is there, right now." Emil stopped himself; he was already taking on enough risk just by *knowing* what he already knew.

"Yes, I'm sure it's very impressive. What are you doing here, Emil? You could have lectured me over the phone," Jill said, getting up and starting a light stretch.

Emil looked away. He wanted to tell her something that would really hurt her: that he'd learned more from Crissy Varner, from the precious times that they'd spoken together and she'd enlightened him, showed him his full potential, than he'd learned from his own mother in an entire lifetime. But he couldn't. Not just yet. Not until the plan had unspooled a little further, and Jill Gudgeon understood that it was her son who was the brilliant one, the patient one, the probing one, the one who understood when to get out of the way of a story and let it happen, even if that meant casualties.

"You know why I'm here, Mom."

Jill Gudgeon straightened up.

"Yes, but I would like to hear it."

"I need money."

CHAPTER **FOURTEEN**

KINDT STARTED OFF driving slowly and sped up as we got closer to the water—the river delta at San Paulo Park. His yellow Mazda, dirty as it was, stuck out from the pickup and sedan traffic on the way there, allowing me to hang back far enough to avoid being spotted. When he pulled into the parking lot of the park, though, I decided to ditch subtlety in favor of getting my shit back. I pulled up alongside him, close enough to prevent him from opening his door. I rolled down my passenger window and waited for him to do the same with his driver's side.

"AC broken?" I asked. Kindt had opened his flowered shirt by two further buttons, and dark streaks of sweat pulled the faded fabric close to his skin. There was sweat on his eyebrows, the liquid glimmering under the cold blue lot lights.

"First you assault me on property that I manage, then you stalk me?" He undid his seatbelt and measured the space between our cars with his eyes.

"You broke into a crime scene and stole a murder victim's personal possessions, Kindt. Give it back."

"What?"

"The box. You followed me because you wanted something in the trailer that you couldn't get at without breaking in. Give back what you took and I'll let it end here, once you tell me exactly why you knew where it was, and what made you want to throw it out. Understood?" I pulled the small Ruger from where it was holstered at my side and rested it on my knee.

"I left something in there myself on a previous occasion when I was repairing the damage that your family member did to the property. Tools. That's what I went in to recover." Kindt moved his right arm, doing something I couldn't see. Reaching for the box and trying to push it onto the floor off the passenger seat, probably. I stopped my finger from moving closer to the trigger.

"Did you put that Cobra Commander sticker I got from a liquidation store on the lid in 1999? Did you sand off the logo from the bottom with rock polishing paper you stole from Bobby Hendricks in the first grade?" I climbed out of my seat, tucking the gun back into my shorts, and circled over to Kindt, barely breaking eye contact. I reached into his passenger window before he had thought to shut it and leaned down, grabbing the blue box. I felt the familiar pebbled surface of the top and the unusual weight of it—if there were only papers in it, they'd been crammed dense—while Kindt looked at me with dull hatred.

"You were gabbing with me pretty good in the trailer, Mr. Kindt. You don't have anything to say now?"

"I say we can agree to call this quits right now or we'll both end up telling the cops different stories, and you don't carry much respect in this town," Kindt said, as though his slumlord proxy status would grant him a stealing-evidence free pass. "I took that outta the property to cut off any more questions or poking around, and that's the truth. Found it on your mom's table right after the shot, when I went in to try to help her. When I saw what was in there, I thought the decent thing was to keep it private."

"So you hid it on a property that any police worth their salary would be turning upside down and over within minutes of you calling in," I said. I opened the passenger door and sat down, Dunkin' Donuts cups and pungent burger wrappers rustling under my feet. If Kindt was armed, I liked being closer to him, better able to close the distance with a couple of the strategic punches Chuck had taught me in the woods behind our trailer, leaving my gun where it was. Kindt stayed quiet. The BB wound in my arm throbbed, and the pain kept me calm.

"Is there anyone else who ID'd Vernon Reilly as being at the scene?" I thought of Officer Maitland's blank, incurious eyes again, and about whether that lack of curiosity came from laziness or from knowing all the answers already, because he'd planned them out himself.

"How would I know that?" Kindt asked.

"You know in the way you can only be sure of a lie: you made it up, so how could anyone else have seen him out there?" A guess delivered confidently can be a useful interviewing tool—maybe it'd work for parking lot interrogations, too. Kindt didn't say anything, clammed up like someone who'd been arrested more than a few times and knew the value of a blank stare and an off-topic response.

"I didn't want to steal anything. I'm not a thief, just someone who doesn't want to be bothered. And who's just trying to do what your mother would have probably wanted. So take your shit outta here and quit bothering me." Kindt put his hands on the steering wheel and stared straight ahead. As soon as I stepped out with the box and closed the passenger door, he reversed and screeched out of the dark parking lot.

Alone there, the box felt heavier in my hands than it had in the car. Checking that my rental was locked up, I walked a few steps over to a park bench, and sat down with my phone's flashlight on to open the box. First I took out the roll of money, which looked like more cash than Crissy had ever held at once in her lifetime. Then I started to look through the Polaroids.

CHAPTER FIFTEEN

———————

Excerpt from Last Victims: The Varner Spree Killings *by Jill Gudgeon. Morris & Connington, 2000.*

People who saw Chuck Varner preach immediately understood how this all worked, Crissy was always explaining to me. I pressed her on it, as much as I could, telling her that I couldn't possibly do Chuck justice without seeing him. I knew there was a tape, one she'd never told the police about, one that she'd probably hidden along with the rifle that she swore Chuck never brought back from the overpass shooting.

It was a smile she had, a tiny suggestion that only a perceptive lens in close-up or a professional gambler would be able to see. I only asked about a potential tape twice. The first time was after I brought Stella to the mall, a trip that I never told her mother about. I think that Crissy will be pleased that I did it when she reads this book—Harlow Mall has banned Crissy from the premises, and every security guard is compelled to memorize a photo of her the day they are hired. After Micaela Abrega, the wife of Peter Cane (whom Varner shot through the liver, the fatal bullet emerging from his back and lodging in a sculpture of Orange Boost mascot Mr. Citruz), caught Crissy Varner distributing cards with Chuck-related slogans on them in the parking lot, Crissy practically became a part of the training manual. So mother can't take her daughter to the site of Chuck's ascendance into immortality.

I asked Crissy if there was a tape when she got back from work that night. "You loved watching him speak so much. I can tell when you're talking to me, sometimes, that you're emulating his speeches, his patterns—"

"Yes," Crissy said, walking past where I was sitting on the tiny vinyl couch to check on Stella, who'd gone to bed without a word of protest or request to watch a few more minutes of television. The girl watched less television than any child I'd met since my son was born and I started noticing such things.

"So I was just wondering if there was a way I could hear him teach. Or see him."

Crissy came back into the room from the kitchen with a drink she hadn't bothered to mix, just gin on ice. And the little smile, which really had almost nothing to do with her mouth: it was a dent in her right cheek, not quite a dimple, more of a line. A straight, temporary wrinkle.

"Sorry, Crissy." I let it go. "Stella was so good today. She really has perfect discipline." I'm still glad I didn't pursue it. She wouldn't have forgiven me if I'd pressed her, not when she was exhausted after work. "I want to drive you up to my hotel, Crissy. You and Stella. Stay the night, I'll get you a room. Not tonight, you're clearly almost done in, but I thought it would be nice. A treat."

Crissy agreed, and I got her the room. Stella stayed in it all night, with an assortment of toys, books, and my permission to use a reasonable amount of room service. Crissy and I waited until she was asleep to use the pool, which was starting to empty out. It was after nine, and I'd lent Crissy my green swimsuit, which looked younger on her than on me. I felt like I was in an old photograph when I wore it, almost two-dimensional, chaste. Crissy filled it out, not coarsely, just youthfully. Seeing her like that made me remember that she'd been only twenty when she had Stella.

We paddled around for a few minutes, returning to our drinks of gin and lemonade in poolside plastic Minute Maid bottles. When we were quiet, it was possible—not just for me, but for her, too, I'm sure of it—to believe ourselves friends, especially in this hotel, this vacation space. This time, I decided not to ask, but to say.

"I know there's video, Crissy. At least one. You're too responsible not to have put Chuck Varner on tape at least once, and we both know it. Even if the police were too slow to ask, even if you were too smart to give fuel like that to the press, knowing they'd just cut it up for TV, it must exist."

"It wouldn't have done the police any good."

"Of course it wouldn't. They just want to collect everything and bury it in a cardboard box in some basement, pretend they're doing the work. That's not what I've ever been here to do, Crissy. I'm here to extend the lesson, but I need to learn it first."

An hour later, we were in my room, which adjoined the one I'd gotten for her and Stella. I'd watched Stella while Crissy went back to the trailer, fishing out the VHS from wherever it rested. The front desk of the hotel sent up a VCR to replace the slick DVD player in my room. I gave the teenager who installed it a ten-dollar tip, mostly for doing his work quietly enough to allow me to crack the connecting door open to watch Stella, who was sleeping in the center of one of the two enormous beds.

When Crissy got back, I moved to shut the connecting door, but Crissy waved me off.

"She sleeps through anything."

We put the tape in and sat on one of the beds together, migrating back toward the headboard and pillows piled there as it played. The camcorder taking the footage was too steady to be handheld, and showed Varner talking to a group of four teenage boys, two with long, beautiful ponytails, the other two with shaved heads. They're in a parking lot, the light is orange, the arid heat almost visible. Three of the boys are white, one is Asian, and as the minutes pass, they start making less eye contact with each other, tossing fewer of the snide looks that define the thinking American teenager. The more Chuck Varner talks, the clearer it is that he has them. He's in profile for most of the video, skinny under a loose black T-shirt, with a sharp nose and slicked-back black hair that keeps falling over his eyes as he talks and gestures. He never touches it, just moves his head in a slight whipping nod to punctuate sentences every now and then, setting his hair just right as he does it.

Chuck Varner speaks to me for the first time.

"Society is slow castration. Do you get me? I know it sounds ridiculous, at first. He's got to be exaggerating. Why would the whole goddamn world be so interested in my dick, a guy asks himself. You usually go around begging anyone TO be interested in your dick, and find no takers. Am I right?" Chuck gets his first laugh.

I didn't think he'd be a comedian, and I didn't think he'd be so effective at engaging sullen parking-lot smoking teenagers, who had clearly been passing a joint moments before he approached them. The crassness gets them, an older man being juvenile with them. The Asian boy, shorter and chubbier than his friends, seems to be the leader, his laugh giving the rest of them permission.

"The world is interested in taking from you what you value most. And when you're this age, right at this moment, all you can think about is fucking, right? But that's not really, really what you're thinking about. It's what your body is coding the message as, and you can, in a way, trust your body. But don't just listen to lust. Listen to the anger that comes with it. Sex is pleasure, yes, but sex is also chaos. Losing yourself.

"And the anger. Don't tell me you don't feel it. Don't tell me it didn't just sweat out of you watching those bands in there, banging your heads off your necks. You, especially—great Bolt Thrower shirt, man—you needed that, didn't you? You need nights like this because you don't know what's going to happen if you don't get them. That contact you get in the pit, when you're throwing arms and you know the bodies are flowing around you because everything is right—that's chaos. It's life.

"You're angry because you need to fuck. You need to fuck because you need pleasure and chaos. Pleasure IN chaos. And you're mad at the fucking gatekeepers, man. Whether it's that girl you can't even ask out because you know it means more to her to say no than it does to just give talking to you and touching you and knowing how good that could be a chance, whether it's the shithead cops and fake cops that our world is infested with—they're castrators, guys. They're so focused on controlling the temporary, the moment, that people like us scare the shit out of them.

"Because we know that life can't last, and we don't give a shit. Because we're into the real message of the universe, the heartbeat that we feel in our brains and in our bodies and in rooms like that when we're tuned in to a truth that some hot chick laughing at you or your dad telling you to focus on the S-A-fucking-T so you can get out of his house can never know. It's all about coming and chaos. You know that and I know that. And we know that the rest of the world is too dumb to get it, except the ones who hear the alarm.

"Know what the alarm sounds like? BANG. Bang. Bang. Bang. That's all that gets their attention. The call to arms in this world, this world we're forced to live in, isn't just a call: it's an armed call. And you know who sounds it? Anyone?"

The boys are rapt, and so was I. They must have remembered this moment in their lives after the Harlow Mall massacre, remembered this parking lot prophet channeling hates that may never have occurred to them and loneliness they may never have been preoccupied with into a pure, solution-oriented message that made them feel so very, very important.

The tape ends with Chuck laughing and leaning back against the car that the camera is balanced on top of, shutting it off with a backward fumble of his hand. And maybe that's when the spell breaks for the boys, too: perhaps they're too smart for him, once the charisma wears off, once they actually think about what he's saying. I don't know. But even if Chuck couldn't convince them, he could certainly convince others. He already had.

Crissy and I stayed silent. When I looked over to my right, there she was, crying quietly. Neither of us broke the silence.

From the next room, Stella, her voice gummy and adorable with sleep, said "Daddy." She said it again, then she woke up and screamed it. Crissy climbed out of the bed and walked into the next room, and held her daughter in an embrace so tight I thought Stella might stop breathing, or that Crissy would absorb her entirely, and they'd turn back toward me as one, new person, a creature equally Stella, Crissy, and Chuck. No longer broken into discrete, partially human artifacts.

Just one breathing, looming, monster.

CHAPTER SIXTEEN

T HE BOY WAS waiting for Kindt in his office. From his covered position on the hill, he'd watched Blanche begin to follow the old man out to the river, as planned. Her shot had come alarmingly close to his head, and if she hadn't panicked, had squeezed off two more bullets, he would have caught one, he was sure. The range was certainly close enough: he'd nailed her precisely with the little BB rifle. She was still a beautiful shot, still had the reflexes that Chuck Varner had baked into her when she was a child. But she lacked his instinct, his strength. Of course she would—that's why The Boy was necessary.

He'd been sitting on Kindt's desk since he got tired of pacing the office to take the tension out of his thighs, which were tight from squatting in the grass. Kindt was one of those men in minor power who was incredibly easy to manipulate with the promise of slightly greater power: after prying into Crissy Varner's business a couple of times, once almost revealing The Boy to Blanche when she was young and not ready for the knowledge, he had become incredibly pliant after Crissy had first thought of enlisting him to carry out small missions.

"Feeling needed," Crissy had said, "is part of what we warn our followers against. It's exactly how they use you, how they bend you. And no one has needed Kindt for a long time. So let's use him."

Crissy had only directly called on the old man once, for a cover story when she and The Boy did a weapons run at an illegal gun store owned by a survivalist two hundred miles north. They'd taken the place down when the man was away and his weak son was watching the home-based store. The Boy had broken his wrist before even asking him for anything, and Crissy had taken it easy on him by only stealing ten handguns. Seeds of Chaos, Crissy had said, leaving them scattered around Stilford when they drove back, dropping a Colt under a dumpster in the alley behind Walmart, a lane frequented by users and dealers. Kindt was prepared to tell the police that Crissy had been with him in his office, that he was helping her with her taxes. But illegal gun dealers tend to leave these incidents unreported.

Just this one passive mission was enough to make Kindt their dog. He had visions of notoriety, of heroism, probably ideas of being a leader himself when Your Life Is Mine entered its next phase: a phase that Crissy was always extremely vague about when she spoke to hopefuls and outsiders like Kindt. He'd wept when Crissy died, and when The Boy told him he was needed so Crissy could be avenged, Kindt had risen to his full, miniature height, pressed the clinging Plasticine snakes of hair he had left back over his scalp, and said, "Anything." The Boy had fed him the first part of the Vernon Reilly story: the part that landed Reilly in jail, that gave The Boy enough time to make sure that every hour of Blanche Varner's return to Stilford was choreographed.

Planning like this, alone, he felt closer to Crissy than he had when she was alive. Closer to Chuck, too. Blanche was correct about this—the family functioned best when the individual absorbed all of their needs and insights, doing away with their weaknesses. Chuck's impatience, Crissy's neediness. The Boy had neither. The best of them lived in him, and the worst had leaked out with their lives.

When Kindt got back to the office The Boy would give him another piece of the plan, wait for it to play out, then give him something else.

CHAPTER SEVENTEEN

I PULLED INTO THE motel lot two hours after Alfred Kindt left me staring into Crissy's treasure box. After looking through the Polaroids, I'd peeled a bill off the roll of cash and walked to a roadside bar where they used to let Jaya and me drink when we were in senior year, as long as we stayed in the restaurant section, and stuck to drinks that could pass as virgin if the liquor inspector came in. For the sake of those particular old times, I had a Long Island Iced Tea and paid for it with money my mother had probably stolen. Then I stared at the tablecloth and drank water refills until it started to get too busy in that place to think, and I could tell the creature in the Men's Wearhouse suit and increasingly reddening skin on the next stool was about to start talking to me. He did, just as I got up.

"You frown a lot. Bad for your skin," he said, pointing at the slight wrinkles next to his right eye. I could have put his own pointing finger deep into his eye and be walking to the door before the screaming started.

"Sorry, yes, I do think the sex offender registry is permanent in this state, sir. Good luck," I said, instead of the eye stab. I made sure to be loud enough that the bartender, both servers, and any table nearby turned to stare at him. I left.

The slot right in front of my motel door was occupied by a pristine truck. One of the few pleasures of staying in a roadside motel is parking your ride four feet away from where you'll be passing out, and I felt every extra step I had to take back toward Room 14 after parking near the office. Dan Maitland climbed out of the driver's seat when I was a few doors away, and I had enough time to put my face on, what Chuck used to call "the street mask." Closed-lip smile, blank and bored eyes. It was easy to slip back into it, and I realized how often I'd used this face without thinking of him and his lessons over the course of my little career, and how useful it had been. Before Maitland could speak I held up a finger.

"My phone," I said, walking back to my car. The phone was already in my purse, but I unlocked the passenger door of the rental and took the holstered Ruger out from under the seat, clipping it back to my belt, then putting on my jacket. I could feel Maitland's eyes on me and made sure that he couldn't see any of these interesting movements.

"Are you all right with me being here? Know you must be tired, but I decided against waiting until tomorrow," Maitland asked, tapping his knuckles against the wallet in his front right pocket. Maitland in his plain clothes looked like an off-duty something, but it was hard to tell what—mailman, radio jock, bartender maybe. Not a cop. Nicely fitted chinos and a dark plaid shirt, tucked in.

"How did you know where I was staying?" I asked, reaching into my bag for my room key but stopping before I got it out, waiting for him to answer.

"It was maybe the third or fourth thing you told me when you came to the station. Arcadian Inn. Just wanted a quick conversation. Out here's fine," he said.

"We've talked a lot today, Officer Maitland. And I got the impression that both chats were pretty reluctant on your part, so this is half a surprise and half annoying. Do you have any new information for me?"

"The 'officer' bit is what's getting in the way of us having a proper conversation. I'm a cop for about three more months, if I have my way."

"What?"

"I've done—I'm finished with my part of this, especially after what's happened with your mom. This is going to be complicated to explain." Maitland had been staring into my bag this whole time, relaxing only after he'd seen my hand loosen to reveal the motel passkey, instead of the recorder I figured he was worried about. He kept talking.

"I haven't been absolutely honest with you, Blanche. The department has little intention of handling this case right. They'll tell you that it's because it's a lock, that there's no time to solve the why when they already have the who, but that's not it. And we both know that the scope you found today is not Chuck Varner's."

"How do we know that?" I tried to keep the combating emotions of vindication and suspicion off my face; I'd known there was something withheld about Dan Maitland, something both vague and familiar. Those predatory eyes that I recognized from my dad's face. Maitland in public was a person who was half made-up, with the important part kept inside. Just the kind of masking my mother taught me, and that Chuck had to use, because there was only emptiness under the mask.

"We know the scope's not his because twelve years ago, you and Crissy Varner broke that rifle down into pieces and you spread the components all over town in places they'd never be found. And I know, even if you don't, that you wouldn't flub a job like that."

This landed the way Maitland had hoped it would. I shut up and stared at him.

"What I found most interesting," he said, "is that you really wanted to believe that it was Chuck Varner's scope. That on some level, you *wanted* to see evidence that he was still alive in the world."

"I don't prefer the idea of someone precisely simulating a Chuck Varner artifact. I find that scarier. Because it means that someone is working to keep him around. Do you get that?" I felt the truth of it as I said it: Chuck, Crissy, the past, these were known quantities. Whoever was doing this out there wasn't. This was Chuck's chaos at work, through someone new, someone better at it than he ever was.

"So do you want to talk out here, or sit down somewhere?" he asked.

"Emil Chadwick," I said. "Fucking Emil Chadwick, that little worm."

"Yeah?" Maitland said, smiling.

"He gave me your card and got me directly in touch with you so I wouldn't talk to anyone else on the department. So I'd come straight to you without stirring anything up."

"It was just timing, Blanche. We wanted to make sure that you talked to the right people first. He wants a story, and knows this is the best way to get it. Crissy told him he could trust me. And she told me that you would want to talk to as few cops as possible, whether you knew it or not—that you were taught, repeatedly, never to trust us."

So Maitland had given me Detective Pargiter's number knowing I wouldn't call it, whether it was actually the right number or not.

"Is my mother even—"

"God, Blanche, I wouldn't lie about that. That would land *me* in prison and also make me a total piece of garbage. I'm sorry to say that your mother is dead, yes. But we have a lot more to discuss."

"I could go to your superiors right now, instead."

"You'd be going to them with questions, Blanche, and we know how that would go. Agitated young woman with a deeply fucked-up past claims that there is a police conspiracy against her? Come on."

Maitland didn't even offer to drive me, but I knew it wasn't out of rudeness—just an avoidance of the awkwardness of my inevitable "no." I hadn't quite trusted him when he seemed like just another ineffective cop. Knowing enough about my mother that we had to arrange a little drinks party to get it all out made him worse than bumbling: it made him dangerous, more specifically dangerous than strange men already are.

I took hold of the situation my own way, taking my cell phone out and taking a picture of Maitland in front of his truck. I took a picture of his license plate, too, and texted both to Jaya, showing Maitland the screen just after I did so. I left Jaya a voicemail telling her exactly when and where I was, and that I was headed for a drink with Maitland, "the soon-to-be-ex cop who wants to tell me something about his concealed relationship to my mother." I didn't tell her that I had a gun resting against my spine, both because she would have disapproved profoundly and because I didn't want to fill Maitland in. The phone started buzzing with calls from Jaya as soon as I finished with the message, but I didn't pick up. I didn't have the time to listen to sensible advice.

"I wish you hadn't said that last part," Maitland said. "'Concealed relationship.' Makes it sound illicit."

"Concealing that you had a connection to the victim of a murder you were investigating isn't illicit, Maitland?"

"It is," he said. "But you of all people must understand the value—the necessity—of concealing ties, sometimes. But fair enough."

Our conversation was already different from any of the others we'd had. Here, in this parking lot, he seemed ready to concede any point.

"That's why I wouldn't be a cop, Officer Maitland. But you are. You're not supposed to be concealing anything. Not that I'm naive enough to think it actually works that way in any department in this country."

"This country or any other one," Maitland said, grinning. "But really, I wasn't being devious. It's just been, you know, sort of undercover work."

"No. I don't know. I have no fucking clue what you mean."

"Then let's go and have a talk so you can find out. Someplace extremely public. This is the best way we can keep anyone—and I don't mean you, of course—from getting hurt."

Maitland promised to drive slowly, and I tailed him closely. A mile from the motel, I realized how tired I was and annoyed by a pain in my ribs, either from my dive in the trailer or the fall I'd taken outside of it. The BB injury had stopped throbbing, and was clean and bandaged after a stop at a Rexall and some brief triage in the bathroom before I'd had my Long Island. I pressed into the injured rib to check if it was broken, then pressed harder to wake myself up.

I overuse the mirrors when I drive tired, which also means I get more glimpses of myself than I'd like. After this many waking hours, my face had indeed collapsed into a nightmare of exhausted meat. I didn't have the time or inclination to fix it, but felt a bit bad about walking into any place, even a dive, with Maitland looking casual-polished the way he did and me looking the way I did.

We ended up in front of a huge multiplex that had been under

construction when I'd left Stilford. The lot was full; blockbuster sea-
son, superheroes pulling in the crowds, a couple of screens left over
for a romantic comedy and a period drama. As far from *Marigny Five's*
little opening in the Carver as possible. Maitland was waiting by his
truck, and we walked to the entrance together.

"You don't have to buy a ticket until you're up the escalator," Maitland said. He did have a cop haircut, but the teenagers who were
streaming toward us, exiting and going on into the night to drink and
smoke weed and make out and generally squeeze out a bit more summer, didn't make Maitland as a cop. They saw a man and his tired girl-
friend going to the movies.

"Wasn't open from when I lived here," I said. He grunted, the
kind of response a non sequitur like that merited. It felt like an oddly
normal conversational beat, which made me distrust Maitland even
further. Chuck taught me to watch adults small-talking, to look for
the real thoughts they were having while they exchanged automated
pleasantries. They were what was used when people were sizing each
other up, Chuck said, or deciding what their next move would be. I
couldn't remember if he was talking to me about approaching women
or recruiting boys.

I sat down in the glowing neon brightness of the concourse while
Maitland went to get us expensive sodas. Behind me was a crane game,
unplugged and dark, the claw grabber inside detached and lying among
the elephants and SpongeBobs it was supposed to gather up. Maitland
had been half-right; it was extremely public here, but that didn't make
me feel safe. Just like at the Carver in New Orleans, I would start to
see bodies around me dropping if I lost focus on the present, even for
a second. And there were still moments, sometimes long ones, where
I walked into a space like this and saw it as Chuck had taught me to:

a space to perform, to make chaos happen. The parents and toddlers who walked in front of me became momentarily blank. That's how Chuck would have seen the people in Harlow Mall before he shot. Nine faceless obstacles between himself and immortality.

Maitland came back with two waxed paper cups adorned with wrap-around masked vigilantes. His face was vivid to me in this crowd, almost seeming to glow from the reflected light and the intensity he was staring at me with, consuming me as though I wasn't staring right back. He sat next to me on the plastic bench I'd chosen and passed me my cup.

I gulped the soda through the straw, wishing there was something stronger than aspartame in it to briefly drown the images on those Polaroids I'd wrested from Kindt. Next to me, Maitland was still rehearsing. I decided to run in on him before he could start the conversation the way he wanted to.

"You spent a lot of time with my mother," I said. His eyes snapped up. This was a tough interview gambit, a play on the cold-reading techniques that sham psychics use, and that Chuck Varner had originally taught me on a teaching-mission day when he'd gotten no less than four teen boys at the Stilford Polytechnic smoke pit to agree to an afternoon meet-up: a probing guess that you're ready to follow up with a half-dozen other probes if you miss on the first, fast enough that it'll seem that you have impossible knowledge once the subject replies with a dazed "Yes" when you score a hit. I didn't have to guess beyond one, though.

"Yes," Maitland said. "I knew her very well." He was looking straight ahead, tracking a duo of teen boys, one in an unzipped red hoodie and the other wearing a Danzig T-shirt and studded punk bracelets, as they walked toward two slightly younger girls. When the girls turned to see them, they hugged and headed for the escalator.

"You were a Chuck Varner hobbyist," I said. Now, Maitland was looking at me. "Came as close as you could to the source to find out more."

"You're wrong there. I didn't have any interest in that aspect of things, and Crissy respected that. I came to your mother for counsel, for advice. There were many different sides to that woman, Blanche. I think that if you'd ever come to know her as a grown woman, your opinion—"

"This is the second conversation I've had this week with a man trying to explain my mother to me. I lived with that bitch for sixteen years and underwent a wash of mental abuse that only a professional asshole like a cop or social worker or nurse or any of the other people who should have gotten me away from that woman could be blind to." Crissy had made me an expert in dealing with the police and family services in the couple of years after Chuck's spree: say as little as possible to the cops, and say exactly these things to the social workers, with as little improv as possible. The reactions had been trained into me by Chuck, then Crissy. There'd been a thorny time in the weeks after Crissy was banned from Harlow Mall for handing out Varner Six cards, but she'd agreed to a few rounds of therapy and had pled residual abuse trauma. I was trained to cry at the right times and in front of the right people when the prospect of leaving the trailer and Crissy behind came up, and a cycle of case workers who didn't seem to share files or opinions with each other eventually just let it all go. So Crissy had me for another eight years.

"That's the deal with you people," I went on. "You don't see what's going on when it is going on, but then you talk about understanding it deeply the moment it's done."

"I knew Crissy. Well enough that I understand why it was smart to be scared of her," Maitland said.

"Why would you be scared of a trailer-living waitress with no family and no friends, Officer?"

"She didn't need friends, Blanche. You know that. She told me as much. She probably told you."

"So you'd talked to her, you'd spent time with her, and you end up single-handedly investigating what happened to her?" I realized I could speak as loudly as I wanted to in here, and the only effect would be to make Maitland uncomfortable. The ambient screaming of advertisements and video games raised the volume on every conversation on the floor, making everyone around us oblivious to what I was saying.

"Your mom had people who listened to her and I was one of them, Blanche. Don't you remember me even a little bit? We were neighbors for a few months. Kindt remembered me right away, but he did always have an eye for kids."

It was when Maitland smiled, a twitch on the right side of his mouth that slowly extended, that I remembered. Remembered specifically holding that face in the dirt with the back of my sneaker while Boyd Sharpton pulled his pants down and sprayed him with a Super Soaker when we were all about ten years old and he was smaller, maybe seven.

"Goddamn," I said. "Dan. Danny."

"Don't feel bad," Maitland said. Danny.

"You changed your name."

"Nothing weird about that. And my hair just got darker on its own, with time. My mom was real disappointed. I just took my stepdad's name after high school, when I was old enough to make the choice and sure enough that I'd never see my birth dad to have to explain it to him. But yeah. Danny Lear, back then. Crissy insisted that you wouldn't remember me, you know. Once my stepdad finally was able to afford a two-bedroom for us downtown, we were out of the park for good. I used to have to bike back to see your mom. And I did, usually at least once a week." Danny turned slightly toward me on the bench, as though he were presenting himself freshly, as though we could meet for the first time once he'd told part of the truth about himself.

"Crissy made sure that we barely crossed paths, once she started teaching me," Danny said. "Plus, you were older than me and I was kinda scared of you. It was your mom who made me feel welcome. Let me come over when you had after-school stuff, when it could be just the two of us in the trailer. Eventually she didn't let me play with you, or with any of the kids that you liked. Crissy used to let me play with your toys while she talked about Chuck Varner and the way forward. 'The Way Forward' is how Crissy said it, you know. You could hear the capitals."

"Yes, I know. 'The Way Forward.' 'Your Life Is Mine.' I know all of it."

Maitland laughed and crossed his legs, rolling up the right cuff of his pants and pulling down his sock. He had a small tattoo. *Ylim*, small but emphatic in Baskerville font. I got a chill that started in my cheekbones and flashed through the rest of my body.

Chuck Varner had given me the same tattoo, but a cheap stick-and-poke version, on top of my six-year-old foot one Sunday morning in the trailer, when Crissy was at work and he was in one of his directionless, black moods. The tattoo was a greenish smear now, but it itched under my sock. What he'd done that day with the needle was to etch the day and the lesson into my mind.

"The physical," Chuck had said, his breath sweet and medicinal from the gin slush slop he and Mom drank on the days they allowed themselves to, "is the scaffolding that holds up the mental. You get me, Blanche?"

I'd nodded, memorizing "scaffolding" to look it up later, bracing for the pain that he warned me would come. He wasn't ready yet, still heating up a needle from a motel sewing kit over one of the burners on the stove, holding it there with pliers. I was right next to him, helping the way he used to let me, by holding something nearby while he did the real work. A technique that Crissy tried to reverse when she took on my teaching, always having me make the speech or hold the gun.

Chuck had dipped the needle into the small pot of India ink we'd found in the crammed caddy of stationery that Crissy kept on one corner of the kitchen table. He started to roll down my right sock, then stopped.

"You choose which foot."

I immediately pulled the right sock down the rest of the way, and Chuck smiled.

"It wasn't a test, baby. But still, good. I think it'll look best there." When he started, the pain blazed up so intensely I didn't have the screaming language for it, so I just stayed quiet. I thought I could feel the needle going right into the most prominent bone on the top of my foot, the part that rubbed against the inner tongue of my Keds when I put them on barefoot. Chuck stopped for a moment, holding my foot in both hands like a salesman, the butt of the tattooing needle between his teeth.

"That's the 'Y,' Blanche. We can stop if you want."

"No," I said. It was in a controlled tone, one I managed by imitating the way Mindy Rawls, a cute black girl in my class who had a voice that I admired, talked. If I'd tried to answer in my own voice I would have at least remembered how to cry, even if I couldn't scream. Chuck didn't notice any difference.

"Good. Because that one was a test." He started poking and dipping again, mixing the ink with the blood in my foot, my blood with the ink in the bottle. "I'm keeping it to initials for when we're famous, baby. When Your Life Is Mine isn't just a slogan on a card. When it's known as the name of the single most important political and social movement of our time. The words and message that brought truth to America."

I guess that was the last lesson I learned that day: that pain could build to a point where you took in the reality of everything around you, without processing, without explanation. Because that was the first time I had an inkling that Chuck Varner was babbling, just saying words without any meaning behind them. I forgot my catechism, and for a second, I forgot that he was Dad: he was just a man who was hurting me and saying nonsense words with his cupcake-and-formaldehyde breath sharp in my nose while he stabbed my foot.

Maitland was still showing me his tattoo when I came back to the present, running the pad of his right thumb over it, fondly. A disciple.

"What do you tell people it stands for?" I asked.

"Yesenia Lisa Isabella Malvar," Maitland rattled off, then laughed. "My first great love. Crissy and I came up with the name together after I got the tattoo, which was the day after I got into the academy. We had a whole backstory and bio, how I'd gotten the tattoo not because I still loved the girl, but to remind me—"

"I don't want to hear it, Maitland," I said. The laughter, which had already stopped coming out of his mouth, now departed his eyes. He blanked out, went to that dead zone that most people only got to in the second before they were about to vomit from booze or food poisoning. And then I actually was meeting him for the first time: Maitland's blankness was his real face, the black in the middle of his pupil deepening and reflecting out the nothingness that my mother had used as a foundation for Chuck Varner's filth. I should have been more afraid of him, but I wasn't; I'd seen this before. I'd almost become this.

"Sorry," he said, when he remembered to port his personality back into his body. "I thought that maybe Crissy had told you about me, even if she didn't use my name, and you were just waiting for the right signal. We never got to talk after her last trip to see you out in New Orleans."

"You knew about that."

"I gave her the cash for the ticket. I thought about telling her it would be no use, but I didn't want to be disrespectful. And I'd been wrong, and watched her be right, so many times over the years."

"You're sick."

"I'm focused, Blanche. So focused you have no idea. I know you have no gratitude and no perception—your mom made that extremely clear to me, and anyone who meets you must realize it within seconds. Do you know how hard it is being a cop here? Unrewarding? I see the charge the others get from rolling up on a domestic, defusing it, or putting the pieces together on some stupid B&E turned murder, and I think, hey, that's a goddamn cop. That's how you do it. You feel rewarded by the work, gratified by the small, the tiny, the microscopic victories. And I didn't get any of that reward crap. Because I wasn't doing any of it for me. I was doing it for Crissy Varner. Everything I did in my career was leading up to a moment that's not going to happen anymore, because she's dead. At least, it's not going to happen the way we planned. She planned."

I moved along the bench about a foot, then stood up and made a stop gesture when Maitland was starting to rise. I watched Maitland's jacket when he settled back down, looking for the shape of a holstered gun. He was close to tears and started smiling to counteract what his eyes were doing.

"You were so lucky, Blanche," Maitland said. "All those years with her. I know it must have been as much of a challenge as a reward, and ultimately it was a test that may have been impossible for you to pass, but—"

"Did you kill her?" I asked. Maitland stopped smiling, and almost looked like he was going to cross the few feet between us and put his hands on me. To shake me, not to hit me.

"I would do anything in my power to have your mother here with us again. I wouldn't ever, ever allow her to be harmed, or to harm her, if I had any power over it. I'm with you on this, Blanche. I didn't want to accept that it was some burnout like Reilly who ended up putting out that light forever, but I just can't see any other way. I've genuinely looked for another answer. No one who followed Crissy could ever do this to her. Never."

"You're a cop, Maitland," I said, trying to pretend for both of our sakes that I meant that he was a good, effective cop. I started to pace, tightly, making his eyes follow me. "Someone put that scope up there in that tree, and knew how much it meant. Either it was Crissy or someone who knew the story of the scope. Had seen photos of it, had taken the time to modify one to look just like it. So you're saying that, what, Crissy did that, just in time for the scope to get stolen? Any thief would have pawned it, not hung it like a Hallmark ornament then fired a gun to get my attention. There is someone *else* out there, Maitland. Another one like you, or someone else that my mother used like she used Emil Chadwick, to get more attention on Chuck Varner's idiocy and whatever she had planned. And I think whoever it is might have another shooting planned. Not like he shot my mother. Like Chuck shot all those people at Harlow Mall. Do you get me, Maitland? My mother's weird coded messages plus her dead body are pushing me into some pretty unavoidable suspicions."

Maitland took the lid off his soda and drank what liquid was left, then took in an ice cube and started sucking it. He looked down for a few seconds, as though he were making a silent prayer, a request for guidance. I used all my discipline to keep quiet, and it worked.

"That's not the sort of plan Crissy would have made, Blanche. We're beyond shootings. There's not going to be another Harlow Mall. And even if she did think that that sort of chaos had a role—she wouldn't have told me. Specifically me. I would have been in the dark about those types of plans."

"Why?"

"I became a cop because your mother told me to, Blanche. She said it would be useful to us someday, and that it was as good a way for me to make a life as any other. She said—I remember this part so well, and it came back to me today in a big way, because we were talking up on that hill where you showed us that scope—she said that it was important to have people like me in positions of respect and authority when the time came, because it would show how multifaceted we were, how much the group has changed since Chuck Varner. And she told me that part of my role was to be clean of knowledge that could hurt us. That's why she was careful to never, ever let me meet any of the other allies she was making."

"Allies? Fucking disciples. Slaves. That's what Chuck wanted, what she wanted. And this Reilly is clearly one of them, don't you get it?"

"No," Maitland said. He drifted for a second, smiled at a patch of wall behind my head, took on an expression that was both beatific and condescending. "Reilly is not the correct material for our belief system as it is now. Not at all. Blanche, your father may have started this movement, but Crissy became its center in a way he never could. She made it possible for people like me, who were horrified by what Chuck did but ultimately understood it, to have roles, to be a part of what was coming."

Then Maitland told me one more thing, and it was enough. The soothing, overwhelming noise of the multiplex had gone silent the second I looked at his tattoo. He was still speaking when I turned around and started walking through the thick, vulnerable crowd, running the second I hit the sidewalk.

CHAPTER EIGHTEEN

——————

THE OBVIOUS THING is to call the police. The only thing. We all think that—that's part of the logic gap that makes true crime frustrating, that I struggled with before I shot *The Marigny Five* doc.

You talk to these people, with their suspicions, with what they'd already noticed, the pieces of a full pattern they've already discerned. You want to shake them, to ask why, why don't you talk to the police, why don't you get this *taken care of,* why don't you get it out of your life?

And of course, there are a lot of reasons. Ask a black man in New Orleans why he didn't call the police and you'll hear a few of those reasons, after he gets through laughing. Ask a woman who's been assaulted and you'll hear more, after she looks into your dumb face and wonders if you're worth talking to, if you'll bother to listen or if you'll repeat the question.

When I finished running from Maitland and was back in the Arcadian parking lot, I took out my phone and I did think about calling the cops. This Detective Pargiter. "Officer Dan Maitland is a member of an unknown death cult headed up by my dead father and dead mother," I'd say. "He was investigating her murder when he told me."

Maybe a simpler "Officer Dan Maitland has ties to the victim in an ongoing investigation, and he didn't reveal them." But how hard would that be to prove? What else would I have other than what Maitland had said to me, which I could have fabricated, something he'd tell everyone I'd invented as part of my mad fantasy that Crissy's death was a conspiracy, not a simple smash-and-grab shooting?

There are always reasons not to go to the cops. Especially if you're going to them with unpleasant news about one of their own. But in that moment, the reason was control. If I let go of this information Maitland had given me, it wasn't going to be mine anymore. It would be theirs to do with what they wanted to. Which would probably be nothing.

But there was a much larger reason. The same one that drives a lot of people who could talk to the police to stay at home, to clam up. Guilt. If I told them what I knew, what I suspected, they'd look at me. And maybe, maybe, they'd find out what I'd kept secret for so long.

This was the reason Maitland was counting on. The last thing he'd said to me was, "I know what you and Crissy did, that night. Just before you left her for good. Crissy told me everything, Blanche. I know you can keep secrets when they're important. I want you to know that I can, too."

I left running, but I knew Maitland wasn't going to follow me. He'd already caught me.

CHAPTER NINETEEN

I COULDN'T NAIL DOWN precisely what woke me up: the pounding at the door, the pounding in my skull from last night's gin and tonics in my room, or Dan Maitland's phone call. I picked up the call as I walked over to the peephole. Jaya was outside, and she looked hot, dusty, and pissed. I opened the door and folded her into a half-body hug, then gestured with the phone. She wheeled her small suitcase over to the bed and flopped into the spot I'd just gotten out of.

"Did you spill booze on the sheets, or is this actually human sweat?" she said as I shushed her.

"There you are," Maitland said when I got out a "What?" in my best been-up-for-hours-but-left-my-phone-on-silent voice. "Crissy's back with us, Blanche. She's at the county morgue—has been the whole time. Computer error, like I thought. And I am so sorry. You can come down and see her at 2:45." Maitland did sound shaken, as though he'd just seen the dead body of his own mother. Probably near-true in his mangled, follower's mind. Another Chuck Varner victim, this one with a pulse and a badge.

"Are you going to be there?" I said. Jaya was staring at me, and I pressed the phone closer to my hot ear to minimize any possibility of Maitland's voice leaking out toward her.

"Of course, Blanche. We have more to talk about, whenever you're ready. And I hope you know I wasn't threatening you last night," he said, hesitating a little before his last sentence. Wondering if I had him on speaker, if I was recording this chat into my laptop. If I had the necessary agility and brainpower to get that setup going, I would have.

"Blanche," he went on, "I'm leaving the force, but that doesn't mean I can't be compromised heavily by what you know about me, just as you can from what I know about you. We share knowledge, right? That's it. I can't hurt you if you can hurt me, that's how I see it."

Jaya was staring at me expectantly now, but I held up a silencing finger. She threw an empty plastic motel cup at my head, but it fluttered to the carpet almost immediately.

"Okay," I said. "Is there anything else right now?" From the silence at the other end of the line I could sense that there was a lot of anything-else coming.

"You can meet with Vernon Reilly today. He's asked to see you before he's processed out, and there's not much I can do to stop you."

"Processed out," I repeated, slowly. I sat down on the edge of the mattress, facing away from Jaya.

"Yes. I'm sorry. All charges are being dropped. Alfred Kindt called in last night and made a deposition this morning to the tune of him being extremely unsure that it was Reilly who was on the grounds at that time of night, and that he'd seen him around the park that afternoon and only inferred the rest. Kindt is willing to face charges of obstructing justice if that's what it'll take to ensure that Reilly doesn't go to jail on his word. I don't—I'm not sure what's happening, now. I don't know who killed Crissy, but I'm going to find out. I promise you this is important to me. You know it is."

"I can't listen to this shit anymore," I said, speaking to myself and to Jaya as much as to Maitland. I ended the call with some excuses and a reconfirmation of our 2:45 appointment, after seeing the time on the bedside clock radio. It was 11:20.

"Hello," I said to Jaya. She pulled the covers over her face then immediately pushed them off.

"Every layer of this bed is grosser than the last," she said. Then she looked at me and stopped kidding around. We did the hug again, this time a real one. My mind went slightly blank from the comfort of it, and I only broke it off when I couldn't stop the thoughts from starting again.

"Everyone's lying, Jaya. This wasn't a stupid home invasion. It's got everything to do with her disgusting Chuck cult, how she never let it go. Whoever she was teaching killed her, and there's other creeps out there either covering for him or waiting to see what happens."

I told her the rest, with deletions. The mystery box I'd wrested from Kindt in the parking lot had to be secret, and so did Maitland's Chuck Varner club membership.

"Kindt rats out this local addict, just some kid, to get the cops cleared out of the trailer park. Now he's taking the identification back, but I don't know if they're going to bother to investigate, at all. No one's going to listen to me. Something really bad is going to happen if we don't find out who killed Crissy, do you get it? I don't care about her except to be fucking terrified of what she was planning with this."

Jaya had me close to her before I could babble any longer. I leaned into her and started crying, then sobbing, then just quietly heaving for what seemed like at least fifteen minutes. It was Crissy that was making me cry, again. This time, because I knew I still wasn't safe.

Crissy wouldn't be dead until everyone who believed in her and Chuck was dead. There was no safety left in the filthy secrets Crissy had built for us in the ruin Chuck had made of our lives and all those others.

"We have to talk to Vernon Reilly. Find out what he knows about Crissy, about all of this. About what's going to happen next," I said, meaning it but also trying to shift the subject away from my tears.

Jaya wasn't having it.

"Even if you hated her, it wouldn't be normal if you weren't upset. This is normal. Whatever you are feeling right now is normal. That's your mom, still, on some level. Crissy was your mom," she started whispering.

"Please shut up. Thanks, and god, I've ruined your sleeve, but no platitudes, I can't take it."

"That was the last one," she said, leaning back from me a little and then getting off the bed. She looked thinner than she had in New Orleans, which with her tiny proportions was actually possible—Jaya looked different whenever she shaved off or gained as little as three pounds, because she was so small.

"You haven't been eating," I said.

"No. I've been worrying about you. I drove up as soon as I woke up this morning, which was pretty damn early, I'll have you know. I want a shower."

"Why didn't you shower at Padma's?"

"Because there is no getting out of my ma's house for at least two hours after I set foot in there," Jaya said. She pulled off one of her shoes and looked at her toes with clinical concentration and deeply felt disgust. "This place is like three miles from Mom, Blanche. She's going to be really hurt unless you make up a really good reason why you didn't just stay at home."

"It was only my home for a couple of years," I said, in what I knew was a whiny tone when I saw Jaya's serrated side-eye.

"Two pretty important years, yeah?" Jaya said. There was a subtle shake to her voice, and she started to take her clothes off as she headed toward the shower. This was normal enough after our years as roommates. Jaya and I kept living together when we went to USC, before deciding that living together and working together was a good formula for starting to hate each other and never having sex with anyone again. What Jaya and Padma had done for me was remarkable simply in how unremarkable the life they gave me was: in the wake of Jaya's dad's death, they created two normal years of teenage living for me, an oasis of regular life that I pretended I understood and fit into until I actually did fit.

"I've been asking people about Emil Chadwick," Jaya said. She'd let the guilt pantomime play out on my face until she knew I'd arrived at a place where I would see Padma without her having to add any extra pressure, and she looked pretty smug about it. "It was hard to get publishing people talking, even though they're supposed to be worse gossips than us. But the poor little boy's been trying to make headway in TV and film for years, and I had more luck there."

"What do they say about him?"

"No one in the business likes him, his first three book pitches went nowhere, he has pretty solid narrative skills when it comes to feature pieces and scripting, and he's floating a Chuck Varner project with a surprise central character." Jaya was in the bathroom now, poking her head out. "I need to wash the highway grime down the drain, like now. Sorry. To be continued."

"No one knows it's me he's trying to sell?" I called out.

Just before the shower streamed on, she answered. "No one but you, me, and him. I think."

I walked back to the bed and reached under it, pulling out the blue box. Lighter without the money, but still substantial. Before Crissy had taken it over, it had been my own Chuck Varner reliquary: in it I'd kept the turquoise bead bracelet he'd given me for my fifth birthday, telling me it was an ancient Mayan talisman, the old pair of sunglasses that I'd stolen from his truck because I liked them so much and then been too scared to give them back when he lost his temper in the extreme at Mom when he realized they were missing, and a handful of shells from the one and only time he'd taken me to the range. He only let me hold handguns and the AR, told me I could shoot something bigger than a .22 when I was a little older. But he was dead by then.

The roll of cash was in my bag. It felt like mine, after all that Crissy had put me through and was still putting me through. Whether I came up with that reason simply so I didn't have to think too hard about where the money had come from, what Crissy had ultimately done for it, wasn't something I was willing to ask at that moment.

The weight in the box came from copper-jacketed .38s, thirty of them in six little bundles held together with elastic bands. The rounds would fit the Ruger, and I put two of the bundles into my bag, burying them deep under receipts, tissue, and a silk scarf that I had bought in New Orleans and kept forgetting to take out. It was moderately filthy by now.

There were twenty Polaroids in the box. The first twelve were real ones from one of the old cameras, the last eight from a modern Instax. I looked at each one for a few seconds, refreshing my drunken memory of staring at each of them and crying last night, then put them in my purse.

The last items in the box hadn't been left there by my mother. Crissy would never have taken off her wedding ring, for any purpose, and she'd kept Chuck's on a necklace ever since getting it back from the morgue. Whoever had put these rings in the box had wrapped them together using an unfolded and then wound-over paper clip. It was almost touching and completely creepy.

I put the rings in the change pocket of the jeans I'd be wearing that day, once I cleaned myself up. They were loose enough for me to comfortably wear the holstered Ruger at my waist all day. I left the box, with its remaining .38 rounds, on the carpet, and nudged it back under my bed.

When the shower turned off I waited a second before knocking. Jaya, towel-wrapped, kicked the door open lightly. She was using a washcloth to get steam off the mirror so she could start on her makeup.

"Hey," I said. "Something Emil Chadwick said kinda got to me. I've been sitting on it and I want to let it out."

"What?"

"You're going to be offended."

"If I'm going to be, saying that won't change anything, sweetie. Go on."

"Have you been trying to edge me into making a documentary about my dad this whole time? Not this whole time, maybe, but for the past few years? Was making the *Marigny* doc sort of your lead-up to ultimately asking me to do a Chuck Varner movie?"

Jaya had turned away from the mirror before I hit the last question.

Yes. She was pissed. She started gesturing at me with her lipstick as I backed slightly away.

"Are you asking *me* whether I've tried to manipulate *you* into doing something you didn't want to? After we both went to USC to direct and you had me coproduce every single thing you ever did in and outside of that school? After you told me that we were better as a team than we ever could be alone, and just sort of hid between the lines that I'd never get to direct anything we ever made together, because you were the artist?"

"I never—I would never say that, Jaya, because I don't think it. This is a partnership, you and me, we've always been—"

"And have I ever even asked you about Chuck Varner, once, after our conversations about him in like, our first two months knowing each other? Other than bringing him up before we shot *Marigny* to tell you that the movie was *not* about him, have I ever probed you for details? Have I ever asked you to share any of that shit with me? Have I ever given you a hard time for never asking about my dead dad, because I knew that it made you think about what a piece of shit yours was?"

"Maybe you should have asked," I said. Blurted, really, speaking before I could think, saying something I knew would hurt, even if it held barely any truth. "Maybe you should have asked me about him because there's no one else in this fucking world I can talk to about what I went through with Chuck and my mom, and I never felt like you cared to listen."

Jaya took another step toward me and raised her left hand. I thought she was going to put it on my shoulder, or maybe slap my face, but she took hold of the door instead.

"We never spoke about those things because you never wanted to. You've always set the rules for us, Blanche, from the moment we met. You let me know how far every conversation was allowed to go. I don't know if that's something you learned from—them, but it's part of you. Control. Now. I'm going to stay in here for five minutes so I don't scream at you for an hour then drive home immediately, Blanche. I know your mom died and that you're as bad at dealing with this as you are with the rest of your life, but you can bet that if I don't hear an apology the second I open this again, we're done."

Jaya shut the door quietly. Crissy used to slam the bathroom door when we had arguments. These were rare, of course—that's one thing about shared faith, even if it's poisonous: if you both truly believe, it can lessen household friction. And we both truly believed in Chuck until I suddenly stopped.

I thought about knocking on the door but went back to the bed instead, sitting down and calling out to Jaya.

"You don't have to answer but if you want you can nod or shake your head, I won't be able to tell. I'm a mess, Jaya, and I know you know that. I'm sorry, too.

"I didn't know—Jaya, I didn't know you felt like I stopped you from doing things. That makes me sick. I want to fix that however you want, whatever you need to make you feel like—Jesus, it never even occurred to me that you didn't think of yourself as a full creative partner. You practically created me. Everything good and functional and creative and worthwhile in me started in that house with you and Padma and—and I'm just nothing. I worshipped a fucking mass shooter in a trailer until I met you, Jaya. That's what I was before you. Do you know how fucked up that is?" Something in the bathroom fell and clattered—a cheap, plastic echo and a crack.

Jaya opened the door, her makeup mostly done, a broken travel blow-dryer in her hand. "I guess pretty fucked up."

"I need you," I said. Before I was conscious of it, I had crossed the room, stooping and pressing my face into Jaya's shoulder, getting it snotty and wetter than it had been before as she stroked my greasy hair and neck. At some point, I stopped.

"Okay," Jaya said. "Okay, sweetie. We're good. We're good." I guess I answered something back before making my own way into the bathroom to get ready, washing off the booze, sweat, and the crusted remains of my sobbing fit. Jaya opened the door at some point to nudge my suitcase into the steam-filled room, so I was able to come out dressed, my mental armor slowly starting to come together.

Jaya was on the bed with my purse, going through the Polaroids. She looked up at me.

"I can't believe this," she said. "And sorry, kinda—was looking for change for the soda machine. I need a Coke Zero like I need oxygen right now."

"It's fine," I said, but I took the purse back before Jaya could dig down to the bullets. I didn't care about her going through my stuff, except maybe if she had the roll of bills, but I worried about this fib. She knew, absolutely knew, that I kept all my change in the pocket of my jeans that currently held those two wedding rings, or on whatever table was nearest the entrance of whatever room I was sleeping in. Never in my purse.

"What are—Who took these? And why do they cover so much time?"

"Crissy took them, as far as I can tell." I walked over to the motel door, letting in light, humidity, and a rotten cocktail of highway and dumpster odors, underlaid by a faint sting of the forest fires burning north and east of us. It was still, somehow, refreshing.

"Not just when, it's the where. These two are LA, Los Feliz I think, this one is at USC—is this one, am I crazy, or is this from when we shot that day on Mrs. Bucknell's porch? Like, week three of the *Marigny* shoot?"

"That's what I think," I said, taking the photo out of Jaya's hand. Ada Bucknell's porch was surrounded by lattice crawling with lush flowers and foliage, purple and green bracketing her face in an establishing shot that I'd needed six takes to capture, making sure never to direct her and ruin the natural fuck-offness of her face. The Polaroid showed me with my arms raised in a gesture somewhere between an air hug and a conductor pulling back on the way to a crescendo—I think that when Crissy had snapped this, I'd been in the process of silently warning my camera assist not to tell Mrs. Bucknell we had the cameras rolling while she stared down two teenagers who were drinking across the street. I'd never seen her face look so perfectly righteous, this old woman who'd accidentally slept with the worst monster her neighborhood was to see in her lifetime—and I had to slot in a visual of her get-off-my-lawn annoyance in place of genuine rage, to capture the truth of how she felt about the Marigny Killer on film.

"So your mother stalked you around the country, taking photos of you, and never tried to contact you once the whole time," Jaya said. She wasn't quite right, but I couldn't explain to her what Crissy had actually been doing, because I didn't know myself. I hadn't been crying out of sadness when I first flipped through that stack of Polaroids the night before, but out of fear for what part Crissy had for me in her plans.

"Let's get out of here," I said, handing the picture back and sticking my head out the door. The maid's cart was two doors away. "I wanna be sure they swap out these sheets before I get back."

"Wait, wait. We can talk about any between-us stuff at lunch, but

I want to understand. Your mom was stalking you but never made contact? Took these photos but never tried to see you?"

"She did once. This day," I said, pointing to the picture in her hands.

"That day. Holy shit. When you were—when you drove off in Jerome's truck. That's what freaked you out."

"Yeah. Can we go into it later? I kinda have to get myself geared up for the morgue."

"Whenever you want. We have a stop before the morgue, so you'll have some extra prep time," Jaya said.

"What?"

"You've got to check in with Padma and so do I. Every minute she knows that we're on the ground here and that we're not in her house is a mark on our permanent records."

I told Jaya that I'd drive, and also that we probably didn't have time for her to blow-dry her hair. Just as we exited the motel room, I pretended that I'd forgotten the car keys, dodged back inside. I pulled the Ruger from under the mattress and strapped it on.

CHAPTER **TWENTY**

JAYA WAS IN the passenger seat of her car with a wet ponytail, deep into her one of her impossible micronaps, when
we pulled onto the driveway of the yellow house on Piccardo. Padma
still had a gray VW, like always, but this one was new and smaller, not
the tanker that she'd driven Jaya and I around in during high school.
She'd downsized the car, but not the sprawling four-bedroom house
that was too big for her and her daughter, remained so when I moved
in, and was now an absurdly large place for one person to live. They'd
bought it the year before Neesh Chauhan died, and Padma would
keep it until she died, too. I let Jaya keep sleeping and walked up to
the door, knocking quietly as I did in the recurrent dreams I had about
this place when I was stressed out.

Padma opened the door and I immediately made a shushing motion, gesturing toward her daughter in the car. Jaya had a slightly

drooling cheek leaned against the half-rolled-down window, and looked as peaceful in sleep as I looked hungover and confused awake. Padma and I folded each other into a deep embrace. She was taller than Jaya, my height, and barely looked older than us, thanks to an annoyingly pure diet and coping skills that were beyond my imagination. Holding her, realizing how much I needed her, I thought for the first time of the danger that I might have drawn here, to her and Jaya, by never leaving their lives after I'd entered them with such insistence, all those years ago. I held on to her and promised myself that if my lies and the parents who had spawned me ended up hurting anyone else, it wouldn't be this woman.

"Jaya, you lazy pack of bones," Padma yelled over my shoulder. She yelled softly; somehow, she could do that. I turned to watch Jaya jerk awake and peel her adhered-on cheek away from the window. She whined "Mom" in the voice she only felt safe using around her mother and slowly began gathering herself and her things.

"Don't—how many times do I have to tell you—don't tie your hair up when it's wet. It's like putting an ice cube on your scalp. You'll get sick. You probably are sick already," Padma said during Jaya's turn for an embrace. I pushed the two of them gently inside and shut the door behind us.

"She wouldn't let me dry it," Jaya said, pointing at me. Jaya regressed in small, appealing ways when she was around her mom, becoming a little more shy, a little more playful. I had never been more on my guard than when I was around Crissy or Chuck—I felt safest, most myself, the farther I was from either of them. I envied Jaya this comfort now, just as I'd envied it a decade ago.

"Sit down," Padma said, taking over herding duties from me, pushing us through the lush plant-lined hallway with its almost cloying odors of jasmine and gardenia. Padma started keeping the plants because she hated the house smelling like any kind of cooking and thought the flowers might help. The collection of greenery had grown into a jungle when she discovered that her kind of perfectionism was ideally suited to indoor gardening.

We sat on a couch I hadn't seen before, part of a three-piece set that looked infinitely more expensive than my apartment's IKEA kindling. Through and after a recession, Padma's accounting services firm had barely suffered, eventually even growing, thanks to her reputation for total competence and a knack for justifying write-offs.

"I'm sorry I didn't come earlier," I said to Padma, who was moving into the kitchen, pulling down a small crystal platter that was reserved for guests. I felt a small pang of offense that she was using it for me, but talked myself out of feeling hurt, as Jaya would be eating off it, too. Even family could become guests under certain circumstances, and I understood what those circumstances were when Padma answered.

"I'm so sorry about your mother. Not for your mother, no, I know you don't talk about her that way, but for what you're going through, for what you have to do. We love you so much, and don't apologize to me in this home again. You've been my daughter for years and I want you to know that that won't change and I won't stop saying it to you ever, Blanche."

She'd always said my name with a bit of a French-Caribbean lilt, which made no sense for someone from the subcontinent with a UK education, but it was the way I most loved hearing it. I'd already cried enough that morning, and the memory of my motel sobs was enough for me to keep dry this time. I was good at stopping emotion when I had enough time to see it coming. Chuck had taught me that, too. But I did need to get up and hold Padma again, tightly. The crystal dish dangled precariously over the sink from Padma's left hand before Jaya noticed it and leapt up, grabbing it away and placing it safely on the counter.

The three of us talked about career matters first, the parts of our lives that we'd made for ourselves, that hadn't been shaped by the violence of other people. Padma waited for the first significant pause before getting right in there and talking about her husband.

"When Neesh died, at the store, you know, the first thing I thought was that it was on purpose. He couldn't have just been robbed by some idiot who got too scared to take his money when he saw what he'd done. It couldn't be that ugly and simple. It must have been mistaken identity, some sort of plan gone wrong, or maybe someone from back home with a grudge. I invented all sorts of stories to explain that bullet."

The shot was point-blank, right outside his optometry shop on Langley, near Ninth and Schwab, a storefront I used to walk past a few times a month when I took myself out for a Slurpee while Crissy worked a late shift at the pub and I was able to wrangle Mr. Paxton's scooter keys in exchange for a promise that I'd clean it and put in a couple of bucks of gas. Jaya's dad took the bullet but kept his wallet—the cops found it in his right hand. The shooter had also put a bullet in the security camera after the shooting, which would have been useful if the camera was hooked into anything other than the building's stucco wall.

I looked over at Jaya, and Padma caught it.

"It's fine," Padma said. "I can talk about this now. I went to—I've been seeing a therapist for years. And I understand now that this is just a thing that happens here. Not just in America, but here, this town. Someone gets in the way of the wrong someone else. No pattern, no thought, just a want for money or drugs. It happened to my husband, to Jaya's dad, and now it's happened to your mother. To that Crissy woman."

She was absolutely back to being Padma with the slightly envenomed delivery of this last line. Some of our first intimate conversations, the ones where I verged on that sisterly-maternal relationship that Jaya had with her mom, were about Crissy's ravings and control of me, with any mention of the cult of Chuck carefully elided. When I moved in, after Jaya's great campaign in the face of Padma's grieving numbness, we were part of each other's resurrections. Padma took care of herself by taking care of us. But Jaya and I became symbiotic, exchanging pain for pain, support for support, until it was no longer a trade, but simply love. We talked about my crazy mother, and we talked, very selectively, about Neesh Chauhan, who briefly made the papers for being shot point-blank by a mugger for no reason other than that he was on the wrong square of sidewalk. Her father's death was then forgotten by the rest of the world in a way that Chuck Varner's never would be, in a way that none of Chuck's victims would be, and the unfairness of that hurt in a way I hadn't figured out how to talk about yet, with Jaya or anyone else.

But I could still be direct with Padma in a way that I could with no one else, even Jaya, because she had the way of asking the right question.

"What are you worried about, Blanche?"

"I'm worried more people will die. I'm worried that the bullet for my mother was only the first one. I'm worried that this is part of something that my dad put in motion a long time ago, or that my mother thought he did. And I'm worried that it's my fault, no matter how much I try to stop it."

"What?" said Jaya. Padma shushed her.

"Don't shush me, Mom, your house or not. What do you mean, Blanche?"

"Crissy—in the house, she talked about how Dad had acted too soon. But not that he shouldn't have done it at all. She thought the shooting was perfect, but it was sort of, sort of a Christmas in July." I laughed at this, and poked at a tissue box on the table. Padma's cat, Ranchero, who had replaced Jaya and me as an affection depository when we'd moved out, jumped onto the couch beside me, immediately falling asleep. The house was immaculately clean except for the occasional dead leaf and endless deposits of Ranchero's tabby-striped fur.

"So you think that—that Crissy was planning another mass shooting?"

"Yes," I said, shuddering, then putting a hand on the cat. I could feel the engine in him move into a purr, the most passive form of vitality imaginable, but still an undeniable sign of life. It reassured me, which in turn made me feel silly.

"I think that whoever killed her was someone she was trying to make into a murderer. A Chuck descendant. A tool for her lessons."

Padma shook her head, then lifted her hands off her lap and looked at them. They were shaking, too. Jaya walked over and held them.

"Don't worry," Padma said, "it's not some awful disease. It's the killing talk. This is what happens when I think of Neesh. It's why I can't watch almost anything on television. Stupid." Jaya sat down and hugged her, but Padma looked at me with intention. She had a way of talking about her own emotions with such clarity that it inspired you to talk about your own. And it was definitely calculated.

"That's really normal, Ma," I said. "It's not stupid."

"Like soldiers," Padma said, still fishing. I could tell by the lack of interjections that Jaya had caught on now—she knew her mother better than I did, of course, and had picked up on the absolute steadiness in her voice. The leading in it.

"I don't know what I have and haven't dealt with," I said. "Crissy, I think I have. When I left her, left our place, I left with only my fear of her. No love."

"That doesn't just vanish," Padma said. "Even if it turns into something else, it's still emotion. Strong. Your mother, Blanche, it turns into something."

"Maybe," I said, and then perhaps because I was so uncomfortable saying even another word about Crissy to the woman who'd done more to become my real mother than I could properly explain, I added something I'd never talked about out loud before, to anyone except Crissy.

"I was there in the mall that day. With my father. Chuck. He told me to go up to the food court and watch while he, while he did it. Killed those people. All of them."

With the words came the pictures. Chuck, strong and tall as he had always been to me, but with a different look on his face, a canted angle to the whole works that started in his eyes and seemed to be a part of the bones themselves as he drove me to the mall. When Dad came back and told us what he'd done to the couple on the highway with his rifle, Crissy thought he would want her to take me out of town. Set up someplace else. I remember her, wearing the tied-off purple blouse that I loved on her and secretly wanted to wear myself, if I thought it wouldn't disappoint Chuck that I wasn't trying to dress just like him anymore, being so happy for Dad and so upset at the same time. Trying to tell him so in a way that didn't look like she was questioning him, and all around us the heat in the trailer becoming stifling because Chuck had shut the doors and all the windows so we could conference.

"Couldn't you have waited, Chuck? I mean, why did you make the decision not to? We haven't finished building what you said we needed to build. We've got—you're supposed to teach, honey, you have to teach these people so they can do what needs to be done. You're too important. You're too important for this."

"This is my teaching," Chuck said, pulling the Beretta out. "This is my staff, this is my word, this is how they will know me. Do you understand?"

His words after that are vague. Instructions to Crissy, I think. It was the adrenalized fury and ecstasy that welded the conversation up until then to my memory. I found myself telling Jaya and Padma, who were watching me with the kind of rapt curiosity you see in children at a zoo confronting an animal they've never seen even a picture of before, but with something else added. Love, of a type so strong and woundingly intense that I couldn't look right at it. I told most of the story to the coffee table in front of me.

"Everything between that and Chuck taking me by the hand to the truck is gone. Then once we're in the mall, I remember every second. Every picture and noise. I just know that he wanted me there and that I was proud, but that watching his face in the truck was the first time that I was scared of him, in a way that wasn't just, you know, awe. I don't think that we'd actually said out loud that he was going to kill himself when he was done in the mall, but he and Crissy must have known it. They must have, it couldn't have been improvisation. My mother wouldn't have forgiven him that."

The more I spoke, the more our dead, both the hated and the loved, filled the room. Neesh Chauhan, Chuck Varner, Crissy Varner. When I chanced looking up again, Jaya and Padma were holding each other's hands, sitting so close they were almost on top of each other, and they had stopped looking at me.

"This is what I was afraid of," I said, talking fast so I didn't choke. "You're—this makes me further apart from you, I know that. You can't believe that I could see something like that and just carry on with my life. You can't. And you shouldn't."

"No!" Padma said, Jaya overlapping her with the same word.

"Let me talk," Jaya said, to her mother and me both. "You're not further from us. We just can't—I can't believe—that you didn't tell me this twelve years ago. You're supposed to need me, you jerk."

"The hours we spent talking about Neesh in this room," Padma added, standing up so quickly that she banged her knee, hard, on the coffee table before she crossed over to me and pulled me into a hug that I couldn't participate in, not yet. "We told you every single bit of what we knew and loved about him, and how hard it was to see that— to see what happened to him. And we didn't ask you once about what you'd seen. Not once. I'm so sorry."

"No," I said. "I always loved that about you. About both of you. You didn't have that thirst to know that everyone else did before I switched schools, before people started to forget about Chuck. You let it be. You let me come to you."

"I didn't think you were hiding anything like this," Jaya said. "These years you sat with this. Witnessing a massacre. Did the police know?"

I shook my head. "When he was done, when he was holding the gun up to his head down there with the people he killed, Dad nodded at me and I left. Walked out of the food court, the mall, all the way home. No one was paying attention. It was the kind of day where a kid out walking alone could pass by without anyone properly seeing her. Everyone was just too scared for themselves and their own."

Padma let go of me and stood up, backing away. She picked up a portable phone from the mantel, where it had been hidden in an elaborate snaking of leaves and stems, and shook it at me.

"You have to talk to someone, now. Not the police, nothing like that. You can't go through life just keeping that sight inside of you. Those people. Your father. It's—it's a miracle you can do anything, Blanche."

"It's not a miracle, it's you. It's you, it's Jaya, it's me. It's my work. Trauma isn't one-size-fits, Ma. I saw it, I was there, and that's that. No conversation can take it out of my head."

"That's bull," Jaya said. "That's too easy."

"Dealing with it has meant turning away, Jaya. Padma. Looking it dead-on isn't going to give me superpowers, it's going to shake me apart. I want to get this over with, I don't want to start it again. I don't want to spend any time at all in that past. I want to look at my dead mother, then I want to make sure that there's an end to all of Chuck's poison, and I just want to go home."

CHAPTER TWENTY-ONE

I T WAS HER.

The bullet had gone in through Crissy's forehead. Her hair was tidily arranged to flow out from the sides of her head, probably to camouflage how flat the back of her skull was from being blown out at close range.

"She only dyed her hair for work," I said to Jaya, who was watching me and emphatically not looking at the body. "Said no one tips an old lady, especially the happy hour business-suit trash she dealt with when they stuck her with just weekdays. Even when she was barely thirty-five, she was saying this. It is so fucking weird to remember that we had normal conversations sometimes, you know?"

I looked at Jaya, who was streaming tears without making a sound. She nodded, and I could tell she wanted to come closer to me, but the hundred-and-ten-pound fact of the body between us didn't let her.

They hadn't taken Crissy out of a drawer. She was just lying on a table, a sheet pulled up over her with her two arms down at her sides, the wax white of her face blending into the roots of her hair. Without her blue eyes open, with her features perfectly still—she looked more like me than I could take.

She was dead, though. Seeing that gave me the assurance that Maitland couldn't. After talking to him I'd dreamed of a stranger's corpse in this white-and-gray room, a sacrifice body that Maitland had used to help Crissy vanish into an anonymity where she'd be more dangerous. Impossible, of course. But it was still good to see Crissy here, contained, limited, gone, on this slab that looked like the zinc bartop of my regular drinking hole in Koreatown. Definitely Mom, definitely dead.

Maitland was outside talking to the whitecoat who'd let us in. I kept staring at Crissy for another few minutes, circling the corpse like a priest conducting some nameless ceremony. I was, I think, looking for movement. Twitches. Life.

"I guess they expect some righteous anger out there. Or tears," Jaya said. She'd kept quiet until the exact second when I was finished and felt ready to hear a voice. She was a master interpreter of silences.

"They can keep thirsting. I gave the cop a good dose of that yesterday. The anger, I mean." All I'd told Jaya about Maitland was what I had to on the drive up: about finding the scope behind the trailer, and that he wasn't doing a good job of the investigation. Nothing about Chuck Varner's cult and Maitland's tattoo. Nothing about what he'd threatened me with.

"Right," Jaya said. "But are you—are you all right?"

I turned to her and laughed out of surprise, the sound obscene in this room. She was facing the wall, like someone in a horror movie.

"What? I just can't look at her even peripherally anymore, I'm sorry. I can't," Jaya said.

"If I can, you should be able to," I said, walking over and poking Jaya in the arm. She kept staring at the wall.

"You have to look at her. I don't have to do anything but be here for you. I already did this in high school, in this exact room, looking at my dead dad on one of these slabs while Mom sobbed outside and two techs joked around like ten feet away from me as though I'd gone deaf or couldn't speak English. That mugger shot him so close half his face was gone. His mustache was just a hole."

"I know, baby," I said to her, though I really didn't. Jaya had lost someone she loved, and I hadn't. All the good that had come out of Crissy's insanity was in my arms just then in the morgue—this connection with Jaya, the girl I'd sought out after her father died, who I moved in with, who I convinced to join me in petitioning the state to let us go to the next grade of high school in a different county, so I wouldn't be the Girl With the Killer Dad and Jaya wouldn't be the Girl With the Murdered Dad. So we could just be a pair of nobodies in the hallway. And that's what we got, more or less, once I had my new name and a new school.

"Let's get out of here," I said, propelling Jaya toward the door with some minor shoves, leaving Crissy behind in whatever void she now existed in with Chuck Varner.

"Wait," I said, turning back. Maitland and the tech were visible through the doorway's tiny window, and they were emphatically not looking at us—probably the hug and Jaya's tears had turned them around. "Make sure you're between the door and me."

All business again, or almost, Jaya positioned herself as told while I went back to the table. I pulled off my boot and extracted the small, flat Vixia camera I'd slid down the side that morning, and shot a minute of silent footage of my mother's body. A slow track that ended on the bullet hole.

"Done," I said, getting the camera back into the boot. Maitland hadn't frisked or scanned us on the way in, but I figured there was a chance that he or someone else might on our way out.

The whitecoat was gone by the time we exited, leaving just an impatient Maitland, tapping away at his cell phone and affixing a look of concern not quite in time for our exit. I took my own phone out of my purse and slipped it into my jeans pocket, setting it to record audio. Maitland looked underslept, but not hungover.

"Ms. Potter? Coping?" Maitland had barely acknowledged Jaya since our arrival, which was fine by her. She'd grabbed her phone the moment we were out of the morgue, taking it out of the little plastic bucket by the door where we'd been asked to leave our electronics, and was likely beating back emails from the production company asking where the hell we were for press on *Marigny* and pretending to be enthusiastic about the Caroline Blackwood documentary we were trying to sell them on.

She was also probably memorizing every word we said. Jaya didn't always like being ignored, but when she was, she made full use of her invisibility.

"Yeah, I'm doing absolutely great, Officer, sure. Still think this was a totally random break-in?"

"Like I told you earlier, Ms. Potter, we're going to have to start from scratch. But yes, there is still no reason to figure this was premeditated," he said. He was looking at Jaya now, significantly, then looking back at me. "But without Kindt to place him at the scene, there just isn't enough to hold Vernon Reilly, no. And Kindt's alibied, too, before you ask. We ran powder tests on him at the time, I interrogated him personally, all of it. He had a buddy with him that evening, watching the game. We've talked to the friend, pinned down his cell signal: checked out that he was with Kindt, that they were in a sports bar a half-mile away from your mother's trailer at the time of death."

"You didn't check up on his location when Kindt told you he'd ID'd the killer, though."

"No. It seemed like a lock. We didn't have much reason to suspect Kindt of killing her at the time, and now he's alibied."

"I can agree with you on that point alone, I guess." Even with a gun, Kindt wouldn't be any sort of challenge for Crissy, even if he came in when she was asleep. She was a light sleeper.

Sharing the secret of our conversation last night brought Maitland and me closer to each other, an invasive, creeping closeness that made me nauseous.

"I owe Mr. Kindt another thank-you visit," I said. "Thanks for ID'ing my mother, thanks for misidentifying her murderer, that kind of thing."

"Kindt never saw the body. Hung around the trailer while forensics was there, though, either right out front or, after I told him to leave, sitting on the hood of his car about twenty feet away. Eating sunflower seeds and sipping Gatorade while he stared." Maitland pointed to the doors at the end of the corridor and we started to walk out of the morgue, Jaya lagging a few feet behind us.

I whispered to Maitland. "One of Chuck Varner's people killed her, Maitland. Not you. One of the others. You *know* this now. This is not random, the trail going cold while this stooge Reilly sat in jail for just long enough. This isn't right. And whoever it was waited until

I got to town to get active again, with the scope, with Kindt flipping his ID. Things are happening too quickly, and it's going to get worse."

Maitland answered at full volume.

"I know it isn't right, Ms. Potter, and I'm frustrated, too. I thought this was locked up, and that I'd done right by your mother, and now I don't know exactly what to do."

"You talk to Kindt again. You talk to him long and hard in a room that's too bright. You do it or I'll make sure a real cop does." We exited the building and stood in the rank heat and sunlight, a combination that enhanced the depth and sharpened the corners of my hangover.

Maitland took sunglasses out of a little case on his belt and put them on. "There's no need to go over my head, Ms. Potter. I've been checking in daily with Detective Pargiter. He'll be contacting you himself today."

"You still think it was a home invasion. With everything that you know about Crissy Varner, every detail, you still think that."

Jaya looked at me sharply, dropping the pantomime with her phone. She knew, in that second, that I'd been holding out on her about Maitland.

And Maitland dipped his eyes. "We'll know what happened when the time comes," he whispered.

I caught it, but couldn't know if Jaya did. My phone, still recording audio, projected an inch or so from my pocket, and I made sure not to drum my fingers on its surface.

"There's still nothing we've seen so far to dissuade me from the home invasion theory," he said. "I can't think of another logical angle on this, and if you can, I'd love to hear it." Behind the shades, Maitland's eyes were narrowed into a simulated Eastwood stare. It didn't work.

"It's not what you've seen. It's what both of us know, Danny. And what the fuck is he doing here?" I yelled this last part, pointing over Maitland's back.

Jaya said, "No way," as Maitland turned to see Emil Chadwick leaning against the hood of a Budget rental Acura, in a parking space twenty feet from us.

I caught the wince that started on Maitland's lips and crawled up to his eyes.

"I wanted to be here to capture the reunion, Blanche," Chadwick said. He was wearing a linen suit with a white shirt that I wanted to stain a deep red. "And to pick up our chat." He nodded at Maitland, who nodded back.

"You know each other?" Jaya asked.

"Mr. Chadwick got Ms. Potter and I in contact," Maitland said. "We were unable to track her down after her mother's death, and Mr. Chadwick had a line on—"

"He's a little turd that's been trying to blackmail Blanche into taking part in his Junior Journalist project," Jaya said. Her meekness in the morgue was impossible to remember now that she was fired up. "You should arrest him."

"For what?" Chadwick asked.

"For being a dick," Jaya said.

Chadwick smiled.

"For riding your mommy's coattails to a career that you still can't make anything of," I added.

Chadwick stopped smiling. "I came down here because a source has been keeping me apprised of key details of the case, and made me aware that we've lost our prime suspect," he said. "I have an interest."

"And what might that be?" Maitland asked.

For now, at least, I had little doubt that he was Chadwick's source, that he was trying to shove the conversation onward from that little reveal. Chadwick had told me he'd talked to my mother once—was Maitland at that meeting, as well?

"Your source is this cop," Jaya said.

Maitland started a retort that died on his tongue when I looked at him. "I've been answering Mr. Chadwick's inquiries honestly, as he's a member of the press, and our department is open with the press. I would have thought that documentarians would appreciate transparency."

At least his answer was almost truthful.

"I think, and I have told Officer Maitland, that Ms. Varner's murder could be the start of a new wave of violence that we should all be very afraid of," Chadwick said. "Don't you agree, Blanche?"

"Yes," I said, even though it hurt quite badly to agree with Chadwick. "The difference being that I'm trying to stop it, and you're staking your career on it happening, aren't you, Emil?"

Both men were stone-faced by now. Jaya put her hand on my wrist and gave me a tug in the direction of her car. "Let's go see Vernon Reilly the second he's processed out, Blanche. Before any cops or fake writers can convince him to bullshit us, too."

Chadwick waved at us as Jaya bundled me into her car and pointed us toward the San Joaquin County lockup. Maitland just stared. As we drove out of the lot, the two men started talking.

CHAPTER TWENTY-TWO

THE BOY WAITED in Kindt's office just long enough to feel stupid, before he started rifling through his memories for something else he knew about the old man. A place he would run to. Kindt was obedient, the kind of obedience that came with absolute faith, but he was also scared. He'd been told to wait exactly six hours after exonerating Vernon Eagle Reilly before even thinking of going anywhere, and by hour five, The Boy was on his way to Kindt's inevitable hiding place.

The Village West Marina was where Kindt had dumped all the money he'd skimmed off tenants and the landlord for the decades of his tenure at the Underwood park. The Boy made the drive out, two miles west of Interstate 5, carrying in his brain Kindt's boat slip number, which had been printed on innumerable bills in the scummy little office.

So The Boy was waiting for Kindt when the old man huffed down the stairs to the cabin of his twenty-eight-foot houseboat, so much tidier and cleaner than the spaces where he spent his landlocked hours. When he saw The Boy, Kindt moaned, a reaction so genuine that The Boy laughed.

"You really seem like a different person here, I was thinking, right up until you made that pathetic crushed-duck noise. A spick-and-span sailor, a retired navy man with a glint in his eye and scads of charm to give away. That's probably how you present yourself to the other lushes and retirees out here, isn't it? Mooning around the bar and telling stories about the job you've made up to fit in? What was it—something close, I imagine, so you wouldn't feel totally lost the minute you got a question back. Building management?"

"Hotel. I owned a small hotel," Kindt said. He sank down heavily on the step. Above him, through the open hatch, The Boy could see Kindt's suitcases perched on deck. Would have to remember to get those down in here immediately afterward.

"You say that so well, Alfred. I would believe you, I think, especially after a couple of beers and some comradely talk of the high seas. Can you pilot this thing, or do you need a helper?"

"I can," Kindt said.

"You're wheezing, Alfred. Old Wheezy." The Boy laughed again, but stopped when Kindt got the old, evil look in his eye.

"You little shit," Kindt said. "Why she picked you I'll never know. To fuck, sure. But as the follower? Chuck Varner's torch in the world? No one understands it. None of us who knew it, who'd seen you, talked to you, could believe it. I knew Chuck. I know what he was, and you're not it."

"So you did used to watch us have sex while you slapped at your limp little maggot," The Boy said, aware of and furious at the quaver in his voice. Kindt heard it and seemed to suck it in with his next mouthful of oxygen, shivering and laying a hand on his forearm, pushing down the rising goose bumps.

"Who'd want to see that? 'Boy' is the only thing she got right about you. They used to call me a pervert behind my back at the park, you know. Happens with someone who looks like me, working a job like that, whether you're an ogre or kind to the kids. Part of the job. But I want you to know that even the nastiest pedo wouldn't have wanted anything to do with you when you first came to Crissy. She barely managed to fix you at all. No matter what you look like, you're repulsive, you know? You repulse people. You will never lead."

"You're scared of me," The Boy said to Kindt. "That's why you're trying to go for this brave speech. You think this is a movie. It's not."

"No matter where she said you came from, I know what you are. Just an incest-obsessed little boy out to shoot up a world that thinks he's not good enough. You don't get anything *about* Your Life Is Mine. Nothing about Crissy, nothing about what Chuck was trying to achieve. You'll give us all a bad name, all because of one mistake Chuck made and a long mistake that Crissy never stopped making."

Kindt started whistling a song, getting a few bars in before The Boy came over and wrapped his hands around the old man's throat, squeezing. He started to bang the body against the steps, and was grateful to see fear and pain return to the rheumy eyes. The suitcases, balanced against the hatch, came tumbling down the stairs as The Boy finished his work. For security, he found a whiskey bottle in the galley and then used it to methodically pound Kindt's trachea flat. The old man didn't twitch. Crissy's careful instruction, his own sharp discipline, and Officer Dan Maitland's careful crime scene management had kept The Boy's fingerprints and genetic traces out of any database, so there was nothing to worry about at the scene. By the time Kindt's body was found, The Boy's anonymity would be of no use to anyone, let alone himself.

Walking back to his car, The Boy hummed the tune that Kindt had been whistling, in an effort to remember it himself. He got it right as he put his hand on the door handle.

"Under the Boardwalk," he said, and laughed. The old man had really rallied at the end there. It was almost inspiring.

CHAPTER TWENTY-THREE

TELL ME PADMA doesn't know anything about this," I said to Jaya.

"So we're not going to talk about that weird phantom-conversation you and the cop were having? Is that it? What the hell is going on, Blanche? What does 'We'll know what happened when the time comes' mean, and why the hell is a *police officer* saying it to someone with a dead mother? We're going to the station to talk to someone sane right after this, and that's a definite."

"Jaya, I can't. Please. Not yet. I can't talk about this. But yes, we'll go to the cops," I lied. Maitland still had me, as I had him—I couldn't tell any of his superiors he was a Varner man without opening myself up to everything he knew about the last week of my life before I left Crissy.

"Look at me," Jaya said.

I took my eyes off the road for a moment to make eye contact, for just long enough for her to register that I wasn't telling her the whole truth, and just long enough for us both to know that she knew it.

"Fine. For now, fine. And, no, I didn't tell my high-strung mother that we're picking up a recently-off-the-hook-for-murder, multiply-convicted-of-crimes creep from prison to ask him a bunch of uncomfortable questions."

We had about a half-hour to kill until the 4:30 meeting, so I took us along the waterfront, pointing out a few Chuck Varner–relevant sites.

"That's the bookstore Chuck used to leave me at when he went drinking at Morley's. There's where Morley's used to be. An A&W now, but trust me, it was very visual."

The bookstore used to be run by ex-hippies who were getting broker by the day. Chuck would leave them ten bucks as a sort of mass-rental fee and put me in the kids' section for two, four, five hours. Days when he had an appointment with a woman that would take too long to leave me with an ice cream at the beach. The woman owner of the bookstore, named Kimberly something and smelling pleasantly of sandalwood and sweat, sometimes took me to the apartment above the store for soup and a nap. I never went back after Harlow Mall.

"How long would he leave you for?" Jaya asked. She understood what I was doing: offering up some intimate information that I didn't usually talk about in place of answering her other questions.

"Long," I told Jaya. "That's the hotel he took women to." I pointed up at the sign, Cabana Hotel, with a palm tree and a well-built hut on a pale blue background that had gone two shades paler since I'd last been in Stilford, and would look white on a less than perfectly set up and color-corrected shot.

"When you were—did he make you wait for him?" Jaya asked. "God."

"I didn't think of it as waiting for him. He trained me to see it as a fun, secret excursion for both of us, a secret from Crissy." I laughed. Jaya didn't.

We pulled over for gas before starting the last push out to the jail. I turned off the AC, letting the dry wind cool us through the open windows. Jaya pushed her loose silver watch up her arm and rubbed at the sweaty constriction mark it had left, but then kept her hands locked on her knees. Years in LA hadn't made her any more relaxed about highway driving than she used to be when we were in high school. Especially when someone other than her was driving.

"What do we know about Vernon Reilly?" she said. "Anything? Everything?"

"Barely any of his convictions are violent. The assaults look like barfight crap. And no sex crimes. So said Maitland, anyway."

"Great. What else did he say?"

"I can show you," I said, thinking of another way I could give Jaya something, if not exactly what she wanted to know. I pulled my phone out of my purse when we hit a stoplight, and started fumbling with the hookup in Jaya's stereo. The light changed and she took the phone from me, patching it into the stereo herself.

We listened to the first conversation I'd had with Maitland, back at the station. Jaya was a patient driver, but an impatient listener. She did laugh at Maitland's plaintive "hope you're not recording this" line, but after a couple more minutes, Jaya switched over to a throwback '90s R&B station.

"I can't listen to him creepily fish for facts about your dad, Blanche."

"I know."

"It's gross. It really is. But he's doing worse and I don't understand why we're not stopping him, okay? You have to explain that to me. He's leaking information to Emil Chadwick, Blanche? This is—it's got to be illegal, doesn't it?"

"Who said leak? He's speaking to press, presumably not spilling anything that he could get in trouble for, because Maitland doesn't strike me as dumb, and Chadwick wouldn't strike anyone as discreet."

"Chadwick has some hold on Maitland. I can see it. Some leverage."

It wasn't a hold, no. It was a bond that I almost shared with them—a connection through Chuck and Crissy. Even if Chadwick wasn't a member of the cult, he was a breed of worshipper. Awed by the past shooting, eager for the next one. Wanting a role in it, even if it was just coverage, absorption, inside information, a seat at the feast of mass death that I worried was days or hours away.

"I don't think either of them shot my mother, Jaya. And I guess that's what should actually matter to me right now, even if all this other shit is wonderfully distracting." I ground my teeth together, almost loud enough to be heard over the radio, thinking about how much longer I could lie to her. I knew, at least, that I wasn't setting the pace, the schedule. Whoever had shot Crissy, whoever had followed me and hung that scope in the trees, was the timekeeper.

Jaya knew that some of my bitchy non sequiturs were a poorly phrased request for silence, and that was the case here. We didn't talk until we were about two minutes away from our exit.

"I'm rethinking the Reilly thing," Jaya said. "We should be doing this more officially, don't you think? Literally everything we know about him is about violence and erratic behavior." Jaya fiddled with the sun visor, blocking my view of the side-view mirror, and I had to gently push her arm down so I could change lanes safely.

"Look," I said, taking a calculated risk. My left hand on the wheel, I pulled my shirt up a few inches, showing Jaya that I had the Ruger holstered on. "I know you hate these things and you should know I do, too, but right now, it's making me feel a lot safer."

Jaya recoiled against the passenger door. "Take it away. Take it away right fucking now," she said.

"It's not loaded."

"You're lying."

"Yes, but only because you're so afraid. Jaya, I know guns. I wish I didn't but I do, and when I have one, it's not a murder weapon," I insisted, glancing at her as I talked to reassure her. "I'm using it to keep us safe, and that means that I probably won't even touch it. We need to talk to him, and we can't go through the cops. Maitland can't be trusted and he's sure to have told everyone else in the department to ignore the crazy bitch who comes in raving about her dead mom and her spree-shooter father."

"You sound like a fucking NRA commercial, talking about that thing," Jaya said, her voice shaking.

I braked to follow the curve of the exit road and put both hands up on the wheel. Jaya reached for the gun and I slapped her hand away with a cracking impact that bounced her palm off the parking brake.

"Don't touch it," I screamed. "You have no idea what you're doing and you have no idea what we're inside of right now, do you get that? These are people who kill people. They killed my mother. Chuck blew apart the spines and guts of nine people in that mall. I know what a gun can do and I know what a piece of shit who has one can do, and I know what I'm not going to let happen to you, do you hear me?"

Jaya sat still. For a moment I thought she was going to yank up on the parking brake, pull the car into a screeching swerve.

"Your dad shot people? Great. My dad got shot, for no reason, by someone who probably was just as confident that they knew what they were doing with a gun as you suddenly seem to be. All I'm saying to you is that if I see that thing in your hand, I'm going home to say goodbye to my mother, right after I tell her why I'm leaving, and then you and I are never going to talk again. Clear?"

Jaya had been angry at me before, of course. Countless times. We'd been as close as friends could possibly be, closer than family, because we chose each other and made the choice to marry our careers together. But, even this morning at the motel, she'd never talked to me with this breed of deal-closing coldness, the tone of someone who was willing to walk out the door and consider the consequences afterward.

"Jaya, I'm sorry. I can't—don't say that to me. There's nothing left of me if you go. That's pathetic but it's fucking true."

"Shut up. Just listen to me and shut up. Don't let me see the gun again." She touched the back of my hand, which was clamped in a bloodless squeeze around the wheel, and spoke softly. "I understand, kind of. We need to get through this, but you need to know that there are places I can't go. I can take anything the world puts in our way, but I can't take you being a different person, Blanche. I can't take you being a person who casually flashes a gun. Don't tell me where you got it and don't let me see it again."

I heard forgiveness in what she said, but also some latitude. She didn't want to see the gun again, but that didn't mean I had to get rid of it.

We got to County just as Vernon Reilly was being put through the last of his processing-out. After Jaya got out, I took the holster and Ruger off and slid them under my seat, in case we had to go inside for Vernon. We ended up waiting in a parking space that the guard pointed us to very specifically, sitting on the hood of the car until a bruised, younger version of the elderly Charles Manson who wasn't vigorous or charismatic enough to look like the young Charles Manson came through. I called him over first, at Jaya's prodding.

"He might not be the most unracist guy," she said. It took about a minute of talking and the word "Denny's" to get Vernon Reilly into the back seat of our car. Jaya and I stood outside for a second after he'd gotten in, taking a breath, staring confidence that neither of us quite felt into each other's eyes. Reilly was a petty criminal. If Crissy had turned Reilly, had brought him into Your Life Is Mine the way I thought she had, it told me something: that I could handle him, too.

While Jaya checked her phone, I got into the car, immediately reaching down and pulling the Ruger out from below my seat, wrapping it in the light sweater I'd been using as a back pillow and stuffing the package into the driver's side door storage panel. I didn't want to risk sliding a gun into Reilly's hands the first time I hit the brakes too hard.

I switched the station to outlaw country as soon as the engine was on and Jaya was inside. She kept taking looks backward that she probably thought were subtle, but were as telegraphed as silent film mugging to an experienced prison body language expert like Reilly. He chuckled, but only once, and Jaya probably thought he was laughing at something in his head. About five minutes into our drive back to Stilford, Reilly politely asked for us to look for some rap on the dial.

"No trap shit, though," he said. His voice was picking up an increasingly cringey hood inflection the farther we got from the jail. "And sorry about your moms, having nothing to do with it even as I do."

"Thanks."

"You know who killed her?" Reilly asked.

"No, do you?" I asked.

Jaya shot me a look, wanting us to save this for the restaurant, where I knew she was thinking she could at least ask Reilly if he minded us setting up a little camera, perhaps signing a release.

"Nah," he said. "I really thought you'd a said something interesting on that, though."

"Why?"

"Because your mom said you killed her."

"You knew her!" Jaya said, and I gave her a shut-the-fuck-up glance.

"Yeah. Shit yeah I did. Was her em-plo-yee. Just not the kind of information I was willing to offer up to any pigs."

Maitland probably hadn't even asked him any questions, probably just intuited that, like Kindt, this man in the wrong place at the wrong time was following orders of a sort in staying quietly in jail until it was time for him to be let go. Crissy's orders to soldiers who weren't allowed to know or speak to each other. A risky but perfect organization in at least one respect: you can't betray someone you've never met.

"But yeah, before Crissy even got shot she was calling you out as the one that did it. She said you was gonna kill her. But kinda nice, like, like she was sweet on you and the idea of you killing her. Crazy. She called you Chuck Varner's true daughter."

"Oh?" I said. I couldn't look at Jaya, and I knew if I looked back at Reilly, my fist would land on his face a second after my eyes did.

"Yeah. Proud, you know? Loved you. Paid me like a grand, gave me a plane ticket to come take photos of you all in NoLa. Said I was the kind who could blend in good in a shitty neighborhood." Reilly laughed. He was skinny and short but somehow managed to take up the entire back seat as he started clawing his hair back into a ponytail. Crissy had had him out there with her when she was stalking me. It was odd to reorient my idea of her taking the Polaroids to Reilly doing it, but it made sense. She always liked having partners or proxies on field missions.

"So you knew her for long enough that you were—following her."

"Not following-following, if that's what you mean, haha," Reilly said, pronouncing the "ha's" and drumming his hands on the back seat. "I wasn't 'ally' material, she always said. And fuck no I did not tell the cops about any of this."

I looked at Reilly in the rearview: past the scrappy beard, there were ropy Egon Schiele tendons around his mouth, a jaw that drooped to show the stumps of teeth burnt out by a decade of various kinds of pipe-sucking, frozen green eyes with unmoving, tiny pupils. His smile looked like he was trying to wink and couldn't do it without moving the rest of his face. Chuck never would have picked him out for any- thing more than a sacrifice errand, and Crissy would do the same. I could see how Crissy and Chuck would look at a particular kind of loser like him: the kind of fake-tough zero whose middle-class back- ground hung around him no matter how much street talk he picked up, how many teeth he lost, and how many scabs he acquired. *Some- one who always pretends and never follows through.* I couldn't remember whether it was Chuck or Crissy who had said that in a lesson. It didn't matter.

"I've seen you," Jaya said. "Around where we were shooting over there."

"You got it. I love NoLa. Was a trip I'd a taken myself without mommy's paycheck but that just made it sweeter. But where you were making your home movies, that was a part of town that knew how to party, you know? You gots to get distance from those tourists if you really want to get deep."

Another of the Polaroids I'd found in the blue box came into my mind: me, crouched in front of Mrs. Bucknell's house, waving to my sweating B-camera op to get into a crouch, too, so he could get the right angle of the old woman walking into her home with the portrait of her dead sister just visible through the open doorway. About an hour before Crissy had approached me. Had Reilly even known she was there in NoLa, following him as he was following me? I touched Jaya's knee, warning her off talking more.

Sitting in the packed Denny's on Charter Way, Reilly opened up further. For food, first, shoveling in a double order of hash browns that he'd crushed two fried eggs and half a bottle of ketchup into.

"She was with you on that trip, right?" I asked.

"How you know that?" Reilly asked, speaking to the potato-yolk slurry on his fork that he was communing with.

"We can get through this faster if the questions go one way," I said.

Jaya snorted assent. Reilly kept talking.

"Just I thought you never talked to her, and I knew I thought it was fucked, her paying for me to fly out then coming herself next day. But yeah, I got to the motel, did fuck-all but drink, she got there the second night.

"Crissy was pissed I hadn't been working. Shooting you, I mean. Knew where to find the motel 'cause she'd booked it." Reilly took awhile to get all this out, because he'd gotten the entire meal off his plate and into his esophagus in between words.

"How did she look to you the last time you saw her?" I asked Reilly, even though I hadn't intended to at all. It was dinnertime, but I stuck with Reilly's breakfast theme, getting bacon and toast. The server saw my look when she set down the quarter-cooked rashers of fat in front of me—she took them back to get them grilled up to crispy and brought my plate back.

"She looked good, man, I guess," Reilly said, licking yolk from his mustache and ketchup from his beard. Jaya was still looking away but couldn't avoid the sounds—this kind of slobbishness stirred violent thoughts in her. She'd once reached into my mouth to pull out a piece of gum that I was apparently chewing "like a fake '70s New Jersey movie prostitute."

"Good how? Healthy? Normal?"

"What are you getting at?" Jaya asked, interrupting.

I ignored her and picked a piece of bacon off my plate, crunching it. Emulate their movements, Chuck used to say. They'll listen to you if they think you're like them but on a higher level.

"Healthy, all that. Little sloppy in the clothes but that was regular for her," Reilly said. "Crissy was only ever real put together after work. That's when we met most—right off the highway when she got back from her job, up until she quit last year. After that we met at bars. Only let me come to her place once."

"You think that was odd?" Jaya asked. She was recording video from her phone, which was propped up against her little clasp purse. She was savvy enough not to ask for Reilly's permission yet, something that always derailed an interview. We'd ask afterward.

"Nah. Lotta people don't want me in their houses. I used to steal shit, I get it." Reilly did look shy about this, smiling in a school-picture wince that was probably cute when he had his teenage teeth. "Probably what made it so easy for Kindt to send me up to County. That and a shit public defender who wouldn't even make a couple phone calls to alibi me once I'd waited long enough. Fucker. Kindt, I'm going to be having a real personal talk with, right soon."

"I don't think you mean that," I said. "And if you do, can you wait? I want to talk to him, too. Actually talk, not beat."

"What do you mean 'waited long enough?'" Jaya said. "You were waiting for something before you made an effort to get out of jail? What?"

"Shit," Reilly said, then went right into answering my question about Kindt as though Jaya hadn't said anything. "No promises on the old man's health and safety." He scraped at his molars with his fork and checked the tines for plaque. There was a lot.

"Promise, so we don't have to tell Officer Maitland," Jaya said. It was odd for her to make a miscalculation like this—she was nervous, more nervous than I'd ever been, and that made me feel calmer. In control for the both of us.

"Maitland." Reilly laughed, and not for effect—out of authentic amusement. "You want to rat on me—and yeah, I was joking, I was joking—tell a real cop, not the kid who begged for this case so he could handle it front to back and get what he needed."

"What?" Jaya asked.

"Maitland let me know that if I kept my mouth shut until the right time came, I'd come out of jail free and richer. And it didn't matter who I talked to about it after a couple days, or nothin'. Weirdest fuckin' cop deal I've heard of, so I guessed that he was one of Crissy's boys. How about it, am I right?" Reilly was asking me, but I was staring at him, through him, at the prospect that Maitland was even more of a psycho than I'd thought. That even when he was being honest with me, he'd been lying about almost everything.

Reilly laughed and leaned back in the booth, knocking his coffee over with his knee. He didn't mind.

"I need someone to start making sense," Jaya said, pulling napkins out of the dispenser and floating them toward Reilly's lap. He did the patting and soaking up, then got up.

"Hold it," I said. "Wait."

"Wait for what? I'm free and you got absolutely no hold on me. Just a ride down from lockup, and now here we are. I could use a good walk." He sat back down, though, as the waitress approached, staring at her body in the black-apron-on-black-slacks-and-shirt uniform as though it were a transparent vinyl dress. She was a small girl, maybe Filipino, and I tried to communicate an apology to her with my eyes. Reilly waited as Jaya paid our bill, and we all left together, Reilly walking faster than us. I tapped his shoulder and got him to stop when we were out the front door.

"I'll give you $500 for a few more minutes and answers, Vernon," I said, doing my best to smile at him even as I ignored his high-beam staring at my tits. Eye-drilling the waitress had broken some sort of creep-dam of lust in him. I didn't even cross my arms while I waited for him to answer.

"Five hundred dollars gets you, say, two answers."

"Did Maitland tell you there was something bad planned after you got out of jail?"

"Wait," Jaya said. "We don't pay for interviews, Blanche, come on."

I turned on her and laughed, but she didn't laugh back—she had her no-bullshit high-integrity face on, and not just the fake one she had in meetings where she was insisting on an edit that we both needed to get past a distributor.

"That's a movie rule, Jaya. This is a murder."

"Nope," Reilly said. "Didn't tell me shit but that I should wait and it would work out for me. It was easy time to do in there, knowing I'd be out soon. I had to wait much longer, I could have called an actual lawyer and I could have gotten alibied by a bar full of people in SF, where I actually was the night Crissy got it." Reilly walked a few feet away from us and started to flick at the hood emblem of a silver BMW, which would have looked out of place in this Denny's parking lot if you didn't know Stilford. People didn't lose their taste for the food they grew up with here, even if they had managed to cash in on the city going broke through smart legal dealing or opportunistic drug dealing. The lot was clear of people, but crammed tight with cars— the capacity of the restaurant reflected the capacity of the parking lot, so people jonesing for all-day breakfast could take a look from the road and move on to the next franchise.

"What were they waiting for?" I was nervous about the car's alarm going off, but it hadn't yet, so all we had to worry about was the owner coming outside to scream at us.

Reilly stopped poking at the emblem and turned around.

"You," he said. "That's all I can think of. Crissy wanted you back here so bad, and now you are here. Guess Maitland, if he was one of her boys—"

"He was," I said.

"What the fuck?" said Jaya. "You know about this, Blanche? It's true? The cop's—"

"Maitland knew he could get you where Crissy wanted you," Reilly said. "Could at least do that for her, if he couldn't keep her alive. And the other kid, too."

"Who? Who's the other kid?" I wanted to shake Reilly, the fucking moron, for just tossing this in. I could tell he hadn't even been with-holding it: he just genuinely didn't realize what was important and what wasn't.

"I guess that's question number three, gonna have to charge you extra. But you look trustworthy so I'll give you this up front. I can tell you this much: he was 'ally material,' like your mom would say. Crissy told me I wasn't good enough to do the most important work. The 'gun work' to come, she said.

"I saw the back of him, once. Skinny fucker. He was in her trailer that time I went by. He wasn't wearing a shirt, and Crissy got between me and him as soon as I opened the door. She was fucking pissed, booted me out right away. He good enough for the 'gun work'? I asked her. She didn't even answer or ask why I swung by. Threw a fifty on the dirt and didn't take my calls for a couple months."

"Oh my god," I said. Crissy had gotten me back to Stilford the only way she could be sure that I'd come. By getting herself dead. She knew I would need to see her body. That I'd need to know.

"Are you sure it was a man?" Jaya asked. "You just saw the back of a person."

"Definitely a dude," Reilly answered. "Your mom never would have let a girl in any of this shit. Only you, Blanche. She missed you so fuckin' much."

There was a faraway popping sound as Reilly grinned at us, scratch-ing at one of the patches on his skin that wasn't bearded or pimpled over. The pop repeated, and this time there was a closer and louder metallic *spang* just behind Reilly. He turned to look at the new hole of blackness in the hood of the BMW, just as one opened up in the right side of his head, and redness sprayed out of the left. For an insane moment, all I could think of was running past him to the car, to the Ruger tucked into that driver's side compartment, the infinite security I could get from the bullets inside it.

Jaya started to scream and I grabbed her, leaning with my arms wrapped around her so I was half-carrying her tiny weight as we ran back into the restaurant.

When we were inside and she put her hands on my cheeks in a half-clutch, half-slap, I felt air push into my open mouth and understood that it hadn't been her screaming, but me.

CHAPTER TWENTY-FOUR

THERE WAS A plastic tarp over Vernon Reilly now, reducing his body to a shape and the red that had leaked from him into a black design that strobed under the patrol car lights. The Stilford cops, experienced as they were with homicides in this banner year, had gotten the parking lot taped off, the BMW into their temporary possession (to the despair of its owner, who turned out to be a Chinese-American bicycle shop owner), and the Denny's emptied out in about eleven minutes. Jaya was sitting in the passenger seat of her car, wearing a metallic blanket over her clothes at the insistence of a paramedic who'd seen her shivering. She'd clamped down on her shock and fear before I had, though, doing what I couldn't—getting it out in those physical shakes, crying on my shoulder.

We agreed that my screaming after the gunshot was a kind of

progress. It was our first post-shooting laugh, coming just as the cops pulled up.

I finally met Maitland's detective. Ron Pargiter was black and the kind of tall that partially ironed out the extra eighty pounds he was carrying, but was wearing pants that he should have moved on from. The zipper crept down every time he stooped and stood up again. He finally answered me on one of my many Maitland questions.

"Officer Maitland has been suspended. For reasons unrelated." Pargiter was scanning windows in the office buildings around the Denny's, looking for one both low enough and close enough to make the angle of the bullets that had ripped into the car and Vernon's head make sense.

"Reasons unrelated to what?" I asked. Jaya had mostly stopped shivering, getting rid of the fear by focusing on work: a uniform was leaning down and speaking to her in the car, and she was doing one of her curious-dummy-to-seasoned-interrogator arcs. The cop would start gently explaining what crime and murder were to her and be defensively explaining his credentials and theories on this particular case within minutes.

"Reasons unrelated to this particular shooting," said Pargiter.

"There needs to be a fat 'As far as we know' in front of that, Detective. Where's Maitland, like, right now? And where was he an hour ago?"

Pargiter stared at me for a long, silent moment. Maybe a full minute, which is longer than people think it is when two people are being quiet. He pulled me aside, but not with his hand, which I appreciated. Instead, he nodded to the far wall of the building, past the logo. I walked there first, with him behind me. Close enough that a bullet that was looking for me would have found him first.

"I'm going to be direct and as open as I can be with you, Ms. Varner, because I think you have more to tell me, and we might as well be direct with each other. And by direct I mean you don't lie to me even once, and if you do find yourself lying, you correct yourself immediately and say 'sorry, Detective Pargiter, for jeopardizing our trust.' And lying includes concealing crucial information, is that clear?"

One of the techs was handling plastic sheeting at the scene around the corner, and I thought of how far it would have to reach to cover all the scraps of Vernon's low-functioning, but still large, pink-and-red brain. I'd seen one piece go at least eight feet.

"Item one, Officer Dan Maitland was taken into custody immediately after returning to the station from the morgue where I was informed he met you, Ms. Chauhan, and a New York journalist named Emil Chadwick."

"That turd Chadwick was not with us. And he's not a journalist."

"He's what? Just a turd?"

"Correct."

"This is what I mean by directness, Ms. Varner. By concealment. If you tell me something about Mr. Chadwick and then immediately bury it under wordplay, all you're actually communicating to me is that I'm not worthy of the information you've got. And that makes me reluctant to tell you anything that isn't directly related to your safety." Pargiter had a way of talking in a slow, teacherly manner that wasn't exactly condescending, and that was patient while expressing extreme impatience with lesser moral samples of the human race, such as myself.

"Don't—if you're going to lecture me on proper conduct, how about you tell me why an untested and fucked-up officer was handling my mother's homicide, and not an actual detective? Not you?"

"We're extremely overtaxed as a department. We were using lower-ranked officers as a proxy on certain cases as supervised training, Ms. Potter. Maitland was making daily reports to me and had never, as far as his record reflects, demonstrated unreliability. In this case, he had been lying in each of those reports. And we are suspending this program immediately department-wide." Pargiter was answering me as though he were on the stand, probably some free prep work to answer this very question from whichever lawyer asked it when the time came.

"Fine. And I am being direct with you. Emil Chadwick is obsessed with my father's crimes, and whatever relation he thinks I have to them, and he is an absolute turd. He told me to contact Officer Maitland directly, and it was clear that they knew each other. That's all I know about him, other than that he's here to exploit this situation," I said, flapping a hand toward the body in the parking lot.

"We brought Chadwick in at the same time as Maitland, but released him. In fact, the arrest was at Chadwick's request: he didn't want Maitland suspecting that it was his call that got us to pick him up."

"Chadwick got Maitland arrested." I didn't think it was this bit of information that got me dizzy, just the accumulated stress of watching Vernon Reilly's skull fly apart a few feet away from me and the only friend I loved. But I found myself leaning against the warm brick of the building, with a second of time blank behind me.

"Breathe," said Ron Pargiter, and I listened. I looked to the side to see if any cops were looking at me—Pargiter noticed and circled me so he was standing between me and any onlookers. After a couple of minutes I was upright again.

"Yes, Emil Chadwick called us to report Maitland's malfeasance.

And Alfred Kindt's false ID of Vernon Reilly. It was easy to verify: nothing about Maitland's handling of your mother's case was done according to department policy or properly reported. Floods of false paperwork. But he was sitting right in front of me at the precinct when those shots popped off."

"Kindt." Kindt had been a Varner believer, too. Of course. He'd felt too crass to have the kind of faith that even a religion of baseless hate like Chuck's would require. But Crissy could work with any sort of material if she really wanted to. The thieving and the perving comments had thrown me off, made me suspicious of him in the wrong way. Kindt hadn't been taking the blue box out of the trailer to steal Crissy's money—it was for the Polaroids. He wanted an artifact of her, of me.

"Did you get Kindt, too?"

Pargiter grimaced. "He was our first homicide of the day. Dead on his boat. Maitland's alibied for that, too. He's not our shooter, whatever you and Mr. Chadwick may suspect—" Pargiter held up a hand, stopping the outburst I was about to make. "I realize you are not a duo, but whatever different or similar suspicions you may have arrived at about Officer Maitland, he wasn't up there with a rifle today."

"Reilly just told Jaya and me that Maitland told him to sit tight in jail until I was here. Me. They were waiting for me to get to town before the next step. Next step being—" I pointed again toward the tarped-over shell of Vernon Reilly.

"Jesus shit," Pargiter said, absolutely to himself and not to me. "Sorry."

"What did Maitland tell you?"

"He mostly talked about you, Ms. Potter."

I bit the inside of my cheek hard enough to taste blood. Maitland wouldn't, not at this point, tell the real police what he had on me. He wouldn't do that.

"Or Ms. Varner, as Maitland insists on calling you." Pargiter said my father's name apologetically.

"You called me that when we started talking," I said. Pargiter closed his eyes and moved his tongue around his closed mouth, as though trying not to scream at himself.

"I am so sorry. It's Maitland's talk still running through my head. Says calling you 'Potter' is disrespectful, no matter what you may think.

"Maitland said, and this is as close to quoting as I can get—he wanted me to record him and play you the tape, but I don't accede to requests from suspects, especially ones that were once supposed to be cops—'That you have nothing to do with what's happening now, but it is all your fault.' And he admitted to having a deep connection to your mother, getting angry at me when I asked if that relationship ever crossed into the romantic, but insisting that the only people who had ever been closer to your mother were Chuck Varner, you, and 'Him. The boy out there.'"

"'The boy out there.' Crissy at least taught him how to talk in those elliptical shithead empty slogans. The—"

"The shooter, I presume," said Pargiter. A young uniform cop came around the corner with a notebook and a self-important look. Pargiter pointed and shook his head. The cop immediately turned heel.

"Then what?" I asked.

"Then what what?"

"What did Maitland say?"

"Nothing. Said he was through talking, and wouldn't be volunteering any more information or answering more questions. Hasn't said a single word since, to me or anyone else. He's just staring at the goddamn wall in his cell." Pargiter had the dignity to look embarrassed by the piece of shit that wore his department's uniform, and I took that into account. I wasn't about to clasp his hand and tell him everything was fine, but it took the gas out of my attack.

"God."

"Officer Maitland was an efficient cop in many ways, and good at working the game. Not quite enough to get promoted, not enough to make many friends, but enough that we gave him a chance on this new program."

I stared at Pargiter and he didn't look down. But he did modify his answer.

"I gave him the chance. When the call on your mother's homicide came in, Maitland told me he'd lived in that trailer park. I did come down to the scene, talked to the witness, saw how open-and-shut everything was. I handed the case to him and told him to keep checking in. And I went home and ate a pork chop dinner with my son."

He said this last while staring full force into my disapproval. I had to admit, somehow taking it made him a little more okay in my eyes.

Pargiter kept talking. "I fished today but I can't get any personal data, any reflection on what he is or was like, from anyone from his academy year or beyond. Even his partners. So I'm at a bit of an informational impasse, and I would be happy to take any statement you have, Ms. Potter. If you'd like, you could start by telling me why you didn't come to anyone else in the department when you had suspicions about Maitland."

I felt the distant prickling of danger at the back of my scalp when

Pargiter spoke, this time. He wasn't just sharing what he knew with me; he was strategically drawing me in, opening me up. This was a man who didn't see clear divisions of criminal and civilian, just gradations of guilt. Guilt like the kind that was coming off me. I decided to tell some of the truth now. I could lie later, if I had to.

"Maitland told me what he told you. Except the shit about all of this being 'my fault.' He suggested that he had a preexisting relationship of some sort with my mother."

"I'm not interested in what he told you. I'm interested in what you know, Ms. Potter. I think you know much more than your mother ever allowed Maitland in on. Just the impression I've gotten."

Before we'd started this conversation, Pargiter had been shifting his legs a bit as he stood in the lot, the way a tall heavy person does when their knees and hips are complaining about a day of carrying the upright weight. But now he was stock-still, except for his scribbling hand.

"All of this," I said, pointing at the tarped-over body, "is happening not because of me, but because of my father. My mother's obsession with his ugly, stupid cult, which was nothing more than a collection of stupid slogans that gave shape to his fucked-up violence. Whoever shot Reilly here is someone who, like Maitland, subscribed to whatever it was Crissy twisted this cult into after Chuck died, and after I left the house."

Pargiter closed his notebook and pocketed it.

"Do you think there's going to be a Chuck Varner–inspired mass shooting in my city sometime soon, Ms. Potter?" he asked.

Every sentence he'd spoken to me since he'd confessed his limited culpability in giving Maitland control of my mother's case had gotten calmer and slower, and because of that, this question sounded absolutely surreal. He could have been asking me whether I liked kale.

"Chuck Varner sniped a couple from an overpass, waited a few hours, then headed to Harlow Mall to finish it. So here's what I think is going to happen: the same person who killed Vernon Reilly is going to want to kill a lot more people. He's going to do it tonight."

CHAPTER TWENTY-FIVE

———————

T HE YOUNG UNIFORM cop, still holding his notebook,
came around the corner again. His voice squeaked a little, but
the words were insistent.

"Detective Pargiter, I'm sorry, but we found part of the rifle, we
think."

Pargiter, still lost in the prospect of an upcoming massacre, took a
moment.

"Who touched it?"

"What? No one did, sir. It's up on the hill."

"Let's go." Pargiter included me in this, and the young cop took to
his squad car, putting me in the grilled-off back seat as he and Pargiter rode up front. Jaya, who was sunk into her phone, didn't see us
passing.

The yellow-grassed incline, just under a billboard advertising Dole juices, was a perfect spot. Chuck would have admired the selection, and so would Crissy. Perhaps she'd even helped this psycho pick it out, someday months ago, when she thought she'd be along for this third act, not in the ground. There was flattened grass in the rough shape of a body, which the officer used his flashlight to pick out for us. In the middle of it was the scope. If not the same one that had been hung in the hills behind Crissy's trailer, it was a perfect facsimile.

I looked at Pargiter and he nodded. "I know about this. The forensics team who went up to your mom's place when you called Maitland said they bagged and brought it back into evidence, but Maitland bullshitted it out of their hands, telling them it was getting sent to LA for some advanced tests."

"He knows who this guy is, Pargiter. That was the lie he was telling me—that he didn't know who else Crissy had enlisted. The other cultists. Maitland got the scope back to this psycho."

"Bennet," Pargiter said to the thus-far nameless cop, whose name I would forget again almost instantly. "Leave the flashlight. Get back to the car."

"Sir?"

"Now."

Pargiter turned to me when Bennet was sitting back in his driver's seat with the door shut.

"You have got to spell out this cult thing for me, Ms. Potter, because right now it sounds like some wild goose tangential garbage that's going to get in the way of us finding this man," Pargiter said. "Chuck Varner have a church? Robes? I know he used to spout garbage around town and hand out little cards, but I thought that was all over when he went on his spree."

"Killing those people gave it new life, Detective. Crissy knew that people, that boys and men, were obsessed with that shooting, that if she found the right ones she could turn them. I don't need you to believe in the message. Fuck knows I don't. Chuck was crazy and I'm incredibly glad that he's dead. But I do need you to believe me. Crissy kept on preaching his antisocial crap to impressionable men like Maitland, and one of them is out there with a gun. A lot of people are going to get killed unless we find him. Him or them." I had a sense that Crissy had kept her following small, intimate, but it was just a feeling. And I'd been wrong on those at almost every turn since I got back, including her enlistment of Kindt. I'd had a feeling that I could handle the Reilly interview, too, that Jaya and I were making progress. His spill of blood and brains was a lot more concrete than that feeling. It was Crissy who knew me, not the other way around—she'd gotten me exactly where she wanted for this final act.

I checked my phone—it was only six thirty, just a couple hours since we'd picked up Reilly.

"I think this is going to be a longer conversation than we want to have up here, isn't it?" he said.

"Yes. But before we have it, I need two favors."

"Stop for a second, first. You're saying your mother had sway over these people, that she had some sort of mind-control grip on them?"

"Nothing supernatural or conspiracy theory about it," I said, having winced when the detective said "mind control," which I associated with the worst of right-wing pundit panic fantasists. "She carried on Chuck's system of belief and found weak-minded people to prey on for obedience. That's it."

"And Emil Chadwick is a coat tail grabber, intimately connected to your father's massacre through his own mother's work, and has had at least one and possibly multiple conversations and moments of contact with your mother?" He looked worried. Damn worried.

"It's not him. I've sat down with Chadwick, and I know—my sense of people, of psychos, can't be that dull, not after everything I've seen. She could have used him, yes, but it would be like Kindt, not for violence. He doesn't have the stuff." I knew what drove Chadwick because he'd told me—and because it was what usually drove me. "Chadwick wants the story. He wants a big story that will make his career and his life mean something. He thought he wanted it bad enough to let people get killed, but I guess he figured differently in the end."

"He knew this was coming." Pargiter raised an eyebrow, and made a gesture down the hill to the target zone in front of the Denny's. I could see Jaya's car, the door now open, her shape standing next to it. With the scope, I'd be able to see her face. The shooter had been able to see us, brush our bodies with his projected vision before ending Vernon Reilly's life.

"Yeah, Chadwick knew it was coming. And I think it scared the shit out of him when he realized how close it was," I said.

Pargiter's furrow was becoming one big eyebrow.

"Look," I went on. "I lived with two insane people for my early childhood and one for what was left of it after Chuck went on his suicide run. I know crazy when I see it, at least. Chadwick is a coward, he's a liar, but he's not a shooter."

Pargiter sighed, calculating what he was going to say next. Jaya would be getting impatient, and if I knew anything about her wildly varying body temperatures, she would have handed her space blanket back to the paramedics by now.

"I don't want to place my expertise over yours for various reasons, Ms. Potter. So I'll ask this way. Can you tell me why, exactly, you'd rule Emil Chadwick out as a potential shooting suspect? If he's crazy enough to let people get killed for a book or a magazine story or what have you, he isn't crazy enough to do some shooting himself?"

"I know Chuck. I know Crissy. And they'd never choose him. They'd call him a mule, a carrier, unworthy. They'd tell their real disciples, their trusted, core members, that some of our family existed to be burnt up around us, a protective layer that kept us safe, pure, and clean for the real work ahead. Whoever killed Crissy is that key disciple, the one who thinks he's the chosen leader now. And it's him that got Maitland to lie to you, to me, to collude with Reilly and get him in prison." I didn't even need to put on Chuck's voice on purpose— when I remembered how he preached, it came naturally. Pargiter looked dry-mouthed and, though he tried to hide it, disgusted. Like he'd taken a bite of bad shellfish but wasn't in a place where he could spit it out politely.

"Right. Chadwick wasn't our shooter today, anyhow, so that checks out," Pargiter said. "I have eyes on the man and he's not here. I won't tell you where he is but I will tell you that I feel like visiting him quite urgently just now. Now, these two favors you want?" We started walking back to the squad car, but slowly, giving me enough time for my proposal and Pargiter enough time to refuse or maybe, maybe, to say yes.

"I need to talk to my friend alone first. Jaya. For about an hour."

"With the time frame you're guessing, a shooting tonight, you think that's a good use of our time? Really?"

"I don't know a way that I can help you directly, Detective. I don't know how to find out who's doing this, if Maitland doesn't want to give him up. You've got to make him talk any way you can, after I've told Jaya what I need to tell her." And what I pray he's not going to tell you, I added silently.

Pargiter nodded. "I told you to be fully truthful with me, Ms. Potter. So I'm going to believe that whatever you're holding back from me is not something that can save my people, in my city, from getting murdered."

"I don't know anything that can help you that I haven't told you," I said, truthfully. "Get Maitland talking."

"They're working on him at the station."

"Then get Chadwick in again. Someone. Warn people to stay inside, I don't fucking know." We were back at the car now, trying to avoid eye contact so we didn't have to see exactly how hopeless we both looked.

"What's the other favor?"

"I asked the first cop on scene to send a car to Jaya's mother's house. Did they do that?"

"Yes."

"Then just keep it there. Keep her safe. She's the only other person I love in this city, and that makes her vulnerable."

We got in the car and started driving. I kept talking through the mesh. Pargiter didn't turn around.

"Get the cop to tell Padma to stay away from the windows, not to leave the place, and not to panic. And that I love her and I'm about to explain everything."

The last part was a lie. I couldn't actually explain everything to Padma without losing her for good. The way I was about to risk losing Jaya for good.

CHAPTER TWENTY-SIX

J AYA DID THE initial set-up on the camera and the two portable lights she'd rented and stashed in the trunk of the car. If I hadn't known her and worked with her for years, the level of prep would have surprised me.

She'd persuaded the doddering start-up on the third floor of One Stilford Plaza, the only office that still had lights on and people in it, to give us the use of their conference room for a quick shoot, a hundred bucks cash. Asking all of them to leave the office so we could have a quiet set was one step beyond, but she pulled that off, too, simply by acting like it was completely expected, intuitive stuff. Anyone who knew anything about shooting should know that clearing out of your own workplace as soon as someone with a camera and spending cash turns up makes perfect sense, right?

"It'll buy all of you dinner," Jaya told the CEO, a thirty-six-year-old man with the misplaced remnants of a punk haircut up top.

"At Taco Bell, maybe," he'd replied, gesturing to the ten-odd people in the room, all of whom had started to look much busier at their laptops when we entered. One of them, a Hispanic girl with a butterfly tattoo just behind her ear, so fresh its turquoise color was still ocean vivid, had a screenwriting program open, toggling back and forth between that and a blank email. She nodded knowingly at us, definitely onside. Jaya handed the boss another couple of bills.

"Upgrade it to Del Taco." The boss, whose name was Chad or Jim, let us into the small conference room, which was flooded with harsh overhead light that was absorbed by a dark green wall on the far side. While Jaya took out the minitripod, I found myself a position, clicked off most of the overheads and got our portables in place, then waited for her to ask me to finish the framing. She did, acting as my stand-in while I got everything right. We switched back, Jaya closing the room's door with a clicking sound of finality before she went back to her seat.

"So why are we doing this again?" she said.

"This is what we do. We record, we shoot, we build the story that we find. I want us to remember that and feel normal for a second."

"I just saw a man's head explode," Jaya whispered, her upper lip moving in the way it did when she was trying to control either rage or tears. There'd been a strange, runny-egg-white look to her eyes since I'd dragged her inside the Denny's and we'd hidden, facing each other in a huddled crouch under a booth. I'd muttered things to her, words I'd forgotten by now, trying to keep us both out of shock and as calm as possible. And she'd held it together perfectly while she was executing the job of getting us into this office and rolling, just the way I knew she would. Work, and her and Padma, were all that had kept me sane after I escaped Crissy.

"I'm not feeling normal," she went on. "I don't think I ever will again."

"You're telling me that handling that douche and herding his team of nerds out of their own workplace in under fifteen minutes didn't make you feel—no, not feel, but know—that you're in control of our shit, whatever else is happening out there?"

Jaya registered this and visibly looked better for a moment.

"We're going to make the movie that Emil Chadwick wanted to make," I said. "That's what we've been doing since Crissy got killed. All this audio I've recorded, the video that you've rolled, the stills we've taken was for a reason." I wished for gum, or a cigarette, anything to put in my mouth to gnaw on while I stopped the wrong words from seeping into the air and onto the digital tape. A purpose, a future for this. A movie would make sense of what Jaya had just witnessed, and what I was about to tell her. That's what continuing Chuck's cult had meant to me, at first, when I was a child who'd watched bodies blow apart in front of her: Mom and Dad had said there was a reason. That it made sense. That's how you keep your sanity in chaos. You pretend there's a good reason for everything.

"Keep going," Jaya said.

"The only reasons you haven't pushed me to work on a Chuck Varner movie are your decency and that you love me. It's something that we're supposed to do, and we're going to run into the question for the rest of our careers once it gets out that it didn't end at Harlow Mall. That Crissy kept this cult going and it earned her a bullet." There were inspirational posters on the walls of this conference room, the manly kind about *Gravitas* and *Beast Mode*, alongside a whiteboard covered with terms like *Monetize* and *Engagement,* connected by marker lines to a swirling dark center.

"We're making that Blackwood movie."

"They won't let us. Not yet. As long as we work together, especially after my name comes out after all this shit right now, I'm going to get the Chuck Varner question, and you're going to have to ignore it to support me, and know that deep down I'm holding our careers back. That eventually we'll be lucky to get enough credibility to make Lexus commercials, but we'll never get to consistently make the work we want to. Because I didn't want to make the movie about my past that everyone wants to see. Does that sound true?"

Jaya had started looking down while I talked, not avoiding my eyes, but absorbing herself into her own thoughts. Putting it together. Admitting it.

"You're right."

"There are two parts to this, Jaya. The first, I told you this afternoon. But I want to tell the camera. But the second part is just for you. For us. It's something you need to know, because if we do a Chuck Varner movie, it's not going to be about me. It's going to be about us."

"All our movies are by us."

"No. About us. Chuck Varner is a part of your past, too, okay?"

Jaya didn't understand, and looked like she was scared to. So she just flicked the camera on and got me aligned in the shot.

"All right, Blanche. Chuck Varner. Go."

And that was all I needed. The name, his name, and the command—from her, specifically. From my best friend Jaya Chauhan, who I'd lied to from before I first met her, who I loved and needed more than anyone else I'd ever met who hadn't fooled me into thinking I needed them.

"I was there in Harlow Mall that day. I watched my father, Chuck Varner, murder those people, one at a time. The cops don't know. The media never found out. I only told my closest friend about it today.

"The only person I ever spoke to about it before today was my mother, who used to ask for the story like a kid asking for her favorite fairy tale. I'd tell it to her when she was in bed after a long shift. She was a server, right? I'd massage her feet for her while she dozed and tell her about Dad shooting those people, how they fell, how it took a few seconds for anyone who hadn't been shot yet to understand that this was real, that they were in the abattoir now.

"That's what Chuck Varner called crowded public places. Abattoirs. He stole most of his lines from death metal lyrics, but it is absolute nonsense that any of his ideas or anger came from there. He was just gathering whatever he could to give shape to his ego. That included me, and my mother. Crissy. She was his first cultist, and I honestly think that they had me so Chuck could try out training someone to worship him from the cradle up. And it worked for a few years."

I gave Jaya another ten minutes of this, the Chuck Varner story that I was ready for the public to know, before I asked her to shut off the camera. She was crying for real, now, knowing more about those years in the trailer than I'd ever told anyone else. And, of course, what would seem like the biggest deal possible to anyone who hadn't actually been there.

"You had to watch him kill all those people. You were so little. A little girl," she said. "Today has been so fucked up that I barely thought about it since you told Mom and me."

"That's not the worst, Jaya. The worst part is that it isn't the worst part, my memory of seeing those people go down, spilling their lives out. I can't dissociate enough from what Chuck told me to actually feel the killings that day for what they were—simple murder, the robbing of life. I'd be lying if I said I did. I still remember them, all of them, as something my dad was doing to become what he wanted to be. It was like visiting him at work. That's the worst part. I still don't feel like I saw people being murdered, even though I know that's exactly what I saw. Does that make sense?"

"No. But it doesn't have to. This—Jesus, this is all so awful, Blanche."

I breathed for a few seconds. Noticed myself doing it, tried to remind myself that I would still be doing it when I finished telling Jaya what I had to.

"I'm so sorry, Jaya. I need you to know, to remember, that I'm not a killer. Just remember that while I'm talking. Please."

CHAPTER TWENTY-SEVEN

J UST WAIT FOR me to be done. Just wait. My father was raising me to be his lead disciple, his lure, his 'high priestess,' he said. He was supposed to keep to the sniping for the first few sprees—stay up on the overpass, move to different buildings all over Stilford—trees, hills, tarped under in the back of a moving truck that Crissy was piloting—he had a plan for steadily unrolling minor, small-scale chaos that would always stop just short of mass chaos. But he couldn't resist the intimate kill, couldn't help himself from getting—this is how he said it—'closer than a handshake' before putting a bullet in someone. We'd drive around town for hours on days he got off work, after he gave me the sign at the breakfast table that I should tell my teacher I had a tummy ache and needed to get picked up. We'd cruise. He taught me how to steal gas by siphon, taught me how to take apart and put together his rifle, taught me how to wait.

But he couldn't teach himself the kind of patience he needed to carry out the plan he wanted to.

"And that's what should have told me the truth, right there. I was a little kid but I was smart, just not smart enough to truly pick apart the kind of boring, average psycho my dad was. That day he went into the mall, where he played out the fantasy that he planned to be a 'high-peak kill,' something he was only going to do after a decade of sniper kills all over California, chaos murders that would attract more boys and girls to his cult. He just couldn't wait another day, let alone a decade. I should have known he was full of shit. That he was just a routine murderer. Like these fucking kids at the high schools, any psycho in the tower with a gun—that was all Chuck Varner ever was. A void of a person who thought he was brilliant and unacknowledged, convinced one woman that it was the case, made another human being with her to guarantee a disciple, then spread his emptiness as bullets.

"But my mom and I—before I ever called her Crissy, before I ever dared to disrespect or disbelieve her—we chose to keep believing Chuck's reality. Reality—that's more or less what he called the cult, what it would have been if he'd become the shadowy leader he wanted to become before setting me up in his place. Not Your Life Is Mine, but Reality. We were the only people tuned in to how fucked up and death-driven the world—not just Stilford, because that's obvious—but the world as a whole, really was. How it needed to be—this was his fundamental, baseline quote: 'Not erased, but corrected. We are the X, we are the checkmark. I go before, then you follow. And soon, they'll all follow.'

"That hill where I found his scope is where he used to teach us. Mom and I, cross-legged, long after dark, when all the rest of the trailer park kids were inside, dinner over, the heat sticking our clothes to our bodies and the grass to our clothes. He'd sort of declaim, worse than any prof you and me ever had, pretending he was Socrates and that the child and the woman he had staring up at him were the birth of a new generation, his legacy. That's why I never wanted to say a thing about him once I got away from Crissy. Anything I say about him is legacy. Anything I say about Chuck Varner is Chuck Varner getting into the world again."

I stopped. I didn't know how long I'd been talking for, how long Jaya had been watching me with a compassion that I was about to stomp all over.

"I'm so sorry, baby," she said. "Why didn't you want to say that on video? Why just to me?"

"I want you to understand what was in our minds when Crissy and I lived the next ten years together in that trailer. How she kept that poison in me. I need you to know that.

"You have to remember, please remember, Jaya, that randomness was the most important part of Chuck's instructional. That's what my mom absorbed the most. Pick disciples at random, pick victims at random."

Jaya was inert beside the dead eye of the camera, and soon the expression leached out of her eyes, too. Her mouth didn't open, but I could see her jaw droop, as her face went slack—not in relaxation, but in shock. I think that in that moment, she predicted what I was going to say. Because, maybe, she'd been carrying uncertain knowledge about it ever since I first pressed my friendship on her in high school, starting us out by telling her that I knew what it was like to have everyone talking about your family and pretending you couldn't hear. That day, outside Mrs. Martin's Applied Math class. She'd looked at me that day with suspicion, but I hadn't imagined she knew what to be suspicious of. She just expected me to make fun of her, or ask an exploitative question. And I didn't. But she was right to be suspicious.

"At random, Jaya. I could never have known. Please stay with me through this, okay? Not because you owe it to me, but because I owe it to you. We—Crissy—picked him at random, but I chose you and your mom myself. I chose to love you myself and try to fix what she'd done. To protect you."

Jaya pulled her legs up onto the chair with her.

"Oh my god. Oh my. Oh. You killed him."

"No. No, I didn't. Crissy did. Until I really saw what Chuck's teachings meant, Jaya—until I saw your dad on that pavement and walked another block and saw you waiting in the back seat of the car while your mom sat up front, reading the paper and waiting for her husband to come back and start the car. But I saw you, mostly. Thank god you didn't see me or we never would have—none of this could be. Nothing we've done together. Nothing in my life. It all exists because Jaya Chauhan convinced her mom to foster the kid who kept bothering her at school, the girl who kept trying to insert herself into her life because she thought she needed to be there. To apologize. To make up for Neesh Chauhan lying on that pavement while you and your mom waited for him to come back."

CHAPTER **TWENTY-EIGHT**

PARGITER HAD AN officer he liked, Clem Broward, following Blanche Potter and Jaya Chauhan from an invisible distance. Broward was on his day off but needed the overtime, and a daylight public sniper shooting had apparently been enough for Pargiter to saw off some extra resources. So there was no risk of losing the two women, if they decided to take off. There was a slight risk of losing them the other way, but Pargiter had stopped Clem before sending him after the two women as they left the parking lot.

"You're following them but also looking ahead of and around. Scan all vantage points. Pretend to be the fucking Terminator. See everything. We don't lose one more citizen today, got it?"

"They're LA," Broward said. "Not really our citizens." He was being bratty, and Pargiter was in no mood, but decided to pretend he was. Kid was in on his day off.

"Even worse. Tourism's bad enough as it is."

Pargiter had left on his own catch-up mission: tailing Emil Chadwick, quick, before getting back to a possibly more hands-on version of his interrogation of Dan Maitland, who remained mute in a cell.

Pargiter had called in Chadwick's rental plates and model, and gotten periodic reports on his whereabouts while he was on scene at the Denny's shooting.

The last report, which came in right after Blanche Potter left to have her little chat with her friend, had Chadwick's Acura in the parking lot of Harlow Mall, booting a talk with Chadwick higher up on the priority list than Maitland. They hadn't had any legal cause to keep Chadwick at the station when he turned in Maitland, but Pargiter was going to invent one or just lock the boy up in a basement somewhere and get any information he had out of him. The car was still there, Chadwick presumably still somewhere in that mall.

"It's important not to panic," Pargiter said on the drive to find him, both talking to himself and rehearsing what he was going to tell the head of mall security once he got there. Pargiter had already sent a couple of uniforms down to walk the halls in front of the storefronts—half of which had been empty since 2008—to keep watching and listening.

"Watching and listening for what?" they'd asked when he radioed them. He'd asked them to call his cell back to keep his answer away from any police scanner hobbyists, a plentiful breed in Stilford.

"Watch for guns and listen for shots," Pargiter said when his phone rang just as he was getting into his car. "I am about absolutely sure that nothing is going to happen there, and I don't want to waste an evacuation order that I may seriously have to implement soon, but I want to be cautious." He described Emil Chadwick to the officers, requested a total lack of interference, and told them he was on his way. He knew that Chadwick couldn't have shot Reilly, but the Potter girl's babble about this goddamn cult had gotten to him. Maybe Chadwick had strangled Kindt on his boat. Maybe there were a hundred of these psychotic motherfuckers about to rain killings down on Stilford.

Pargiter drove as though he had the cherry on top of his car, darting through traffic. He made good time to the mall and parked near Chadwick's Acura in the south lot. There were papers and a white T-shirt in the back seat, two Starbucks cups in the cup holders up front. No lipstick on either, not that that meant anything. If Chadwick drank coffee at the rate of the reporters that Pargiter dealt with, it meant he drank as much coffee as cops do, and both cups were likely his.

The mall was quiet, as it normally would be on a weeknight. News of the shooting at Denny's had echoed all over the city already, of course, but the Harlow Mall shootings were over a decade ago. More important, they were dozens of mass shootings ago—connecting a murder in the here and now to Chuck Varner's spree would make as much sense to the average Stilford citizen as drawing a direct link between Vernon Reilly's headshot and JFK's.

A woman in a loose red T-shirt pushed a shopping cart with a toddler and five Walmart bags by Pargiter as he walked down the sidewalk to the south entrance, past the empty patio of the Fuddruckers that he used to take his kid to some Sundays. Chocolate milkshakes and cheese pizza, until Eric had exhibited prediabetic symptoms and they'd stopped allowing him anything sweeter than fruit. By now, Eric was ten and slim and seemed to have forgotten what candy tasted like through a sheer desire to obey his mother, Harriet. Eric asked him for kiwis when he came over on a visit, and Pargiter didn't dare tempt him into cheating with some Twizzlers or even a Mounds bar, which had so much coconut in it that it justly should have been counted as a fruit, if it was his call. Eric would have told his mom, and he would have been right to, Pargiter had to admit: he would be offering the kid treats to sway his loyalty, to hurt his bond to his mother, not out of pure love or a desire to see his son have fun.

"I'm a sick fuck," Pargiter muttered as he pushed the doors open and entered the frigid halls of Harlow. He brought his thumbnail up to flick against the outside of his blazer, checking to see that the weight of his holstered service piece was resting where it should be, ready to be pulled out. An Asian family of four, a young black couple, and a few Hispanic kids were walking in front of him, as though they were milling around waiting for a multiethnic advertisement for Harlow Mall: The Reinvention. They'd gotten the blood out of the tile but not out of the reputation. Even people who didn't remember the shooting itself hadn't forgotten that something bad had happened here. Something that had left a stain.

Pargiter took the advice he'd given Clem Broward and started Terminator-scanning the stores he passed, looking for Chadwick. He also couldn't help looking for Harriet and Eric, even though he knew she was at work and that Eric was at basketball camp. It was this talk of cults and mothers that Blanche Potter had brought up, and the threat of the shooter, of course. Divorced men who never managed to sort out relations with their ex-wives wanted to see these women as controlling, maybe even deranged: Pargiter had arrested enough men who'd screamed about their exes while they were being cuffed, processed, right up through the trial, that it had snapped him out of the worst of his own bitterness. Blanche had no reason to snap out of hers, from the vague shape of the situation that he'd been able to grasp so far. Her father was fucked and her mother was, too. Which often led to an obvious conclusion, but not always. And Blanche did not seem fucked up to Pargiter.

Pargiter stopped in front of the Gap, looking at the back of a man seated on a bench facing the store opposite, a brightly lit Microsoft Store with white, digital-screen-covered walls and a snap laminate floor. It was Chadwick, sitting with both arms extended along the back of the bench, as though he were waiting for two women to join him. His hands were empty and far from his pockets, so Pargiter continued to extend him the privilege of doubt as he circled around to the front of the bench.

"Hey, Detective Pargiter," Chadwick said when he refocused his eyes and saw the big cop who'd obscured the video-game-playing kids he'd been watching in the Microsoft Store. "Should they be in school or what?"

"It's August. And nighttime."

"Oh, yeah," Chadwick said. He scratched his nose, which was dry and flaky, skin turning to dust in the summer air, a long way from the humid New York neighborhood where he belonged, and his eyes glazed over again.

"Yeah," Pargiter said, trying to hide his impatience by speaking more slowly than usual. "There's been a shooting, Mr. Chadwick, and we want to make sure—we want to ask you some questions because we think you can help us, and not because we suspect you of any wrongdoing. In fact, we know you can't possibly be directly involved, based on when I last spoke to you and when the shooting happened. I'd just like to talk to you."

"Was it Blanche?" Chadwick asked. He straightened up, alarmed, and looked almost heroic for a moment, in his pure concern for someone else. It was a strange, naked moment that Pargiter noted—it was a special kind of weirdo who concealed the better part of his nature and let the wormy aspects take up most of his living stage time.

"Ms. Potter and her friend are fine. It was the man that Maitland had hooked up for the murder of Crissy Varner."

"Reilly," Chadwick said, nodding and looking relieved. "He's the kickoff. I get it." He slouched again and patted the seat beside him, inviting Pargiter to sit.

"You came to us with information on Officer Maitland, Emil," Pargiter said, switching to first names to try to make Chadwick more comfortable, to pull him into a more responsive state. "You told us that he had undisclosed connections to Mrs. Crissy Varner, that he had conspired with Alfred Kindt—"

"What did Kindt say? I met him a couple times. Weird old character." Chadwick grinned, then lost the smile just as quickly, staring back into the store and its bright screens.

If he wasn't doped up, Pargiter figured he was fading into a mental break where he wouldn't be much use to anyone. He resisted the urge to slap Chadwick awake and kept talking.

"Never mind Kindt. Look, you gave me all this information, Emil. You backed it up with text messages that Maitland must have been unhinged to send you, but that he confirmed he had when we had him in lockup. You know things, Emil. We want to know those things, too, so people can stop getting killed. That's what you want, too." Pargiter wasn't sure about this last, but it always helped to flatter a perp's, or citizen's, self-perceived better instincts.

"I didn't know what he was going to do next. Not Maitland, but the one out there. The one making the shots. I really didn't," Chadwick said. His eyes were glistening now, slightly more with it. "I just wanted the story. I thought I was getting out of its way, letting history happen, but I was just—helping these guys. I don't know what I'm doing."

Chadwick stared at Pargiter. He looked like a little boy, despite the gym meat on his bones and his sharp, handsome face. "Like Blanche has probably told you. Like my mom's told me. I don't know what I'm doing, right? You pick up the data, you talk to the people, but what happens when what you find out scares the shit out of you and you just want to go home and forget all of it?" Chadwick's eyes went from glistening to tears and he wiped at them. Pargiter wished he was able to pity him instead of being disgusted; it said something about the limits of his empathy.

A tour bus group, no doubt disappointed to be touring this part of California instead of whichever region their Chinese vacation planner had promised them, walked past the bench on both sides, temporarily giving the mall the illusion of a pre-recession, pre-shooting population. Chadwick kept crying and Pargiter gave him a moment before snapping his fingers in front of his face.

"Emil, I know how you feel. But we need to focus. You can help me do my job, and that's what's most important here. The lives. Now, you said you didn't know what *he* was going to do next. Who's *he*?"

"I don't know who he is," Chadwick said, wiping his nose and eyes with his sleeve, leaving tracks of liquid on the blue cotton. "Crissy was the only one who knew. Maybe Maitland, he was slick. Found stuff out. I've seen him, seen his face, but that's all."

"You've seen our shooter? Where?" Chadwick was silent, glassy. If Pargiter was any more patient with him, Chadwick would have time to start looking at his trembling hands and continue with the goddamn ethical dilemma he should have had before any of this crap started, about whether or not he was an accessory to all the bad shit that had already happened, and all that bad shit that was potentially about to happen. And that dilemma was usually followed up by the sobbing crazies or a sober headshake and a request for a lawyer.

"Chadwick. Right, fucking, now, you need to help me to save some lives, man. You have that power." Chadwick didn't move, just kept staring straight ahead. Pargiter got off the bench, kneeled in front of Chadwick like he was proposing, clasped the man's knees, and looked right into those increasingly absent eyes. A couple of teenage girls behind him laughed at a quiet-but-you'll-hear-us-and-be-embarrassed volume, which may have had more to do with Chadwick coming back to reality than Pargiter's grip did.

"I saw him coming out of Crissy Varner's trailer once, when I turned up an hour early for an interview. For our last interview. It was when I was finally ready to drop it on her. My big reveal that my mother had been the one who wrote the Chuck Varner book."

"No shit."

"Yeah," Chadwick said, looking normal if a little puffy-faced now that he was annoyed. "Turns out she knew already, though. Probably had Maitland check up on me as soon as I contacted her. But I came early that day to see if I could, you know, pick up anything beyond trailer park ambience. Didn't expect to see him. The Boy. That's what she called him, when she was telling me that he was the one she'd been talking about, the one Blanche needed to meet."

"What does he look like?"

"Like Chuck Varner. Like he's trying to look like Chuck, you know? I'm bad at describing features, I'm sorry."

Pargiter sat next to Chadwick again. "I thought you were a writer."

"We all come with different skills. I can work with you on a sketch but I think I'd need to see him again, you know? It was far away. He had glasses, I remember that. Otherwise I just have a feel for him, how he moved."

"How old?"

"A little older than Blanche. But maybe that's just me guessing in retrospect. Crissy told me about him, you know? She said that Blanche has seen The Boy, too, but she doesn't know it."

"She's seen him?"

"Right here," Chadwick said, tapping the bench. "He was right here."

"I'll get as many officers as we need going in as many directions from this place as need be if you'll—"

"No, he wasn't *just* here. He was here on August 17, 1996. He watched Chuck shoot all those people, and so did Blanche, but he was absolutely hooked. 'A messiah born before his forerunner had even died' is how Crissy put it. That's a quote. Chuck's greatest follower, and Crissy found him. Found him and trained him until he was an even more perfect machine of Chuck Varner's message of death than Chuck himself."

"Why this kid? What the fuck was wrong with him that he went looking for the relatives of the man he'd just seen kill a bunch of people?"

Emil smiled, the smile of a small man with a large secret.

"I didn't believe this at first, but Crissy really did. And you can see it in The Boy's face."

"Go on."

"He's Chuck's son. The Boy is Blanche Varner's half-brother. Crissy didn't keep a harness on Chuck when it came to fucking around, as long as he kept any of the other women away from her and Blanche. She made it seem like that, anyway, that it was mutually decided.

"The Boy wanted Blanche to come back real bad, and so did Crissy. They had a plan to make it happen by putting me in touch with her, I think. But The Boy must have gotten impatient. Killed Crissy to be sure Blanche would be here. You see how *clever* these people are? They really should write this book themselves."

Pargiter stared at the lights in the Microsoft Store. He thought he might let Chadwick go just then, let him drive himself back to the airport and from the airport back to New York or whatever asshole city he wanted to wash up in. What was being floated here but speculation, believable babbling? There wasn't anything solid enough to arrest him on, but there was a reason to keep him, Pargiter's limited empathy aside.

"Alfred Kindt's dead, too, Chadwick. Are you going to let me keep you alive, or are you going to try to take a walk on me?"

Chadwick didn't answer. He just started looking at his hands again, resting on his knees, and then allowed Detective Pargiter to lead him out of Harlow Mall, over what was once a liquid, red floor.

CHAPTER TWENTY-NINE

JAYA WAS TREMBLING, a shake that had started deep inside, not the surface shivers I had from the gales of AC cutting across the conference room.

"You killed him," she whispered. "You killed my dad."

"No, Jaya. I could never. Crissy did."

"You're both fucking murderers. You could have told people back then—she would have been in jail for it. My mother and I could have slept."

"I didn't shoot him, Jaya." I resisted doing what I wanted to most, which was to touch her, take her in my arms and stop her from shaking. She would have spat on me if I tried.

"I was supposed to shoot him. A decade-plus of poison from my mother and father made random murder my entire project in life. But I didn't go through with it. I couldn't. He was killed with a handgun, right? You know that. I had a rifle, I was lying under a tarp, waiting. Mom, Crissy, she was on the street, doing rounds, ready to buzz me on my cell if there were cops anywhere close. That was the first phone I had of my own—a little Motorola. I was supposed to shoot whoever turned up in my sights first, and then she was going to get into the truck cab and drive us away. The bullet is the lesson, and the teacher leaves when the lesson is delivered, Crissy said. Not that Chuck followed that rule." I caught my hands moving independently of my thoughts, and realized they were Crissy's gestures, the rolling chop in the air she'd do to punctuate sentences.

"Can you please," Jaya said, her breaths audible and spaced out, like she was taking drags of oxygen that was running out whenever she couldn't help it. "Can you please skip the fucking details and tell me what you did. Tell me about my dad."

She was right. Thinking about Chuck and Crissy for longer than I had in years put me right back into their patterns of speech, the way Chuck would circle a point with suggestions, let you find it first before repeating it to you as a slogan. Crissy had absorbed his cadence, his charisma, his bullshit. *Each of them is praying the bullet comes for them, so they don't have to be around afterward to think. Not just about death, but about anything.* That sort of blather. I felt so full of secrets and love when Dad would talk to me in these ouroboros loops of violent nothingness—his big hand wrapped around mine, telling me things that no one else was allowed to hear, that no one would understand until the bullets hit them.

"Crissy shot your dad, Jaya. I was across the street from his optical place, lying in the flatbed of our Datsun under a tarp, the barrel sticking out an inch from the circular port Chuck had made—just large enough for 'the gun and your eyeline,' he'd say. I was supposed to shoot whoever turned up on that stretch of sidewalk, alone, with no one in sight around them, just once in the side of the head."

Mr. Chauhan, whom I'd seen for the first time twenty seconds before he died, had an unshaven patch below his lower lip and a small wart to the right of his nose. Ugly, squash-goggle-looking glasses, I remembered thinking, surprised afterward that an optometrist had a pair that looked like it was off a drugstore spinner rack. Crissy was visible in the mouth of the alley when I first spotted him, walking from a car parked in the next block and directly into my sights. Crissy was staring at the invisibility that was me in the truck's bed. I was only thirty or forty feet from both of them, and I started to tremble in a way that made me feel afraid of Chuck and Crissy, but not so much that I could stop shaking. The shake came from realizing what I actually was, or, at least, what I wasn't. I wasn't a person who could shoot that man. Eventually the stock of the rifle clanged down, the whole thing slipping out of my soaked hands.

"I remember when I made the noise, your dad looked up. There was an echo, it was that kind of wood-on-metal clang that seems to come from everywhere on an empty enough street."

Jaya had stopped breathing entirely. The rolling office chair she was in was rotating imperceptibly from the controlled force in her body, and it made a tiny screeching sound.

Crissy came out of the alley with her handgun and shot Mr. Chauhan in the center of his face, while he looked into the dark sky above the shop he'd built for his family for the source of a sound he'd never identify. I watched the bullet and part of his skull leave the back of his head in a tiny, significant launch, a spray that ended in a fall.

"Crissy shot him. I just watched."

Jaya was barely breathing now, moving herself and her chair with frame-shaking, quiet sobs. When she made a sound, I knew it would be a loud one. I waited a second before trying for an arm across her shoulders, taking her in a hug when it was clear that she was going to let me, that she needed contact from someone, even if it was me.

"I am so sorry, Jaya," I said, meaning it more than I'd ever meant anything, my first chance to verbalize the apology that I'd been acting out since I'd seen her father die in front of me. Saying it was the first time I fully understood the immense emptiness of ever trying to atone for something like this, with anything short of suicide. But I said it again.

"I'm sorry." After that, there were a few minutes of silence—Jaya with her right forearm across her eyes, her core and jaw tense, processing and burying emotions at a speed that would seem impossible if it wasn't something that I did every day. When she surfaced from that position, it was with her game face on, one that I'd had on my side of the table many times but never had turned on me.

"You need to be really, really straight with me on this next thing, Blanche."

"I'm always straight with you."

"I would have agreed with that an hour ago, but we can't ever say that again. I think it's more that you've based our entire friendship on an enormous, homicidal lie, and then been pretty honest about other stuff that came up after that. Right?" Jaya didn't react to my full-body flinch, but waited for me to nod until she went on.

"Did your mother keep doing this after my dad? Did she keep killing people in the street, at random? Because—" Seeing that I was going to interrupt, Jaya held up a finger as straight and commanding as a conductor's baton, quivering with tension. "Because if you kept your mouth shut and people died, one thing is going to happen, and it's going to be my favor to you. I'm walking the fuck out of this building, going back to the motel alone, cleaning my shit out and ending any contact with you, personal or otherwise. Dissolving the company will happen through proxies and email. I'm not spending another minute talking to you if you've let people be murdered because you weren't willing to be truthful about yourself and your twisted fuck of a mother."

"Jaya, she didn't," I said. I was on the street again, where I'd found myself after wriggling out from under the tarp in the back of the truck after the small gunshot, ignoring my mother's whispered *Blanche, the plan, Blanche* when I walked past her, Mr. Chauhan's dead body, and then past a younger Jaya and her mother, who were just starting to get out of their car to check on Neesh, walking fast but not too fast until I sat myself down at a Chick-fil-A, ordering a small fries when they politely harassed me to get something or move on, sitting under the burning cheer of fluorescents while regular families, bachelors, high school kids milled around me and I thought of the man whose life had melted out in front of me.

"She didn't keep killing," I repeated.

"I'm going to need a little more than that," Jaya said. She looked the smallest bit relieved, and I saw how deeply she wanted to believe me, was willing to take me back if I could just prove to her that it would be all right, that she could. I caught her up with the past.

"I didn't go back to your store until three hours after the Chick-fil-A closed," I said, when I had the story at the right place. "I'd been walking since then." Walking with my camera stuck in my purse. Chuck had told us that it was important to get documentation on every act of chaos, so both Crissy and I had cameras that night. Hers was a dispo, I took the real one. A Rebel that some drunk had left at Crissy's bar by accident. Crissy said I was the better photographer so it was best that I had the camera. I didn't take a single photo all night.

I remembered our planning week better than the night itself, maybe because the adrenaline was lower. Carefully assembling the rifle, freeing it from its PVC pipe and dirt grave. The rifle that had taken George Dillon's face off when Chuck Varner shot him from the overpass, before picking me up for our day at the mall. We'd been practicing with another rifle all these years, but I still remembered the feel of this AR-10, the fit of it. Crissy absolutely insisted on resurrecting the AR for our first new kill. Even if my hands had changed size in the ten years since Chuck had died, the gun still felt like it was growing out of my skin when I had it loaded and in position. It was only when I had a human being in the sights that the AR began to feel like a foreign growth.

"I was going back to tell the cops that I'd done it—I thought that was a compromise my mother and Chuck could have understood. I was still so fucked up, Jaya, you have to understand that. I thought I could feel better, at least, by going to prison quietly and leaving Crissy free to carry on Chuck's work. I thought—I thought that you would be gone by the time I got back."

"No," Jaya whispered. Two a.m. or so, and Jaya had never left—Padma was near catatonic, taken away by two cousins in a car, part of the extended family that had become my own in the next few years. Jaya had been impervious to appeals from anyone when it came to leaving the scene—she'd told me this herself when we first talked about the murder, a conversation that luckily took place in the dark, in a sleepover in her bed, where I listened close and clenched my right hand around my left wrist to keep from shaking or crying, digging so deep that I woke up with crescents of blood on the sheet and bits of skin under my fingernails. More evidence.

"I found Crissy in our truck, after circling the block, then widening my orbit, finally finding it parked in front of a Walgreens. She'd covered over the little hole that the rifle barrel stuck out of with the bit of metal and putty she'd had me put together out of scraps from the metal shop at school."

"Enough with the details," Jaya said. "Just, enough." She got up and started walking for the door of the conference room, and was about to leave when the office crew started coming back to their desks. Our time was up, and then some. Jaya packed up the camera and lights and left, while I tried to make some small talk with the forgettable men in their forgettable office. I was glad Jaya was gone by then; it would upset her more to see me sliding so easily into business-casual talk after the depths we'd just opened up, the canyon that had always been the foundation of our relationship.

She was in the lobby, holding the bags of gear right by the elevator banks. She started walking as soon as she saw me, making me jog to catch up, but that she had waited at all was an enormous positive. I'd worried that once we left the vacuum of that temporary confessional upstairs, Jaya would realize how it made absolutely no sense to continue having anything to do with me.

"I'm sorry about the details," I said. "I'm sorry for filling in what must seem meaningless to you, but it's real to me and I need you to know that. That evening is the marking night of my life, Jaya. It lit up everything I'd been denying about my father and it brought us together and put us on this—on this whatever-we're-doing together, which I think is a life's work."

"Heartwarming," Jaya said, stopping and shoving me once, hard. I staggered back a pace, looking around to see if anyone had noticed. "Oh, there's nobody fucking here, Blanche, don't be embarrassed. If you think that making appeals to what we've made out of you murdering my dad and lying about it—"

"I didn't kill him!" I screamed, losing it for the first time that day. It seemed to calm Jaya down.

"My father wasn't a fucking insect like yours. He built lives for all of us in this city that wanted no part of me, my mom, or him, before you and Crissy snuffed that out and made my mom do the whole thing over again. Not just for herself and me, but for *you*. Do you realize how fucked up that is? You ditched your own broken shithole of a family life so you could, so you could—"

"So I could be a parasite in yours."

"Yeah, that's it. So why should I listen to any more of this? Why do you get a single second more of my time?"

"Because there's more to say. Because—because Crissy had decided to stop the shooting that night, but she was still scared." I focused for the next part, looking down because I knew I couldn't look Jaya in the eye while I said it. But she knew what I was trying—Jaya put a finger under my chin and pushed it up, until we were eye-to-eye, until I had to look at her and say it.

"She wanted to kill you and Padma, too. You and your mom. I came—I had to be with you to stop her. To keep an eye on you and her both. It was a sort of bargain, do you get it? I stayed with you to keep you safe, for my mother to know that killing you both and the risk of it being connected to your dad was too much, that I'd never say anything as long as she left us all alone."

"I can't take in another grain of this. I just can't," she said, stumbling outside. "So stop."

"Forever?" I said, following her.

"For now."

The heat, even if it was dry, had caught us again, and my antiperspirant was absolutely defeated after this many hours, and Jaya was staring at my armpits. I looked at her.

"I should have worn primer," she said. "Fucking melting."

Nothing was over except for this part of the fight, but we stopped talking there. I wanted to touch her arm, her hand even, but I settled for trailing along behind her when she nodded to the car.

CHAPTER **THIRTY**

⎯⎯⎯⎯⎯⎯⎯⎯

I GOT PARGITER'S CALL when we were on our way to Padma's house. Jaya was driving, this time. I thought she might be a little too shaken for it, but she gave me a look that I didn't want to argue with.

"Let me be in control of this, at least," she said. I held my hands up. The Ruger was back at the base of my spine. I'd loosened my belt to accommodate it. Jaya had watched the process with distaste, but didn't say anything.

Pargiter told me there was more to say once we were all in the same room, but that he had one thing for me to think about on the drive. I could hear wind and his breathing as he spoke, the sound of someone who usually moved slowly moving very fast.

"I've got Emil Chadwick here, and he says that you've seen our shooter before. Says that Crissy just called him 'The Boy.' That tell you anything?"

"Not at all," I said, after a second of thought. Crissy's bullshit out in New Orleans had a lot of cryptic phrases in it, but not "The Boy." It did make me bite my bottom lip in what I was forced to recognize as fear, though. Had the innate ring of a Chuck Varner formulation—part white trash, part ominous and silly heavy metal lyric. The Boy. The Boy prophet. The Boy murderer.

"Chadwick said he's your half-brother. The shooter, I mean," Pargiter said. I couldn't even answer this, and Pargiter kept talking after a pause.

"I don't have any memory—and I don't think we have any record of this—but were you at Harlow Mall on the day of the shooting?" Pargiter asked. "I do hate to ask you. Must be like when people ask me if I've ever had to use my sidearm on someone."

I didn't hesitate this time. "I was there, Detective, yes. Crissy wouldn't let me tell anyone at the time, and after a while, it seemed like there was no use revisiting it."

"Jesus Christ. You poor girl."

Before I could find a way past Pargiter's sincerity and get annoyed at the condescension, at how he'd infantilized me just because I was talking about something that had happened to me then, I closed my eyes and saw The Boy.

I could picture him there. And I knew it wasn't pure illusion. There was someone across from me when Dad sat me down at the food court, told me to wait and see. A boy, sitting at another otherwise empty table in the food court, with a perfect view of the concourse below. Like mine. I remembered now because Chuck had smiled at the boy. Nodded, given him a thumbs-up. I was watching the boy and he was watching me when the shooting started, and then that was all I could see.

That day and what had happened became a rider in me, a parasite that was along every day, shading everything even if I never let it define my life. When I was little, I made myself and the version of Chuck's bible that I'd internalized into my therapy, my way of—not using that horrible psychiatric word *processing*—my way of owning what had happened, of making those people dead in the wash of blood that Chuck made with his Beretta into a logical progression of actions. Righteousness. And my memory had helped out by blurring across the parts that couldn't help me and that I was capable of forgetting. That woman in her oversized Minnie Mouse T-shirt carrying a blue Slurpee, going down after Chuck seemed to hug her when really he was shooting her—it wasn't an option for me to forget that. But the boy with the lopsided fringe of hair, fascinated and watching my dad becoming something powerful and meaningful in that mall, and later on in the culture: on TV, in the papers, in Jill Gudgeon's abominable book—I'd forgotten him.

Chuck's ultimate hope wasn't me. And I wasn't Crissy's Disciple Zero. The Boy, now the man, was the future of this cult, the killing future that he had started with his former goddess-avatar. My mother.

"I have seen him," I said. "He was around my age. So twenty-eight, dark-haired—I don't know, god, this was twenty years ago, so much about him must have changed—"

"Hold on to the picture of him in your mind, Blanche," Pargiter said. "Let your friend get home—we have a uniform posted at the Chauhan house, and one inside—"

"Padma must be plenty pissed," I said. Jaya looked at me and I made an it's-all-okay gesture. Before she could stop herself, Jaya squeezed my knee, then immediately withdrew her hand and stared back into traffic. I could have cried with gratitude, knowing that if even this one part of her body was willing to betray some sign of forgiveness, I could make the rest of her follow eventually, maybe.

"I think she's fine. As much as can be expected. Get Jaya in there and then just wait outside your vehicle. I have an officer, Clem Broward, tailing you. He'll bring you right to the station and we can discuss your recollection with a sketch artist in the room. Between you and Chadwick, I think we can put a face on this Boy."

CHAPTER THIRTY-ONE

J AYA PULLED UP next to the squad car in her mother's driveway and grinned hugely when she saw Padma waving from the picture window—the front of the smile was all happiness, but the twitching profile that I saw was just trying to project reassurance.

"You want to come in?" Jaya asked. It was as though she was asking me to come up after a terrible first date that still left her feeling obligated to be polite. I spared us both.

"No. I don't want to—I don't want to make this any worse for you by making you pretend you're comfortable with me in front of Padma. Not yet. Get me?"

"Yes." Jaya had her hand on the door handle, and I was about to push my way out, too, when she started to speak again.

"I won't be telling her this, Blanche. Any of this. I'm not going to ask that of her. She loves you too much, and knowing that—that you were there when her husband died, it would cost her too much. It would cost her you. Her second daughter. That's why I'm not telling her. Because it would hurt her. Not because I give a single emotional crap about you right now."

"That still means a lot, Jaya."

"Don't say my name like that. Just stay safe, and when this is over, we are going to have a serious talk about what happens to our partnership and whatever our—us, what we are—moving forward. Right?"

Jaya was up and out of the car before I could answer, heading for the house. A uniform let her in and Padma waved at me before Jaya slammed the front door shut. I got up and walked to the end of the driveway, facing the street, waiting for Pargiter's cop. The street was quiet, sodium streetlights giving off a cool glow. Jaya would remember to bring the camera equipment in from the car, I was sure, but probably it didn't matter when a squad car was parked next to us.

I stared into the lights and thought maybe Crissy had talked to me about The Boy, in a remote way. Maybe worth telling Pargiter about. When I'd been about twelve and we hadn't talked about Chuck all weekend, a rarity, and were eating some mint chip Häagen-Dazs she'd gotten on discount late Sunday, she started talking marriage.

"I like those cultures where they just let the parents do it for you, you know? I mean, I never would have found Chuck if my own mom had been looking, but some families are different. And that's the one place you don't want chaos, like Chuck said."

"Mom, come on," I said, licking ice cream from a papery sugar cone Crissy had unearthed from the back of the cupboard over our fridge. I wished that I had a bowl, and I also wished for a Chuck-free weekend, something I couldn't have admitted back then.

"No, hold on. He really did mean that. Family, the core, nuclear family, is one of the few things that America started to do right and then started to do wrong. That idea of adding one or two more points of stability to your life and accepting the chaos that awaited outside every time you opened the door to go out or let someone else in: that was really pure Chuck Varner, his late period. If only he'd had a chance to write this down, you know? I think that especially would have resonated. But some of these turban people, they have that part nailed. They know that family's where you keep the order established, and that you look to elder judgment to continue that lineage of stability. It should be inherited, right? That's what you get from your parents. A center. The ability to be calm, to provide calm to the only people you should care about: your family, and your followers." Crissy ate her ice cream out of a certain coffee mug she favored, one branded with a Heathcliff cartoon, now faded from orange catness into a peach-and-gray brocade with an unreadable joke slogan.

"So you got someone picked for me?" I asked. She'd looked at me with a shifting expression, going from surprise that she'd given away too much to pride in me that I'd figured out where she was going.

"I think I might have a boy in mind. A fellow. You'd like him if and when I let you meet him."

Even when Crissy said it, turning one of the evaluating gazes she'd learned from Dad on me, a high-beam stare beneath lazy eyelids, I had a vague shape of the person she meant in my mind. She got up, with her mug, and waved at me to follow her. It was late, which is something I just remembered—well past midnight. She'd woken me up, as she sometimes did when she was lonely, telling me that I could have some ice cream and skip school if I wanted to stay up and talk a little.

So we were walking through the trailer park and up into the hills when I asked her for the first and last time, and she told me one of her many lies, but perhaps the most important one. We often didn't wear shoes on summer walks like this, stepping lightly so we could pivot fast if we felt the first gnaw of broken glass on the soles of our feet. That was another skill Chuck had emphasized: "Walk softly. Be invisible. Only let them be aware of you when it's too late."

That night, Crissy looked oddly like my dad—he was good at turning on a glow of pride or approval every time I did something right, which meant, of course, following his orders exactly. For Crissy, pride only emerged when I intuited something with a certainty that she then had to prick into doubt.

"When you're older, when you're ready to start this work as a real leader, Blanche, you'll know everything I know. I promise."

We walked back to the trailer, Crissy placid while I boiled in a silence that I knew couldn't be broken by me, only by her. That's what total obedience feels like—being in thrall to someone, not just being a good daughter, but ceding majority ownership of your soul and brain to her, the way I had to Chuck.

And that's trauma, too. Crissy and Chuck owned me while the bit I kept for myself throbbed at a lower level, keeping any ideas of existence that were mine and mine alone alive while I figured out how to break free of what my father had forced me to see and what he, and my mother after him, had forced me to live.

Turns out it took another bullet. Just one, to break that last level of silence between Crissy and me, the one that let me leave her for Jaya, for Padma, for a future.

Across the street, a blue sedan pulled up, and the window rolled down. A dark-haired man leaned out, calling to me.

"Clem Broward, Miss. You want to get in?"

I walked over to the car, Broward nodding at me professionally and badging me before looking straight ahead. He had glasses, a borderline Aryan-Pride haircut, and a young face, one that could have used a mustache to keep him from getting mocked too harshly by other cops.

I opened the door, saying, "You took awhile. Pargiter said you were following behind us."

"Pargiter asked me to do a circuit of this block and the few around us to get a read on any suspicious people or vehicles and just, you know, let anyone who's in the know understand that the police are here and that the Chauhan household is not to be trifled with. That kind of thing." Broward mispronounced "Chauhan" but smiled as I got in, immediately getting us moving. I took a look back at Padma's house as we pulled away. No one was in the window anymore. Probably the cops had told Jaya and Padma to limit their visibility.

We drove quietly for about a mile, at a steady thirty-five. I wasn't about to speak first, after the explanation I'd just been through and the memory-spill that was waiting for me at the station. I was about to risk closing my eyes for a few seconds when I felt wetness seeping up through my jeans, and reached down to the seat below me. My fingers came up red. Broward, watching me even while he seemed to be fixated on the empty side street we'd just turned into, spoke up.

"You ever kill a cop, Blanche? Just did my first, and it was a true thrill, like I thought it would be."

The Boy's fist caught my temple just as my hand closed around the Ruger at my back, and I would have felt the pain in my neck if the bounce of brain on inner skull hadn't immediately shut down anything my body had to tell me.

CHAPTER **THIRTY-TWO**

———

CHADWICK PERKED UP a little after the mall, the security of Pargiter's car and calm conversation having something to do with it, probably, Pargiter thought.

Bennet, the uniform kid who'd driven Pargiter and Blanche up to the abandoned scope above the Denny's, met Pargiter and Chadwick inside the station. He was about to open the door of the interrogation room as Chadwick took a long, bracing stare inside, but Pargiter stopped him with an upraised hand.

"You good?" Pargiter asked Chadwick.

"Of course. I just saw him a few hours ago. I'm not scared of him," Chadwick said. "It's the other one out there who scares the shit out of me. And Maitland should never have kept helping that freak after he killed Crissy."

"Like she's a victim. You still want to write a book about this?"

Bennet asked. The rough outline of what had been happening and the potential massacre ahead had been passed around the station. "You need people to get killed so you can get a fucking advance?"

Pargiter looked at Bennet in shock, seeing an expression he'd never seen on the timid cop's face before—something like sass. "Officer, shut up," Pargiter said, inwardly slightly proud of Bennet. Bennet was oversensitive but a solid cop, and Pargiter had always been a bit mean to him, though he didn't quite know why other than that it was mildly fun. He'd have to revise his approach.

"I don't want there to be a shooting, do you understand?" Chadwick said. "I'm the one who's trying to put a *stop* to this, is that clear?"

"Fine," Pargiter said. "Let's not waste any more time, then." Bennet swung the door open.

Maitland was wearing a different kind of city-issued clothing than his usual uniform, but otherwise looked the same as usual. Too calm. He looked Chadwick in the eye for twenty seconds, neither saying anything. Pargiter didn't want to disturb the balance in the room and knock out whatever information would be willingly offered without any questions being asked. Bennet was following his lead. And Chadwick looked not embarrassed, but—Pargiter had to search for the word, finding it finally in the extracurricular Christian reading his father had forced on him as weekend homework: like the Devil, Chadwick was abashed.

"We're both so weak, Emil. Doesn't it just make you sick?" Maitland said, finally.

Bennet hustled Chadwick into a chair across from Maitland, and Pargiter stayed standing at some distance from the table. Bennet shot Pargiter a questioning glance and he nodded, letting him stay. Bennet posted up in the corner of the room.

"I mean it," Maitland said, still ignoring everyone but Chadwick. "We're absolute molds for failed men, as Chuck saw them. Prototypes, if there hadn't been ones exactly like us earlier on."

"Chuck was wrong about the shooting," Chadwick said. "Even Crissy said that. It was his job to stay and teach, not to shoot. And don't listen to him," he added, turning to Pargiter. "I only pretended to Crissy that I was into the cult shit so she'd open up to me. It was an interview technique." Chadwick had reverted to his mall persona, abstract and scared. Pargiter stayed quiet, and Maitland laughed.

"Oh, that's your take now, Emil? Pargiter, you should have seen how enraptured this New York fraud was when Crissy would talk Chuck Varner to him. He is a True Believer, and never think otherwise. And Emil, Chuck was only wrong because he killed himself at the end. Because he put himself in a position where it was suicide or jail. The *shooting* wasn't wrong, not a bit, we know that. You do, I do. Because I should have done one by now. You should be back East right now, counting down time until the ideal moment to do one there. Times Square, maybe. We fucked those both up, though, didn't we? Fooled ourselves. I don't have it in me to really do chaos. And you definitely don't. Coward."

"Shut up," Chadwick said, getting up. Pargiter didn't quite slap him back down, but that was only because he'd mastered this particular hand-placed-on-shoulder shove so many times that the only impact was between ass and chair, not palm and skull. Chadwick let out a small squeak when he landed back in his chair and Maitland laughed like a frat boy watching a pledge endure initiation.

Pargiter turned to Maitland. "You talk a lot about a shooting on the horizon, Officer Maitland. I want you to, for a moment here, remember the years of duty you put in with this department, the people you helped, the lives you saved. No matter whether you were doing that as a pantomime act, those things happened, in life, in fact. You were a cop. That's why you didn't go through with this spree-killing shit. You don't kill civilians. You're not the kind. That's not weak. It's not strong either, it's just sane. Decent. That's who you are. So tell me what you know, and tell me right now, so I can save some lives, and you can save yourself from being an accessory. And then we can talk about your beliefs."

"You're right, Detective. I didn't go through with the killing because I wasn't the kind. Everything else you say is off, your reasons, but you can't help that. You're a drone. A castrated drone who listens to his mother and his God and his captain and does the best darn job he can." Maitland laughed, stopping when Pargiter took a step forward and put his full weight on the right foot of Maitland's prison-issued canvas shoe. Then he screamed.

"Sorry," Pargiter said. "This shithead over here seems to think some clown named 'The Boy' is going to shoot people in my city, soon. Maybe today. Is that right?"

"Yes," said Maitland, holding his foot off the ground, not knowing what to do with the pain. He was cuffed to the table, so couldn't squeeze it and hop around.

"Yes I'm right or yes today?"

"Yes to both. He wants to do it today. But I bet you're wrong about something else."

"What is that?"

"He's going to do it with Blanche. That is very special to him, to him and to Chuck. Can you uncuff me? I think you broke my toe."

"I misstepped, and I'm sorry. You need to tell me more, immediately."

"This first."

"How is undoing your hands going to help with your toe?"

"It will allow me to skip the part of my pretrial where I have my lawyer tell the judge that this interview was conducted under duress, and therefore void," Maitland said, squeezing the pain out of his voice and filling it with professionalism.

Pargiter hesitated, then gave the nod to Bennet, who walked the few steps over to Maitland and keyed his cuffs open. As he was straightening up, Maitland grabbed the front of Bennet's belt, pulling him over his lap. Emil Chadwick screamed, upending his chair, as Maitland went for Bennet's gun. Maitland had his left hand on the holster and was thumping Bennet on the back of the head with his right. Maitland knew Bennet's department-issue holster as well as he knew his own, of course—he released the thumb break and kept moving toward the trigger-guard release. Then he started to slide the gun out, smiling.

Maitland wasn't going to do it. Pargiter knew it. He knew he wasn't going to shoot Bennet, or him, or Chadwick. He knew. He just couldn't risk it.

Pargiter put two bullets into Dan Maitland's head at close range, and when that was finished, Dan Maitland didn't have much head left.

CHAPTER **THIRTY-THREE**

———

J AYA CHAUHAN LEFT her mother behind with two police officers in their home when Pargiter called her, telling her to get into her car and drive straight to the Dunkin' Donuts at Alameda and Elm. He was in the parking lot with coffees when she arrived, and offered her one as she got out of her car. It was black and she usually took milk, but she said nothing and started drinking it.

"The officer I had following you and Blanche Potter is dead. His car's gone, and he was found behind the bush where he'd last parked it. A block from your house. That's what we know. Are you all right? I mean, functionally all right?"

"I'm not, but I'd be worse if there weren't two police officers with my mother right now instead of just one." Jaya lost her words after this, staring at a Technicolor oil stain in the parking space between her and the detective. Pargiter gave her a couple of seconds before continuing.

"I'm not insulting Clem Broward. He was very good," Pargiter said. "Any of us can be surprised."

Jaya stared at him.

"But yes," he went on. "Surprising two cops isn't going to go as easily as creeping up on one and shooting him in the back."

Jaya felt a burning sensation on her chest and looked down, realizing that her coffee cup was tilted toward her body, and that her body was tilting toward the pavement, just as Pargiter slapped the cup out of her hand and set her down to sit on the hood of her car. "Blanche," Jaya whispered.

"He took her. But I mean took, not killed. She's not lying where Broward was. This psycho took her somewhere, and I have to believe that it's where he's planning to do his shooting."

"Why? Why do you have to believe that?" Jaya asked.

"Because it gives us a chance, that's why. A chance to stop this. And I need to believe we have that chance. Jaya, do you have any idea, any at all, where they would be?"

CHAPTER **THIRTY-FOUR**

T HE BOY WAS Crissy's bullshit, as I'm sure you can guess," said The Boy, as I woke up on a strange, U-dented mattress in a room with the shades drawn. I straightened up then lay down again when the pain in my skull seemed to flower into all of my limbs and torso. My arms were tied behind me, tight, with something that wasn't rope. Electrical cord, maybe. He'd left my clothes on, but taken the gun. Before I had laid back down, I saw a rifle, burnished and sleek, mounted on a tripod just beside those drawn curtains.

"Maitland gave me the scope back," The Boy said. "He'd be disappointed I'm not using it. It was just a mock-up, you know. Same model but I built in the scratches from Chuck's old one out of some photos Crissy had. But I left it up for you by the Denny's. Little souvenir. I wanted to use this goddamn beast tonight. Full auto."

"Don't," I said, my voice an actual croak, more toad than frog.

I thought of those green amphibian bodies on the New Orleans pavement, the rich air and their hot living flesh, so small and crushable.

"I'm Seth," he said. "Seth Howell, born, but truly Seth Varner. Crissy wanted an official name change, and I had to talk her out of it. Said it'd make me too easy to find, and she knew it was true. Really she couldn't stand that some other woman, even if it was a dead meth addict—R.I.P., Mom—had given Chuck a child. But I'm Seth Varner, that's for real. You remember me?"

The face came nearer to me than it had been since the car, and this time, Seth was looking at me full in the eye. He even took off his glasses. Chuck's narrow nose, for sure. The eyes, a deep green, came from that woman he'd called a dead meth addict, because there was nothing that beautiful in our shared gene pool. But the forehead, the chin, the lips, they were Chuck's. I was still staring when he kissed me.

I spat back the saliva he'd put into me and Seth wiped his face, backing away. He looked apologetic.

"Sorry," he said. "Too much information meets too much action. We're half-siblings, Blanche. Half. The good half. I think that carrying forward that connection to Chuck is as much a duty as this is," he said, pointing to the rifle. "You know this place? I guess you never saw the inside. Historical for us, and also handy—I got you up the fire escape. Would have been questions if I carried you up through the lobby, asleep as you were.

"Chuck, half the time he left you at the bookstore or whatever, he picked me up from my mom and we came and watched TV here, before he talked to me for hours. Just hours. The shootings, you have to know, they weren't spontaneous, it wasn't a that-day decision. He'd told me about them weeks before, told me to be in the Harlow food court at an exact time, and he turned up with you right on the god-damn money. And I got to see everything. Just like you.

"We were his plan, Blanche. You and me together, carriers of Your Life Is Mine. Us and these bullets."

The Boy, Seth, tossed a handful of bullets into the air and let them clink onto the filthy carpet. He turned off the lights in the room, but I could see him moving, still. The shape of him. Then he drew the curtains open, slowly, showing me what was outside: the board-walk where Chuck Varner used to walk with me while he trawled for women, one of whom was this creature's mother. It was a beautiful, busy summer night.

There were a lot of people, but Seth had a lot of bullets in the clips that lay alongside his gun. Enough for all of them.

"Forget my name. I want you and everyone else to call me Chuck. Chuck Varner."

CHAPTER THIRTY-FIVE

J AYA NURSED HER coffee-burnt hand and watched the pavement while Pargiter waited, feeling his desperation.

She thought back over the decade of truths that made up her friendship with Blanche Potter, all the conversations, all the work, all the silence, all the need and give-back and simple fun. And the lie under them all: her dead father, lying in the street like a dog that had been run over, a hole in his mind. And Blanche, lying under that tarp in the back of a truck with a rifle, brainwashed by more abuse and trauma than she could imagine, still unable to kill an innocent person.

"They're saying the shooter is her half-brother. I know that sounds nuts," said Detective Pargiter. "That's what Dan Maitland told us, that this man is Chuck Varner's son with another woman."

Jaya took the only fact she could think of, wondering if it was because it was the most recent, because it was the only chance she could think of with a mind this taxed.

"We drove by a place where Chuck Varner used to take women."

———————

It was just after eleven p.m. Jaya's phone was on Padma's bedside table, where she'd left it after helping her mother to ease into sleep with a combination of ginger tea and half-truths. Pargiter was driving at a terrible speed, but Jaya could still see people on the sidewalks, in bars, bystanders animated as if for the first time for her as possible victims. There were so many of them, out.

"Getting the last of summer," Jaya whispered.

"What?" Pargiter said to her. She shook her head. He went back to his conversation.

"Yes, Cabana Hotel," Pargiter said into his cell phone. "It matches up. Tons of teenagers out there drinking above and below the boardwalk, along with couples ending dates, panhandlers. It's a goddamn ideal vantage point. You use no radios on this, got it? Shooter could be listening. I need bodies out there, everyone we have, the ones who have a full understanding of the risk they're facing out on the boardwalk in plain clothes with badges, quietly getting it clear. Post up uniforms out of scope-sight of the hotel, seal off anyone else from getting on the boardwalk. We want it clear. Phones only, keep it quiet, and I want eight cops who can shut their mouths and walk softly to meet me a block from that hotel."

Pargiter waited for the amount of yeses he needed, and was gratified not to hear many questions back. Just one, exactly.

"Yes. He has a live hostage. Reason to hope she's alive." Pargiter hung up and remembered Jaya was beside him. "Sorry."

"No. I mean, that's just it. We have reason to hope."

Pargiter nodded. Blanche was only alive, if she was alive, because of how crazy this kid was. But she was only in there with him because of how crazy he was, too. There was a joke in there somewhere, and if he had time, he would figure it out.

The lights of the boardwalk came into sight, and soon, so did the people on it. Pargiter drove faster.

CHAPTER THIRTY-SIX

S HE DID TELL me about you, you know," I said to Seth's back. He was at the rifle, swiveling it back and forth as he looked through the scope, and he didn't answer me when he spoke again—he took a photo out the window with his cell phone, and brought it over to my bedside.

I looked and saw, just in that frame, a middle-aged Asian couple holding hands. Two teenagers in the universal huddle that means a joint is being sparked. A younger boy, maybe twelve, too young to be out, holding a skateboard and drinking from an enormous fountain pop cup. He had a *Jurassic Park* T-shirt on. Seth would aim right at the center of it, if Crissy had passed on Chuck's sniping advice. *Use logos as a target if the faces start to distract you.*

"Crowd's thinning out," said Seth. "Usually stays busy even later than this, but I guess the temperature's dropping a little. Might only get twenty, twenty-five bodies down. You impressed with how quick I had things going once you got back to town, Blanche? It was part impatience, part planning." He laughed, looking at me like a boy expecting praise, but not needing it. He was proud enough of himself without it.

"Crissy told me about you. I didn't know exactly that she was talking about you, but she dropped enough hints that I figured it out. Just didn't want to believe you existed," I said. I was sweating against the cord around my hands, but the knots were tight and didn't slip.

Seth looked at me, and I could see him smiling. With the light coming in from the lampposts along the boardwalk, there was an orange haze in the room so we could see each other. I was straightened up against the headboard behind me. Seth came over and sat at the foot of the bed.

"Bullshit, Blanche, but I'll hear you out."

"She said Chuck probably had bastards around and she was fine with it. That she had me and that was what was important. That's why she put so much into training me up—it's the only reason that makes sense, right? She knew about you, but she knew you didn't have *it*. That you were second-rate. Or else why, why in fuck would Chuck and Crissy let a *girl* in on his plan? And train her to lead?"

"Bullshit. Bullshit once again. But clever." It wasn't quite light enough in the room for me to see if there was any doubt crowding around those green eyes, but he did turn his face away.

"Chuck never taught women. He always went for men. Boys. Always. Crissy, too. They were *stuck* with me because you couldn't cut it. They knew you were a loser. No matter what she told you, Crissy knew it, and she did her best to fill you with the confidence in yourself that she didn't have in you."

I slouched, moving lower down the headboard so it would stop vibrating with my back. I was shaking.

Seth was quiet.

"There's even proof, Seth. You fell for it. The getting-me-back here, the we-have-to-do-this-shooting-together. Don't you understand? Crissy engineered all of this. Even knowing that you'd jump the gun and kill her. She knew that was the only thing that could get me back here, that could get me to take this operation out of your childish, useless hands. You weakling. You pussy."

Seth spat on me, the hot liquid landing in my eye, before he started to yell.

"You fucking dumb *cunt*," he said, his voice pushing through the walls around us and behind me. Immediately there was pounding at the door, loud. Seth leaned right into my face, shoving my father's nose right into mine, and I turned my head and opened my mouth. I could see the corner of his eye, the surprise in it, a glimmering second where he thought I was seducing him in some aggressive way that was foreign to him.

I bit into his cheek, gathering as much of it as I could get into my mouth, pushing my teeth together and through his flesh as Seth screamed. When I pulled my head back and spat out his skin and blood, I could see his teeth through the hole I'd made. He grabbed my throat with both hands and started to squeeze so hard that I was sure his fingers were going to go right through me.

The door burst open and people came through. Men and women in black. In vests. In armor, with guns. Seth jumped up, turned, and every gun in front of me illuminated, making me deaf for the second before I closed my eyes.

CHAPTER **THIRTY-SEVEN**

Excerpt from Last Victims Redux: Chuck Varner's America *by Emil Chadwick. RedPillMega Press, 2019.*

AFTERWORD

I never appreciated what my mother did for me until I saw what she did for Chuck Varner's family. She's gone now—by which I mean, she doesn't ever want to speak to me again, and I doubt she will suddenly start reading me now. Jill Gudgeon never watched, heard, or read anything I made. She was afraid she was too much of a critic to read me without it changing her opinion of me, "perhaps permanently," she said. "I love you, and I usually respect you. Do you know how rare that is, Emil? Do you know how precious?"

The first time we met, Blanche Varner told me that my mother got her right in her book, *Last Victims*. That made me so mad I could barely think, but Blanche wasn't perceptive enough to see that. She didn't inherit Chuck Varner's ability to read people, or she would have known that I was about to flip the table, to tell her how it really was. That her child's memory of her father, of herself, couldn't help but be massively flawed, victim to the same ugly brainwashing that every child undergoes from his or her mother.

Increasingly, that's how I see child-rearing in this country. A process of brainwashing, an erosion of all that is purely moral, innately known, and remarkable in children. In boys. Women like Jill Gudgeon and Crissy Varner are flatteners of the messages that we are born with and the great teachings that are revealed by the prophets, holy and otherwise, that we're lucky enough to come into contact with.

These parents, and yes, most of them are mothers, are giftwrappers, presenting the promise of acceptance and approval in exchange for the erosion of everything that's remarkable in the self. That's what my mother gave to me. And it's what she gave Chuck Varner's daughter, as well. Blanche Potter, as she proved in erasing her last name, touting the truth of my mother's version of her past, and her complete repudiation of the good parts of Chuck Varner's message, the core truths that violence has unfortunately obscured.

I haven't abandoned the truth that I came to understand in Stilford. I really, truly believe in Your Life Is Mine. In the fifth rule of Chuck Varner's code: There is no justice or peace in civilization. Only in chaos. Some of the other rules, particularly number three (Obedience = Faith) require careful unpacking, and may come to reflect the opposite of what they seem to at first. But what philosophical text doesn't transform in front of your eyes when truly awakened minds unlock it for you?

Blanche Potter—I call her by her chosen name because she just doesn't deserve the Varner, not because I'm a slave to her wishes—also called me "misogynistic." Such an easy word that is, for these people, a skeleton key that locks every conversation shut. It's just more evidence of how little she understood anything her father said to her, despite having the privilege of direct education from the man himself. I don't hate women any more than I hate everyone. I don't hate everyone more than I hate her in particular. You in particular. The idea of focusing hatred is as foolish as the idea of focusing love. Focused love turns into the kind of poison that Jill Gudgeon fed me. Focused hate becomes a distraction that prevents us from getting in tune with the total chaos of a free universe, the greatest gift we've ever been given.

Chuck Varner gave me that gift, and I hope that after reading this, I've given it to you, as well. You have to remember that the bullets are a distraction, yes, but they're also a pathway into the only future that the ignorant and asleep deserve, and a welcome escape from an ungrateful world for men like Chuck Varner and Seth Howell.

On some level I wonder if stopping Seth Howell is the worst thing I've ever done with my life. It's a thought I have every day, and I wish he were here to answer it for me. We don't have enough true teachers in this world. And, thanks to me, we lost one more.

———

Note: The print run of Emil Chadwick's book was withdrawn and pulped pending the resolution of a lawsuit against him by

Revisioniste, the production company run by Blanche Potter (née Varner) and Jaya Chauhan. Revisioniste's lawyers claim Chadwick serially fabricated his accounts of the August 2018 events in Stilford leading up to Seth Howell's failed mass shooting.

Documents submitted to the court, including official police reports, suggest that Chadwick did indeed exaggerate his role in stopping Howell, and failed to completely admit to his foreknowledge of the shooter's plans. A criminal legal case was launched after the civil lawsuit, after suggestions in Chadwick's book led to his email and phone records being subpoenaed, and it was discovered that Chadwick had been in regular contact with an email alias of Seth Howell, as well as with two other suspects who communicated in language redolent with allusions to Chuck Varner's Your Life Is Mine cult.

Chadwick hanged himself in a Los Angeles holding cell on August 17, 2019, while awaiting the arrival of Stilford Detective Ron Pargiter, who was set to interrogate him that day. Chadwick's two anonymous correspondents remain unidentified.

CHAPTER **THIRTY-EIGHT**

WE DID OUR small premiere for *The Empty Men* in LA, exactly two years and three days after Ron Pargiter and seven other cops blew Seth Howell into pulp. None of them grazed me, and most of my medical worries came from the bite I'd taken out of Seth's face. The blood tests came back clean.

The official premiere was at Sundance, and over the next several months we would be at TIFF, Tribeca, all the festivals that had said "maybe next time" to us with our previous movies.

"You were right," Jaya said, hanging up the phone in our tiny office space after we got confirmation that we were running in competition at Cannes. "I don't know if we were supposed to make this thing, but everyone wants to see it."

"We were supposed to make it, Jaya. I know it." I smiled and hoped she would, too, but she just nodded, looking at the ground. It had kept us together, the making of this digital creature of light and sound, our shared decisions of what to conceal, what to say. We could be honest with each other, completely, by knowing exactly which lies we were going to tell together.

The premiere was on the studio lot at Fox, in a beautiful screening room booked by the streaming overlords who had bought *The Empty Men* and guaranteed us budgets for our next three projects. I watched pictures and video of Chuck and Crissy on the screen, and felt no fear, only the cool remove I always felt when I looked at my own work. They were mine, now, mine entirely, and would always be. I wore the same skirt and top I'd worn in New Orleans, forgetting that the cigarette ash stain had never fully washed out, so I had to keep a light jacket on all night. I was sweating a little, but Jaya wasn't. With the movie out in the wild, she was herself again, introducing her mom to all the execs, true crime writers, and directors who'd gently begged for tickets. Jill Gudgeon had tried to get in touch with me, to come out to this and to interview me for her swipe at a late-career masterpiece book about Chuck, her son, and me, but I'd replied with a restraining order.

We'd had Padma out in Los Angeles for the past couple of weeks, using some of our production budget to get her a rental apartment that was out of all of our price ranges. On the second night, which was the first night ever that I'd seen her have more than three glasses of wine, I almost thought about telling her about that night, of what happened with Neesh, Crissy, and me. It wasn't in the movie, but I thought, for a moment, that she should know. About how little I deserved to be free, let alone in her presence, let alone part of her daughter's life. She certainly deserved to know. Maybe Jaya saw what I was thinking, because she looked at me for a long moment from the kitchen, where she was trying to solve a broken cork issue.

I kept my mouth shut.

Instead, we talked about Seth. About the parts that had made it into the movie, the enormous battle we'd had in editing it to make sure that Chuck Varner, Crissy, and Seth emerged as pathetic, without even a trace of glamour or that weird celebrity glory that is almost impossible to separate from mass violence.

I controlled every word or gesture Chuck made in the movie, every piece I allowed to be shown. I owned him now.

"I can still—sorry, Ma," I said to Padma, "I can still taste his spit."

"You can't. That's just a memory that you're mixing with a sour taste from another memory. Old milk, bad breath. It's nothing to do with him. He's nothing. Like that man," she said. "That man" meant Chuck when Padma said it in that tone.

"Maybe."

"Do you ever feel safe?" she asked me. She had the same way Jaya had of asking a question that was meant to start a conversation leading to a sort of thesis statement, a mutually agreed upon life philosophy.

"I did when I heard the guns fire. I thought that even if the bullets hit me, at least it wasn't him killing me, you know? Sick." I touched her arm to remind her and myself that I was here, that neither Seth nor any of the others had killed me.

"No," Jaya said from the kitchen. "You're not sick, you're a sane person reacting to a sick situation."

Padma nodded, and I went on.

"But right afterward, I didn't feel safe. Because that's Chuck. And Seth. And the rest of them. The Chadwicks and the other worms."

"Complicated," Padma said, and then laughed. I laughed with her, remembering how I'd dealt with all of these feelings for the first time, after the mall, and for the second time, after Neesh. I'd just put the feelings away and never looked at them again until I was forced to.

And that's what I would do after this documentary run was finished, after the interviews were wrapped, after everyone knew where I came from and what I'd done. I would make that woman who made the movie and talked to the reporters into myself. I would be that person who wasn't bothered any longer, who could look deep into the past and come out with a piece of documentary art and an effective set of sound bites in a junket interview.

I'd pretended I was a totally different person twelve years ago, and eventually, it came true. I would just need to pretend again, and someday I would wake up as myself.

ACKNOWLEDGMENTS

Laurie Grassi, Rakesh Satyal, Loan Le, David Brown, Lauren Morocco, Nita Pronovost, Adria Iwasutiak, Jessica Rattray, Ellen Whitfield, Michael Heyward.

Samantha Haywood and Stephanie Sinclair.

Kris Bertin, Mark Morrison.

Chris Ferguson, John T. Edge.

Andrew Sullivan, Patrick Tarr, Chris Harper, Sam Wiebe, Chris Brayshaw, the Ruthnum family, Raj and Vindhya Rathore, Buddy, Ashley MacCuish, Martha Sharpe, Ben McNally, Type Books, Book City.

ABOUT THE AUTHOR

Photo by Ian Patterson

NATHAN RIPLEY is the pseudonym of Toronto resident and Journey Prize winner Naben Ruthnum. *Find You in the Dark*, Ripley's first thriller, was an instant bestseller. As Naben Ruthnum, he is the author of *Curry: Eating, Reading, and Race*. Follow him on Twitter **@NabenRuthnum**.